Praise for *Adam's List*
(from goodreads.com)

"The detail and emotions that are brought out with *Adam's List* keep you on your toes and wanting more. The main characters and their instant connection makes you swoon. I loved that the rules seemed to be reverse from the normal romance books..."

"Jewels was quirky, and her personality was perfect. She was just on the edge of craziness that Adam needed."

"The passion is palpable and drives the story forward, making you crave more of the characters' interaction. I almost wish she strung it out longer."

"Amazing story with great characters. Adam and Jewel's story was raw and real. The main secret was completely unexpected. It made for an interesting and unique new adult romance."

ADAM'S LIST

Book #1 in NYC Love Series

JENNIFER ANN

This is a work of fiction. The names, characters, places and incidents are products of the writer's imagination or have been used in a fictitious manner. Any resemblance to persons, living or dead, actual events, locales or organizations is entirely coincidental.

ADAM'S LIST © 2014 Jennifer Naumann. All rights are reserved. No part of this book may be used or reproduced, distributed or transmitted in any form or by any means without the written permission of the author.

FIRST EDITION

Cover design by BESTOFYOU
Cover image © dundanim
ISBN: 978-0988390218
Library of Congress Control Number: 2016902176

BY JENNIFER ANN

NYC LOVE SERIES
Adam's List
Kelly's Quest
Chloe's Dream

KENDALL FAMILY SERIES
Brooklyn Rockstar
Midwest Fighter

JENNIFER ANN ONLINE
www.JenNaumann.net
Twitter: naumannbooks
Facebook: AuthorJenniferAnn
Goodreads: AuthorJenniferAnn
Pinterest: AuthorJenniferA

For my incredibly sweet cousin, Hope,
one of the strongest,
bravest people I know.

One

THE OLD HOUSE BUZZES WITH ANGRY rock, brazen laughter, and occasional screams from girls; it's an audio explosion of brass sounds that once again make me question my agreement to come in the first place.

Smoke irritates my nose, some of it smelling like the green variety. The "no smoking" sign near the entrance is clearly more of a loose suggestion than a rule as I'm pretty sure I've seen over a dozen people with lit cigarettes in hand, some of them among the guys hosting the party. A thick haze drifts through the room above the crowd, the smell even more robust than the cheap keg beer.

Sticky goop, probably a mix of spilled beer and strawberry margarita mix, covers the bottom of my newly purchased wedges, making a sick, sucking noise whenever I move my feet. Empty red solo cups litter every crevice of the room, apparently because we're in college and no one can make us follow our parents' rules.

The crowd's an odd combination of jocks, hipsters, preps, and kids who don't belong, like me. At least not anymore.

An oversexed freshman who's built like Jonah Hill—pre-diet—grinds up against me every few minutes, even though I'm nowhere near the area designated as the dance floor. I'm not amused. Clearly, my desire to be alone isn't obvious by standing in the least active corner of the house.

Ladies and gentlemen, *this is my life*.

Or it has become my life anyway, ever since the powers-that-be decided I was way too happy and secure, deciding to give me a healthy dose of reality to choke on.

My reflection stares back at me from an old beer sign on the wall. The narrow nose and dark blond eyelashes I inherited from my mom appear exaggerated in the warped glass. The cornflower blue eyes I inherited from my dad have lost their luster, although it could just be the low lit room overpowering their normal vibrance. But who am I kidding. My lips are perpetually cracked because I don't care enough to drink enough water or keep applying balm. The long, curly locks spilling well past my breasts are in serious need of not only a brushing, but also a touch-up at the roots. Because I'm too lazy to call the salon for an appointment, and quite frankly, I don't give a shit.

I wasn't *always* a fun hater. I had it all in high school. I was a cheerleader with shining blond hair straight out of a L'Oréal commercial, and a killer body that every guy wanted to sack. My long-term sweetheart, Jason, was at the top of the girls' lists for hotties, and just happened to be the star quarterback. Every girl either wanted to be me, or hated my guts because of my perceived perfection. The social world was at my fingertips. I was living the high life as our school's queen bee.

I don't think anyone was neither sympathetic nor surprised when I was so unceremoniously knocked down.

I look away from the mirror, down to the cup in my hands filled with flat beer. Until recently, I was usually among the typical party girls you see at these kinds of things, slamming down shots of vodka and tequila just as quickly as they're handed out. I would've possibly hooked up with some random guy, and woke in a strange room the next morning.

Then my depression meds were kicked up a notch at my mom's request. Now I'm just kind of numb to life. Taking a pill doesn't magically make a person's mental health better. It doesn't take away all the hurt and anguish over something that forever changed you. The alcohol doesn't mix with the drugs—I know this—but sometimes I just need to mask the pain of my past.

I simply go through the motions of each day, going to classes, work, and letting my best friend drag me to these stupid parties, meanwhile waiting for a booty call from my current fling. I have no drive, no vision of what I want to do with my life. Some days I really don't care if things ever change. Other days I think I'd be doing the universe a favor if I just didn't wake up in the morning.

You will become what you deserve.

Did some ingenious poet with a MFA say that, or was it something I saw on Pinterest?

I dump my drink into a half-dead fern in the corner that's doubling as an ash tray, and check my phone for the billionth time in the last ten minutes. As usual, my best friend/roommate/wing-woman, Kelly, has become MIA, most likely hooking up on her way to the bathroom.

Before I can leave in search of her, I'm approached by someone so incredibly tall that he's possibly headlining in the circus. His dark eyes fall on me, filled with that drunken haze most guys get after a healthy dose of hard alcohol. His short, reddish-blond hair looks messy from some kind of playful scuffle with a buddy. The gray t-shirt he dons with the school's logo and mascot plastered across the front looks wet from mid-chest down, most likely the result of a spilled beverage.

"Hey, beautiful," he coos in a deep voice.

Yep. This is about to happen.

"Hey, random, drunk guy," I answer, folding my arms over Kelly's red shirt that shows far too much. One of these times I'll stand up against her brash orders on what I can and can't wear to these nightmares. These days I'm most comfortable in things that cover every inch of my skin, like a moo-moo or a snowsuit.

He leans against the wall at my side, grinning in the cheesy way really cocky guys do when they think they're being charming. "What are you doing here all alone, sweet thing?"

"Oh, you know. Trying to avoid anyone who thinks because I'm standing here alone that it's an open invitation to come hit on me."

His eyes narrow like he's trying to focus. The smell of booze blasts off him with all the appeal of a skunk in heat. "I haven't seen you around. You probably know who I am, right?"

When I shake my head, he touches his chest with both hands. "Cal Howard? Starter on the basketball team?"

"A baller?" I fake a gasp. "*Shut. Up.*"

The kind of foolish, drunken smile that can make a guy look like a complete moron appears on his lips. Though I've never been to a game, I'm sure if his coach knew he could easily blow a .3 about now, he'd be on his way to developing a healthy dose of bleacher-butt next season.

"A pretty little thing like you probably doesn't know much about basketball. I could take you down to the court some time, teach you how to shoot. Maybe play a little one-on-one?"

I send an SOS text to Kelly, hoping she'll give up among her throws of passion to save me.

Where r u? I've exceeded my capacity 4 douchery

"You textin' someone?" Cal asks, leaning down to get a look at my phone. Leaning way too close, I might add. The only thing worse than a sloppy drunk is one who's big enough to fit me in his pocket, and even worse yet, determined. How exactly did I let Kelly talk me into coming here?

These parties are the worst.

"My boyfriend," I lie, nodding. "He's head of security for the Vikings. Big guy, about six four and three fifty. He should be here any minute. I'm sure *he'd* be into talking sports with you if you want to stick around."

Cal sways on his feet. I can literally see his intelligence shrinking as he tries to think. "Do you have a problem with me?"

Taking a deep breath, I fight the urge to roll my eyes. "I would actually have to *know* you before I could make such conclusions."

His eyebrows raise clumsily as he takes a step closer. "Maybe you should take the time to *get* to know me." The stench of his breath about knocks me over when he moves in to grab my arm.

"Hey!" I yell, trying to shake him off. "Let *go* of me!" Quite frankly my new buddy Cal seems too inebriated to have a full understanding of what country he's in at the moment, but I take a step back anyway, ready to bolt.

Out of nowhere, another guy steps in at my side. Nice build with short, dark hair, casually dressed rather than some of the pretentious guys in sports jackets and pressed button downs. The fragrance of men's body spray, spearmint gum, and something else musky and manly follows him. I hardly notice anything else once his piercing, steely blue eyes fall on me.

"Hey," he says, his voice deliciously deep and smooth. A nice row of white teeth appears behind his easygoing smile, slight pucker of dimples popping onto his cheeks.

I throw my own version of a sexy smile back his way, but it probably looks more like a five-year-old meeting her first Disney princess in person. "Hey."

He tips his head at Cal, his eyes never leaving mine. "Everything okay?"

"She's *fine*," Cal answers, finally dropping my arm. "We were just getting to know each other."

The two guys study each other with their chests out, chins lifted, gazes hard. My money would go on the baller by freakishly unnatural height alone, but the new guy doesn't seem threatened. The intensity between them pinches my lungs.

"It's fine, really. He was just telling me he had to leave," I finally say, not wanting to see the hot guy get his ass kicked.

Cal glares at me a minute before he finally turns, stumbling as he mutters "*bitch*", and disappears into the crowd. There's nothing like the shunning by someone whose morals are clearly higher than yours, especially when they're too blitzed to remember it in the morning.

The new guy shakes his head, irritation visible in his expression. His clear eyes are so beautiful, they about take my breath away. "You okay?"

I bray in a nervous giggle. "Guys like that with a shoe size bigger than his IQ? It takes a lot more than that to fluster me."

He chuckles, scanning the crowd like he's looking for someone. I take the opportunity to give him a good once over. Broad shoulders, square face, thick eyelashes, strong cheekbones, straight nose. Dark stubble covers his jaw, matching his short hair, the slightly longer stuff on top styled in a precarious 'do. He looks out of place here in his gray raglan shirt, slightly stretched from the muscle underneath, hole-covered jeans, brown leather bracelet, worn-out Chucks. He'd be better suited in the crowd at a rock concert.

When he turns back to me, I about die as I'm staring intently at him while biting my lip.

"I'm Adam, by the way."

Underneath his approving gaze, I suddenly feel ten times sexier than normal. "Jewels."

He raises his thick eyebrows, smirking. "Want to get out of here?"

I sigh. This hottie is probably just another guy looking to hook up—bump uglies, no questions asked. It seems that kind is easier to find than a condom dispenser. A few months ago during my careless stage, I totally would've been down for a romp with this gorgeous man. Now that I'm somewhat committed to Levi, however, I can't let myself go down that path again. "I'm kind of seeing someone."

Adam glances over my shoulder. "Is he here?"

I grunt to myself. It doesn't really matter that Levi works all the time, or that he's way beyond his college years. He still wouldn't come. "No, these kinds of parties aren't his scene. They're not exactly mine either, but yet, here I am."

Adam shoves his hands in his pockets. "I just meant we should get some fresh air. This place is pretty thick, and you don't really seem the smoking type."

"Yeah, sure. I guess my lungs could use a cleansing."

One of his hands falls to my lower back while he uses the other one to keep people from bumping into me as we fight our way through the sweaty bodies. It's a sweet gesture, one that Levi wouldn't make in a million years. My imagination kicks into overdrive, picturing Adam's hand dropping lower to my butt, the other reaching for my—

No. I shake my head. I can't allow myself to go there.

Jesus, Jewels. Get a grip.

We finally break through the pack of loud drunks and through the front door, letting the cold fresh air of the dark night fill our lungs. The remaining cold leftover from winter chills me to the bone. I suck in a shaky breath. "Yeah, that's definitely better."

Leaning against a stone retaining wall at the edge of the stairway, Adam rests his hands behind his back, looking up to the dark sky. I stare at his relaxed posture, realizing he's probably the type I could get along with. The type I probably *should* be with. Easygoing. Fun. Relaxed. The way his arms bulge just the right amount and his t-shirt bends around the muscles of his stomach, he definitely works out. Probably not for looks, but to stay in shape. Ex-football player in high school maybe. A flush climbs up my neck when I start to envision him naked. My eyes are trailing from his chest to the surge in his jeans when I catch him watching me.

"Where you from?" he asks.

"Here. I made it a whopping fifteen miles from home. You?"

"I live here too." He thrusts a hand at the house. "I mean, not in this place, but in La Crosse."

The intimate way his beautiful eyes peer into me have me even more intrigued, and majorly turned on. "You don't go to school here?" I ask, looking down at my phone to avoid meeting his gorgeous gaze.

"I dropped out last semester. You?"

Sliding my phone back into my back jeans pocket, I find the courage to face him. Once again, the way his eyes drink me in is toe-curling amazing. "Sophomore. Undecided."

Chuckling in his deep, succulent voice, a puff of white air falls from his lips. They're a nice set of lips, dusty-rose colored and as full as you would want lips on a guy. The kind that would be delightful to suck on. "You mean you're in your twenties and don't know what you want to do with the rest of your life? What's wrong with you?"

I grin, excited to play along. "Indecision runs in my family. My mom went to college when she was my age to be a teacher. When I was five she went again to get a nursing degree. Any guess what she does now?"

Under the house light, I catch his eyes sparkling with amusement. "Exotic animal wrangler?"

I shake my head with a hiccup of a giggle. "You were *this* close. She's manager for a chain of discount clothing stores."

Adam chuckles loudly, clapping his hands together. I love the sound of it, and want to make him laugh like that again. I suddenly want to know everything about him.

"I'm probably the only one in this school whose parents don't really care if I *ever* declare a major," I tell him. "They're more concerned that I get as many *life experiences* as possible."

Adam tilts his head. "I feel like I've seen you before. You work on campus?"

"The library. Work study."

It was one of the less creative conditions my parents threw at me after they discovered Levi. While I was less than thrilled when I discovered he had a little boy with an ex-girlfriend, I've gotten over it. But it totally put my parents over the edge when they discovered through a friend of a friend that I was seeing a much older man who's also a daddy. They're always trying to find creative ways to keep us apart, anything short of locking me in a closet.

Adam's expression lights up. "That's it. I think I saw you stacking shelves a few times earlier this year."

"What can I say? It's cutting-edge work."

A few giggling girls saunter between us. In matching slutty tops that show half their bras, and jeans so tight their butts contort with unflattering rolls, it's no surprise when they throw their long hair of various colors over their shoulders and pass Adam sultry looks. The smell of an actual brewery wafts after them.

Adam's eyes flicker to the sky once they're gone. "So, cataloging books and drinking keg beer. How's that life experience thing working out for you so far?"

We pass knowing smirks. "Invigorating. Who knew life could be so vivacious?"

"Your parents sound like mine." He gazes past me to the darkness. "I always figure they're just trying to relive their younger days through me."

"How old are *you*?" I shimmy my way up to the top of the stone wall across from him, pulling my knees against my chest to keep warm.

He turns back to me, stuffing his hands back in his pockets. "Just turned twenty-one last month."

"So if you're not wasting your days away in an institution, preparing for your shiny bright future in the corporate world, what do you do with all your spare time?"

"The past couple weeks I've been crashing at a buddy's, trying to decide what I want to do next." He raises a shoulder in a lazy shrug. "You know, invigorating stuff."

"Sounds like hard work." I giggle in the carefree way I used to before my life went south. It feels good, as if I've shed a heavy weight. "So what have you come up with? Sailing the world? Mission trip to Uganda?"

The soft dimples pop back into place with his grin. "Something like that."

My smile sizzles away. "Wait, you're not joking."

"Life can be short." His beautiful eyes become filled with intension. "I want to do something profound."

A pang strikes deep in my chest. I once saw that same level of determination in Jason's eyes when he uttered nearly those exact same words. Our senior year, after we'd been dating for almost two years, he enlisted in the Marines. I always knew he was really heavily into the military stuff because he came from a family who had all served—his mom, dad, grandpa and a couple of uncles—but it still felt like a blow to the stomach when he didn't choose to go to college with me as planned. My nearly 4.0 average would've given me my pick of schools, but I chose to stay local so I'd be close to Jason's family, and wouldn't have to rearrange my school schedule whenever he was on leave.

"You okay?" Adam asks, dragging me out of my thoughts.

"Yeah. What do you mean, like join the Army?"

His lips pull off to the side in a crooked smirk. "No, I don't think I'm cut out for the military. They'd chew me up and spit me out."

Even though this guy's still a stranger, his words are comforting. Nervous laughter bubbles out before I can filter it. "Yeah, you don't really seem the type."

His smirk grows. "What *type* do you see me as?"

I rest my chin on my knees, pretending to turn all serious. "Hmmm, I see you as the type who would find your way up to the front row at a concert. Or the type who would feel comfortable zip-lining over the Grand Canyon. Maybe the type to paddle board in the ocean, maybe even braid some bracelets on the beach and save some sea turtles when you're done."

"Impressive list." He casually crosses his arms, amused. "You're saying you see me as some kind of granola hippie?"

I lift just one eyebrow, a trick I inherited from my dad. "Am I right?"

With a chuckle, he shakes his head. "I haven't done any of those things."

Glancing at the thick leather bracelet on his arm, I snort. "Here I thought I had you totally pegged."

"I'm not saying I'd be opposed to any of them." His teeth gleam in the darkness behind his flickering smile. "It's just that my parents kept me pretty sheltered. I haven't been out much."

I lift my head from my knees. "It can't be that bad."

He glances at the ground before shrugging, as if I've hit a sore subject. "We crossed the Minnesota border a few times. Otherwise I've never been out of the state."

"Wow," I say, thinking of all the vacations I've been on with my family. "So no rides on a jet plane?"

"Nope. The most excitement I've had involved the public bus."

"You can file *that* accomplishment under lame. If you're attempting to procure a list of more invigorating caliber, I'd definitely add conquering the skies. Once you've arrived in a new airport and walked into a city you've never seen, one begins to feel pretty invincible.

Everything about traveling puts your senses on a new level." I lock my fingers around my legs and sigh dreamily. "The millions of people, the ever changing scenery and sights to explore, the fluctuation of weather, even the choices of restaurants. I can't ever get enough. You know the saying: once you've flown through the skies, you never want to walk on the ground."

"Don't think I've heard that one."

I wink. "That's because I just made it up."

His eyes bore into me with heightened interest. Again, I feel as if he's undressing me with a simple look. And I really wish we could cut to the chase so he actually would. "I take it you travel a lot?"

"My dad's a pilot for Delta. I'm kind of like the B version of an Army brat. You know, gets to see the world, only we don't actually ever move."

"Who needs college? Sounds like you're on your way to becoming a travel agent."

Giggling, I say, "I could be yours, anyway."

Our eyes catch with the double meaning of my words. After a strangely comfortable pause, he says, "What else do you think I should add to this list?"

"Well, you *have to* experience a rock concert from the front row. Nothing too crazy though. You need black belt training to conquer the mosh pit."

His lips tilt in amusement. "You like the kind of music where there are mosh pits?"

"It all depends on the level of idiots you're dealing with. The biggest jackholes usually make an appearance at the heavier rock concerts. I'll only go to those if one of my big guy friends comes as our bouncer. My friend was nearly flattened last summer at Lollapalooza."

"Sounds like you have no business being in a mosh pit. You must weigh, what, a hundred pounds soaking wet?"

I glance down at my fit frame, blushing. Though I rocked the cheerleader's uniform in high school, I've packed on a lot of muscle. I like to run with Kelly to stay in shape, and even did a few 5k runs freshman year. I was lucky enough to get my mom's high metabolism and been able to eat whatever I want and still stay in a size 4, except for the time when I packed on the freshman 15.

Looking back up at him, I roll my eyes. "At least we know you can exclude a career in professional weight guessing at the carnival."

His head tilts back with a deep chuckle. Then he's pinning me down with his sexy stare again. "So what kind of concert *would* you recommend?"

"For you? What do you listen to?"

"Whatever's on the radio." When my jaw drops, he laughs. "What? My parents listened to a lot of jazz and blues when I was a kid. That's all the musical influence I ever got."

"*Dude*." I throw my hands out to my sides. "Your parents *seriously* sheltered you. Child services should've been notified of the travesty."

He gives another easygoing shrug. "I'm open to anything."

I huff as if he personally offended me by not having any special taste in music. "Fine. I'd start out with some Bastille or Mumford and Sons. Everyone likes that shit." Grinning, I add, "Or we could take you to New Orleans to hear the kind of music you're more familiar with."

"Okay, fine." He bites the inside of his cheek like he's trying not to smirk, like he's letting me know he's taking this seriously. It makes him *drop dead* sexy. "What about zip-lining? Is that something you've tried?"

Laughing, I nod. "I was tricked into going a few years ago when we were visiting Arizona. They told me we were going spelunking when they handed us helmets. I'm scared to death of heights, but I'm telling you, there's nothing like floating through the air at fifty feet off the ground. I don't know if it's the fear of plunging to my death or what, but it's quite the trip. I'd definitely take you white water rafting, too."

"So, extremely dangerous activities in Arizona, check." *All dimples.* "After that, where would you take me paddle boarding?"

I space out with the memory of Jason trying to paddle board when he came along on my family's vacation to Oahu our senior year. He was so athletic, even before he buffed up in the Corps and became a surfing addict in San Diego. Those memories seem so far away, as if in a different life. It's been over a year since I broke up with Jason, but the gaping hole of guilt and regret in my heart makes it feel like just days ago.

"Hawaii," I answer quietly, squeezing my eyes shut.

"Are you sure you're okay?"

"Yeah." A cold breeze flips my blond curls into my face. Shivering, I rub at my prickly legs. "I'm one of those who's prone to a coma once the booze stops flowing. Give me another hour and I'll be out for the night."

He leans away from the wall, his eyes worried. "You want to go somewhere else? I mean somewhere *public*? You look...cold."

"As much as I'd love to blow this place, I came with a friend," I say, motioning to the house. Kelly was totally hammered the last time I saw her. She's most likely making out with one of the preppy guys who always seem to fall for her wild spirit and large, chocolate brown eyes. She's like cat-nip for studs.

With his hands still in his pockets, Adam shrugs. It's so reserved, just like all of his other mannerisms. I can see him hanging out in bed on a Saturday morning, his hair ruffled, no particular plans in mind. "Tell her you'll come back to get her when she's ready to go."

Weighing the options in my head, I pull my phone from my pocket. Blowing Kelly off for a guy I'm majorly attracted to seems like a horrible idea. That side of me hasn't reared its drunken head since Levi and I became a *thing*, whatever that "thing" may be. Plus, I really should make sure Kelly isn't so drunk that she's doing something she'll regret in the morning. If only she had looked out for me like that the night I met Levi.

I push off the wall. "I should probably go inside and make sure she's okay."

His eyebrows lift as he takes a few steps closer. "You want company? Just say the word and I'm all yours."

I pull in a sharp, stuttering breath. There's an undeniable force pulling me to him, unmatched to any draw I've ever felt before. I just can't walk away and pretend we never met. I can't ignore the tingle in my stomach, or the fluttering of my pulse. While I have no intention of giving my heart to another guy after what I did to Jason, it's still impossible not to envision myself wrapped around this beautiful man.

He takes a step back. "If I'm making you uncomfortable—"

"You're not," I blurt, reaching out to touch his arm. When my fingers connect with his skin, dynamite shoots through me. "I mean, I'm kind of seeing someone."

"You mentioned that." The dimples reappear, giving him almost a boyish quality. "Several times now." When he gleams at me like that, it's almost impossible not to smile back.

"Sorry." I drop my hand from his arm to nervously slide my phone between my fingers. "I mean, it's not like he's got me bugged. It's not even that serious."

Adam seems to be standing much closer when he asks in a low voice, "It's not? Serious, I mean?"

The tingles I feel in this moment are so out of control, I consider leaping into his arms and taking him right on the freshly mowed lawn. "We haven't even reached the 'in a relationship' status on Facebook."

Adam shrugs. "So simply hanging out with me wouldn't be considered *cheating* on this guy, right? Just because you're seeing him doesn't mean you're exclusively committed to him for life. Especially if he isn't smart enough to claim you as his girlfriend."

The only sound aside from the muffled voices and music from inside are my ragged breaths. His lips are so close, so *edible,* all my thoughts become a jumbled mess. Levi isn't here, and it's not like I have plans to marry him one day. So—

I jump when my phone vibrates in my hands. A message from Kelly flashes across the screen.

Where r u?

I look up and sigh. "My friend's looking for me. I should probably...yeah, I'm going to go." After three steps I pause to look over my shoulder. "Are you coming, or are you set on holding that wall up for the rest of the night?"

Adam brightens in response. Although I really know nothing about him, I feel a thrill for what's to come.

Two

THE BEGINNING OF MY FRESHMAN YEAR when I was still in constant touch with my high school friends and still with Jason, I was religious about hitting these house parties. Jess and Lauren, two of the girls I was especially close with from the cheerleading squad, would come back on the weekends from their colleges to join me, and I'd introduce them to guys like some kind of match-maker. I was still in my element, still the popular girl who guys wanted to date, even though it was common knowledge I was off limits.

The last time Jess and Lauren came to stay with me, Kelly was home for a sister's wedding, and I was beginning to fully understand what it would be like to date Jason all four years of college. He had just been sent over to Afghanistan, and I wasn't dealing well with the fact that he was in harm's way. I wasn't able to handle the reality that we would see each other in person maybe once a year. It was that much harder to watch my friends flirt with a group of cute guys.

That night I scanned the busy room as I sipped my beer. At first when I chose to go to the local college, I was afraid I'd constantly run into people I knew. Not that it would've mattered, because I was on friendly terms with pretty much everyone by then, but I was looking forward to a fresh start away from the old gossip and drama. I was pleasantly surprised when I only saw two classmates my first semester. But having Jess and Lauren with me made me realize just how much I was starting to miss my old life.

"You're like, *really* quiet tonight," Jess said as she joined me. "Everything alright?"

"I miss him," I told her, fighting back tears. "And there really isn't anything I can look forward to. I don't know when I'll see him again."

Jess pushed her long, straight black hair behind her shoulder before she hugged me. It was a sincere hug, the kind that said "I'm here for you." She was always the most level-headed of my friends, always kind. She pulled back, her eyes bright and glossy from drinking.

"I'm sure it's tough. I can't imagine starting out college tied down like that when you don't even get to see him. You should come hang out with me and Lauren. These guys are eating out of the palm of her hand. They're kind of funny, too. It wouldn't hurt anything if you flirted with them a little, would it?"

I agreed with her and joined them as she suggested. Innocent flirting was all I ever intended to do, but half a dozen beers and a few jello shots later, I found myself alone in a corner with a guy whose name I didn't even catch. He was tall and lanky with an accent that my foggy brain had a hard time understanding. I remember how he stood close as we talked, his whiskey tinged breath falling across my face. I remember when his fingers brushed against my arm, I told myself it was time to walk away.

What I don't remember is who initiated the intense kiss, or how I had become entwined with a total stranger before Lauren intervened, pulling me away.

For many days to follow, I was wrought with a crippling guilt. I knew telling Jason was probably the right thing to do, but I just couldn't make myself do it. I kept picturing him sitting in front of a computer, thousands of miles from home, surrounded by violence, listening to his idiot girlfriend confess that while he was away, fighting for his country, she was off kissing another guy. So I did the next best thing I could think of, and broke up with him instead. I was ashamed, and started to realize that I wasn't good enough for him anyway.

Jess and Lauren didn't return my calls or answer my Facebook messages after that night. Before long I realized they didn't know what to say to me anymore. They were probably even more disappointed than I was that I had cheated on a hero.

SEARCHING THROUGH THE PACKED house, stopping everyone I know to ask if they've seen Kelly, I realize just how totally over this scene I've become. I'm done with the leering guys, the eager girls trying to hook up with them, the mindless conversations, and the rancid stench of vomit in random places. It was kind of fun in the beginning, before I cheated on Jason, but now it's just kind of sad and makes everyone seem desperate to get laid.

I push my way past the sweaty bodies, not even bothering to look up at their faces. Kelly's wearing sparkling flats from my closet, so there's no way I'll miss her feet. Adam's just a step behind me, his spearmint breath on my neck, his warm hand on my back whenever we have to stop for someone in my way. I don't miss the way every girl in the place leers after him.

"Maybe you should try calling her again," Adam suggests.

I nod and find my way to a relatively quiet corner to dial her number, holding my hand against my free ear. It rings half a dozen times before I'm greeted by her obnoxiously spirited message. "Hey, it's Kel! I suck at returning calls, but leave a message if that's your thing!"

Nights like these I feel like her unpaid bounty hunter. "Kel, I'm still here, but you seem to have vanished. Call back or I'm telling your dad all about the sushi buffet thing you did last weekend!"

Adam's baffled expression matches my mood. "You think she'd leave without you?"

I stuff my phone back in my pocket, huffing. I hate to call my friend out like this, but... "It's possible she's in one of the bedrooms."

His eyes cast down as he nods like he completely understands. "Stay here, I'll check." When he steps away, I grab his arm to stop him.

"And what does she look like exactly? Oh, that's right, you don't have a clue. Looks like I'm coming with you."

His eyebrows stitch together. "These guys aren't going to like it when you come knocking on their door. What's her last name? I'll try calling her out."

"Just take me with," I insist, shaking my head. "We'll say we're just looking for a place to work off a little cardio." Excitement stirs in my lady parts with the idea of the two of us together, pretending to want a room. Does it get any hotter?

A spark passes behind his eyes just before he gives in. "Fine, but let me do the talking."

He slips his hand into mine. Every nerve in my hand jumps to life, shooting up my arm and settling in my already unhinged brain. My cold hand feels so small and insubstantial in his. Sexual energy pulsates through me.

Adam stops at the first door in the hallway. "Ready?"

I squeeze his hand and nod, my heart flapping like a crow's wings. Danger signals pang against my skull. It's like I'm walking right into the forbidden garden of flirtation. Then again, Levi probably wouldn't even fight for me if he was witness to my womanly ways. Last time a guy flirted with me right in front of him, he just turned his back, even though I wanted him to pull the guy off me.

Adam twists the knob. Suddenly, we're inside the low-lit room that smells like incense, witnessing a couple making out on the second bed in. They're both so drunk they don't seem to notice us watch as the pant-less girl with frizzy red hair straddles the guy stripped down to his underwear, his chubby hands yanking at her skin-tight shirt until it's over her head and lying on the ground.

They each grunt when their lips come back together, their artificial moans sounding like B-grade porn stars. The girl begins to grind her hips against him like a cowgirl getting aroused by a saddle. His mouth almost totally covers her, leaving a glistening trail of slobber across her cheek. It's like watching a couple of middle school kids trying to imitate something they saw on TV. And failing. Miserably.

Hold on a second. The girl's quite overweight with bright red hair. Definitely not Kelly. We've been continuing to watch the awkward couple for no reason. The guy slides a hand beneath her bra, lifting it.

I push at Adam's chest, ushering him to the safety of the hallway. "I may have forgotten to mention Kelly's a skinny brunette." A *hey, look at me, I'm embarrassed for being such a perv!*

flush burns my cheeks. "Something I probably should've told you before we were forced to witness that debauchery."

A pinch of color rises to his cheeks, too. He clears his throat before turning to look over his shoulder. "Let's try the next one."

Still holding hands, we each take a deep breath of innocent air before slipping into the dark room. Low moans float through the room, met with tiny, breathless screams. I become rooted in place. We just walked in on someone actually having sex. I can even smell it among the stench of pot.

I turn to whisper in Adam's ear. "Let's go." My breath catches in my throat when I realized that I just brushed his ear with my lips.

He squeezes my hand, and we tiptoe back to the door.

"What the fuck?" a deep voice barks.

A small light flips on, revealing a guy twice the size of Adam, fueled with dozens of tattoos and arrant rage, hovering completely naked over a small blonde I know from my psych class. "Were you pervs *watching* us?"

I greet the girl with an awkward wave. "Hey, Shalia."

She yanks the sheet over her body, gaping.

I snuggle into Adam's side, resting my hand against his chest that feels *totally* amazing.

"Sorry, we were just looking for somewhere *private*. You know. To *get. It On*. Kind of like what you were doing just now."

Adam curls his arm around my back, holding me tight. From the bulge pushing against my leg, I wonder if he's forgetting my suggestion is only a cover story. It does nothing to ease my hormonal rage that began when we met.

"*Get the fuck out!*" the tattooed guy yells.

Something sails through the air at us before he springs from the bed. We both hop out of the way, narrowly escaping a size 14 Vans. Adam yanks me back to the hallway, slamming the door behind us. We sprint for the stairway with shouts from naked guy falling behind us. Once we're safely out the front door, we're both breathless and laughing.

I hold my stomach. "Omigod, I just saw my directionless life flash before my eyes."

"I told you it was a bad idea." He tries to sound serious, but his smirk stretches up to his ears. He glances down at our still intertwined hands.

"Can I give you a ride back to your dorm?"

I pull away. "I really should find Kelly. She's infamous for making choices of epic proportions. One time she brought a ferret back to our room. I mean, seriously, have you seen those things? They hide in your shoes. They're just creepy."

"I get it, but you're not going back up there."

It's not a question, and I actually don't even mind that he's telling me what I can and can't do. It just adds to his overall charm. It'd be nice if Levi would show that he cares about my well-being like that every now and then.

"Fine. I'll try texting her again."

Adam paces at my side while I type.

Srsly, u need 2 call. I have your parents on speed dial.

Adam runs a hand through his hair, shifting his weight. "Maybe you and your friend should find some other way to spend your Saturday nights. Guys at these parties are always slipping stuff into girls' drinks. Seriously. You have no idea."

I barely have my phone back in my pocket before it buzzes. Relieved, I whip it out. But the message isn't from Kelly. It's from Levi.

Miss u babe. ***Want 2 FaceTime*?** **Here alone thinking of what I want to do 2 u.**

"What's wrong?" Adam asks.

I twist at one of my curls, a nervous habit I developed after I grew my hair out to the middle of my back. "Maybe we should go back to the dorms. Kelly could've found her way home. She could be so passed out she can't hear her phone. Besides, I don't want to hang around this house of fun any longer than we have to."

"Okay. My car's down a block." Adam rests his hand on my lower back again, steering me to a two-door car that looks pretty sleek in the moonlight. As we pull away from the curb, I text what I get the feeling will probably be the first of many lies to Levi.

Kel's sleeping. Talk tomorrow.

MY DORM HALL, A LARGE BRICK BUILDING four stories high on the west side of campus that houses both guys and girls, is covered in darkness, save for a few who must be cramming in homework. It's pretty typical this late on a Saturday to see lights out as everyone is either at a party, working, or in bed. All of campus looks cold and barren from a recent rainfall—the safety lights over the sidewalks are the only sign of life. While I've always regretted staying local instead of going to a bigger city, I have to admit there's something about being in my hometown that gives me a touch of comfort. My senior year we went to a few parties on campus, so I vaguely knew my way around.

Adam stares at the building, drumming his fingers against the steering wheel. "Want me to wait, in case she's not in there?"

"It's late," I say, conferring with my phone to see it's well after midnight. "If she isn't here, I guess she'll have to find her own way back."

I feel like a failure as her friend. If I had been in the right state of mind, I would've known better than to let her wander off by herself in the first place. It certainly isn't the first time this kind of thing has happened, and I know it won't be the last. I've done everything short of threatening to get her one of those kid leashes.

"Okay." Adam says, his voice tinged with disappointment.

Quite frankly, I don't want him to leave either. I can't remember the last time I enjoyed talking with someone this much. But what other options do we have? He can't come in the dorms, and I'm not going to sit out in this car with him all night.

"You didn't tell me what you majored in before you dropped out," I say, looking for a way to stall the inevitable goodbye.

"Give it your best guess."

"Theatre arts?" I ask with a smirk.

Adam snickers quietly under his breath. "Philosophy. At one time I considered being a lawyer, but only because my dad was pushing it. It wasn't for me. It's totally my little brother's kind of thing." He rubs at his neck with a shy grin. "I'm not really sure what I'm cut out for. I'm still trying to figure it out."

"Yeah, you don't seem the lawyerly type," I tease. "I would've put my money on acting."

"You wouldn't be totally off base. I could get behind the whole production of movies and television thing. My uncle directed a sitcom back in the 90s. It only ran one season before it was canceled and didn't pay the best, but he loved his job. I just have a hard time wrapping my mind around the idea of reporting to the same place every single day. I guess I need to look into something that has a bit more flexibility."

"You never know until you try, right?" A moment of silence follows. I shift around in my seat. "How about I give you my number, you know, just in case you ever decide you want more help on that list of yours."

His beautiful eyes glow in the dashboard light. "Is that the only reason I can call you?"

"No, unless you're secretly some kind of stalker."

With a deep chuckle, he pulls his iPhone from his pocket and hits the screen a few times before handing it to me. "Good. I was hoping we could hang out some time."

Our fingers are electrified when they touch. There's something happening between us whether I want to admit it or not. My throat pinches. "I—"

"Enough with the *seeing someone* thing," he huffs, looking both pained and annoyed. "I just want to hang out. Guys and girls *can* be friends."

"I was going to say I have to work tomorrow until five, and I have a few assignments I need to work on." I giggle, typing my number in before handing his phone back. Our eyes catch. "But I'd love to *hang out* for a little bit after work if that's cool with you."

I don't know where this offer to meet up came from. It's like there's a pull between us, and I can't pretend it doesn't exist. Since I don't really believe in all that soulmate crap, *especially* with Levi, there can't be any harm in exploring my options.

A grin slowly makes its way across his face. "In that case, can I take you out for pizza? Say around five? I'll pick you up here."

"Hmmm. Sounds suspiciously like a *date*."

"It's *pizza*, Jewels." He glances at my number before tossing his phone on the dashboard. "I had fun tonight."

"Me too," I say, reaching for the door handle. "Thanks for the ride."

His warm smile makes me flush. "I'll see you soon."

From the sidewalk I watch his car take off down the road. I'm completely blindsided by this stranger who just waltzed into my life. Everything about him will stick with me for a long time: his deep voice, his steel gray eyes and the way they seem to bore right through me, the way I felt exhilarated just sitting next to him. For longer than I care to admit, I've been bored by my mundane existence, numbing it with alcohol or drowning it out with movies on the couch in a ratty t-shirt and yoga pants. Maybe it's just another sign that I shouldn't be with Levi. If he was good for me, wouldn't that void have been filled?

Tonight it was like I woke up long enough to see the proverbial light at the end of the tunnel. I finally feel *alive* again.

AFTER A RESTLESS NIGHT, I WAKE TO the sound of voices shouting in the hallway. The sun shines brightly through the window overlooking Kelly's empty bed. Our room is small, like the other doubles in the hall, but always orderly. Pictures of our adventures the past two years line a metal wire strung on the wall running along our two miniature sized desks that are hardly ever used for anything other than folded laundry. When we're working on homework, we either take our laptops to our twin cots, or huddle on the couch at the end of my bed.

The white brick walls make for a sterile atmosphere, so we counter it with my collection of concert posters hung in cheap plastic frames of assorted colors. Kelly always has some kind of scent burning in the electric candle warmer, this week's a combination of coconut and spring in anticipation of the upcoming summer break.

Freshman year was a different story. I was on a different floor where I roomed with one of the strangest people I had ever met. Sarah had shifty eyes and showed very little emotion. I'm pretty sure she didn't have any friends as she was always around when not in classes. She wouldn't let me put anything on the walls, or play music while she was studying. Kelly and I made it our mission to find ways to irritate Sarah so that she would retreat to the library, giving us free range to crank our favorite tunes and become the place where all our hall-mates wanted to hang out. After I hit the wall of depression, however, Sarah eventually resumed studying in our silent room. Kelly still came around, but it wasn't the same.

I bolt upright, glad I didn't drink enough the night before to have the usual brutal hangover. Finding Kelly will require a clear head. I could start at the party house, but what if that big guy who kicked us out of his room recognizes me? Would Adam come along if I asked? He has wheels, which would be a major bonus if Kelly's too hung over for the long walk back, or if I need to get away from that big guy in a hurry.

I've been up all of two minutes and I'm already thinking of Adam. It's not just that he's incredibly good looking, but there was an invisible connection drawing me to him that *felt* so right. I could've talked to him all night long if it hadn't been for my conscience dragging me down. While agreeing to meet him again may have been a mistake, I can hardly wait for the chance to talk to him again.

Meeting Levi was a completely different experience. There was so much alcohol involved that I only remember bits and pieces of the night. He was hot, I was horny. What we probably both thought was going to be a one night stand suddenly became me wanting more of the great sex he delivered. It filled the empty void. The next time we got together it was awkward because we were virtual strangers who had barely said more than a few sentences to each other. We still don't get into deep conversations beyond sex.

I untangle my sweaty limbs from the bed sheets and grab my phone before springing to my feet. The mirror next to the closet shows dark circles underneath my normally bright blue eyes. Without eyeliner and mascara, they seem deceivingly innocent, reflecting confusion and regret. My blond hair sits in a rat's nest above my head where I must've pushed on my pillow in the night. Even my skin looks a pasty white.

Holy hell. I look one step away from death. I fell asleep shortly after Adam brought me back, and the usual nightmares involving Jason followed. Sometimes the dreams will start out bittersweet, a replay of prom, or homecoming, or one of a thousand other things Jason and I did in our happier days. Sometimes, if I'm lucky, the dreams play out as if Jason and I got married and had a gaggle of kids while living in a suburb.

But I can always count on the dreams turning dark and terrifying. Too many times

Jason will appear distorted, yelling at me in a voice that doesn't sound human. I can never understand the words he's saying.

For a time I was on sleeping pills that would quiet the dreams, but they really messed me up in the mornings, making me too groggy for early classes, so I convinced my doctor I was past needing them. Only I wasn't, and the nightmares resumed. My mental health has waged a delicate battle this past year between what I can handle, and what makes me appear sane. If it weren't for the pills, I doubt I'd be functioning in a way that's acceptable to my parents.

Then again, if it weren't for the pills, maybe I'd be able to cry again. Maybe I'd be able to feel some kind of emotion instead of this dull static that I mask with humor and feigned happiness.

Sometimes I hardly recognize myself anymore. My mom tells me that when I was a baby and toddler, people always stopped her because I had the biggest smile they had ever seen on a child. In elementary and middle school, I was always getting into trouble because I was unable to be quiet or sit still. I was voted "most likely to go places" in high school because I was always so full of energy and positive vibes. When I first signed up for college, I was determined to find a career filled with the most amount of interaction because I loved being around people.

I'm still studying my disheveled reflection in the mirror when there's a knock at the door. Hopeful that Kelly forgot her key again, I bound toward the door and swing it open.

Levi's smoldering gaze waits for me on the other side.

"Hey, gorgeous. Miss me?"

#

MEET LEVI TRAVIS.

Twenty-five, never been married, estranged father of one toddler. Thin leather coat, black button down, dark jeans, black boots. Dirty blond hair hanging loosely around his chiseled jaw in slight waves from his helmet. Intense brown eyes that pierce right through you, straight nose, full lips. He oozes sex appeal. No, *seriously*. I have this theory that he bathes in pheromones.

Sometimes it feels more like a physical thing between us. It's not like we've ever sent each other love notes or read sonnets, and he's never called me his girlfriend. And the two of us really don't have anything in common other than sex. There are times when I'm hanging with him and his buddies that I even wonder if my role in the "relationship" is to look pretty so he can brag.

For the record, bikers have never really been "my type," but somehow I fell hard and fast for Levi. Maybe it was the "older" guy thing, or maybe it was because he's just so damn good looking. Or it could've been the three shots of Patrón that gave me the courage to approach him in the first place.

While anyone who watches *Sons of Anarchy* would melt in his presence, my heart does a series of flips for different reasons. Why in the hell is he here?

"It's after *noon,* Jewels. Did you just wake up?" When I don't move, he tips his head back, irritated. "So you going to let me in, or what?"

I finally snap from my stupor and rise to my tiptoes to give him a quick peck on the lips before opening the door all the way. "Yeah, sorry! What are you doing here?"

He breezes past me, slipping out of his jacket before flopping down on my bed with a shallow laugh. "I can leave if you want." Throwing his jacket on the couch, he gives me an annoyed stare.

I roll my eyes, sitting on the edge of the bed at his side. "Shit, Levi, you surprised me is all. Give me a minute. I just got out of bed."

"Well, get your ass back *in*."

He grabs my arm, yanking me down on my back next to him, making it clear he's here for a booty call. Flipping over to linger above me, he brushes his dry, wind-burned lips over mine repeatedly, with urgency. His hands trail up underneath my night shirt, immediately cupping my breasts, rubbing rough circles around my nipples with his thumbs until they're hard. His tongue darts around in my mouth, tasting like old copper and Mountain Dew. I try to kiss him back, but my heart isn't in it.

Before today I would totally be into him at times like this. He's a skilled lover, making the sex pretty hot, even though I've never had an orgasm with him. Or *any* guy. Still, my body would pang in a delightful way, and I'd help him strip off his jeans so we could get down to business. Now, however, his wiry facial hair is annoying, his favorite cheap cologne mixed with the lingering scent of leather suffocating. Amid his low moans, I feel him growing hard against my leg. He's like an animal in heat, ready to ram anything that moves.

All at once I feel as if I'll suffocate with him in my already small dorm room. I don't want him here. He doesn't fit into my life.

Wait, where is this coming from? Is it just because of Adam?

Just as Levi's calloused fingers slip into my underwear and between my legs, I push him away, turning my head. "Dude, you need to shave."

He rolls to his side, resting his hand against his head, giving me a full view of the complex mural of tattoos spiraling up his forearm. He rubs at his jaw, frowning. "Rough night last night? You look like shit."

"Thanks," I snap angrily.

"Why do you act like you don't want me here?"

"I work in a couple of hours. You should've called."

"It's a nice day." He flashes the mega-watt smile that reeled me in so many months ago. "I figured I'd take the bike out. I don't have to stay long."

"Just long enough for a quickie?" I ask, my eyebrows shooting up.

His brown eyes cloud over as he sits, reaching for his jacket. "Jesus, Jewels. You make it sound so cheap. What's up your ass?"

I bring my fingers up to my temples, rubbing methodically. Am I really going to stop seeing Levi because I spent a couple hours with a guy I thought was hot and incredibly interesting? Adam said something about guys and girls just being friends. What if I'm reading too much into whatever it was that happened between us?

"It's just...I didn't get much sleep last night," I say, stepping in front of him. "I'm sorry. You were sweet enough to come see me, and I'm being a total bitch."

He gently pulls me down to straddle his lap, and brushes my cheek with his thumb. "Baby, I've missed you."

His other hand slides up and down my thigh. Hunger flashes in his eyes, and he cranes his neck to kiss me. The familiarity of his mouth and warmness of his tongue distract me for a moment. I clutch at his face and lean into him, humming softly into his mouth when his hand climbs further up my thigh. Turning me onto my back, he pins me to the bed with his knee between my legs and devours my mouth like it's some kind of all you can eat buffet. His impatient hands return to my breasts, none too gentle.

My thoughts randomly return to Adam, the sweet way he touched my back, how he opened the door, the sexy sparkle in his eyes when I made him laugh, the amazing way his hand felt around mine. There are so many other things I want to discover about him—how his lips feel, the way he tastes...I imagine he'd be a gentle lover.

It occurs to me I'm fantasizing of another guy while my lips are attached to Levi's. I quickly shove him away.

Levi gapes down on me like I punched him. "What the *fuck*?"

"I think I'm going to be sick," I say, bolting from the bed and flying out the room.

It probably qualifies as a white lie, because it's partially true. My insides are a mess. I can't stop thinking about Adam, and I really don't want to.

I run to the row of sinks in the community bathroom and splash my face with cold water. As I'm patting my face dry with a paper towel, a couple of my hall-mates greet me with a "hey" before I'm all alone.

Swishing a handful of water through my mouth, I stare into the cracked mirror, taking a hard look at myself. What *am* I doing with Levi? My mom's voice enters my head, ready to lecture on what I've done wrong this time. *You wanted this thing with Levi. You're the one who approached him that night.*

I spit the mouthful of water at the mirror. "Get your shit together," I tell my reflection, wrinkling my nose.

As I approach my room, a bout of high laughter seeps out. I walk in to find Kelly standing across from Levi, wearing the same low cut blouse and leggings from the night before. She looks ten times better than I do, her dark brown hair strategically pulled back into a sloppy bun, her makeup perfectly applied on her sharp cheek bones and pouty lips. It's rather infuriating how she doesn't look even the slightest bit hung over when I know she was doing jello shots half the night. And who *knows* where she slept.

This is my best friend.

We met the first day of Spanish class freshman year. When our professor said we were only allowed to speak to each other in Spanish, Kelly turned to me and asked if I wanted to drink tequila in the bathroom. It was supposed to be a joke, but I totally got her humor. She turned out to be borderline genius, and became my tutor for nearly any class I struggled in.

We became inseparable almost immediately. She was always around, driving my assigned invert of a roommate insane. Kelly may, at times, be a bit wild, and I can't always count on her to be there—like when she disappears from parties—but she was there to pick up the pieces after the depression nearly crippled me, when none of my "friends" from high school stepped up. She spent countless hours at my side when I didn't want to talk, brought me food when I didn't care if I ate. It would've been easy to completely give up on everything if she hadn't been there.

Her big brown eyes flash wide when I clear my throat. "Jewels, holy shit! What *happened* to you?"

I scoff. "I held up a bakery downtown. Didn't you see it in the news?" When Kelly puts on her pouty face, I sigh. "I don't know for sure. I hardly drank anything last night. Maybe that seafood sub I had for lunch was bad," I say, not wanting her to think I'm contagious. Because unless she's seeing someone who she's thinking of breaking it off with, she won't.

"You're *puking* sick?" Levi asks, backing away like I just told him I have the Ebola virus. "I have to man the shop by myself this week."

"You know, I'm not really sure. I guess it could be the stomach flu." For an added dramatic effect, I even touch my forehead. "I do feel a bit flushed. There's something really nasty going around campus. Kids are dropping like flies."

"Why didn't you say something earlier?" It's almost comical how fast Levi skitters to the door. "Babe, I want to hang out, but I can't afford to close the shop for even a day. You know how it is."

"Don't worry, I *totally* understand."

After a quick glance he's out the door, no goodbye or kisses. He wouldn't want to risk the chance of catching my *disease*.

"*Bye*," Kelly sings after the closed door. "I take it he spent the night?"

I reel on her, reminding myself that literally strangling someone is considered *assault*. "Where in the *hell* did you go last night? We looked all over for you!"

In typical Kelly style, she rolls her eyes, snorting. "Would you relax? I lost my phone right after I sent you that last text. I couldn't find you so I went over to Krista Slaytor's place for an after-party, figuring you'd end up there. I passed out on her floor. And you said *we*. Are you saying Levi *did* come here last night, or do you have a little friend in your pocket?"

"Damn it, Kel!" I yell in her face. "One of these times you're going to hook up with the wrong guy and end up behind some dumpster! If for some *idiotic* reason I ever agree to hit a party with you again, I'm not letting you out of my sight! You're like a freaking toddler!"

"Alright, alright!" she concedes, dropping her shoulders. "I'm sorry. Now, will you tell me what just happened between you and loverboy? I don't believe that you were actually throwing up. I've only ever seen you do that when hung over, and I know you weren't *that* drunk last night."

Laughing a hallow sound, I saunter over to my bed. "For all you know, I was pole dancing all night."

Kelly reaches for our little fridge with her long arm, pulling out a bottle of water. "The old Jewels would've drunk everyone else under the table, but the new and yet-to-be-determined, *improved* Jewels is worried she'll get too drunk and cheat on her steady fuck buddy."

My face burns hot. Even though I was on the sober side, Levi was constantly on my mind while I was flirting with Adam. And now I've done everything I can to turn him down and push him away. My head's a mess.

"Is that it?" Kelly asks with wide eyes. "Did you cheat on him last night? I won't judge. Seriously. It's not like you two are an official thing anyway." She crosses the room to sit on the mattress beside me, taking a long pull of water while still watching me like I'm one of her stupid reality shows.

"No, *god*." I steal the water from her for a swig. "It wasn't like that."

She pulls in a sharp breath. "Wasn't like *what*? What happened? *Spill*."

My lips grow tight. Kelly's the best friend I've had in a long time. Yet somehow the thought of telling her about Adam makes it feel like I'm validating the fact that I actually see myself having a *relationship* with the guy, and that shit is forbidden as long as I'm with Levi. I made the mistake of cheating on someone once before, and I'm still dealing with the consequences.

"It was nothing." I look down at my hands, folded in my lap. "I met someone at the party. We're going out for pizza tonight." I tell her all the details of my night with Adam, except for the part where we watched other couples getting it on because in hindsight it seems incredibly voyeuristic.

"Hole. E. *Shit*!" she squeals, jumping to her feet and doing her crazy little excited dance. "You're totally going to end up with someone your own age who doesn't already have a kid with someone else, and who doesn't just use you for sex because you're hot!"

"Feel free to tell me how you *really* feel about Levi."

She reaches down to slap my leg. "Like you don't already know?"

"I just *met* a guy. Doesn't mean it's time to start a wedding board on Pinterest."

"Think about this, Jewels. You and Levi have been going out for *months*, and he's made it crystal clear that he's never going to get serious with you." She grabs me by my shoulders. "Would you stop and look at yourself? You're young, and funny, and sweet, and drop dead gorgeous. There's no reason you need to stay with Levi. I mean, I get it. He's incredibly hot, and you say the sex is great, but is it really worth it?"

"Are my parents funding this conversation?"

She laughs joyously, stopping to lay a wet kiss on my cheek. "Damn it, I love you, but sometimes you're pretty dense. If you're attracted to another guy, give it a chance, woman! No one is saying you have to stop seeing Levi just because you're going to meet with this guy. Besides, you've been all mopey and shit for way too long. And look at you now, you're actually excited about something!"

"It's possible I'm just really attracted to this Adam guy, and the feelings aren't' mutual. Maybe he's looking for a friend."

"Whatever helps you sleep at night." She pats my back real condescendingly-like. "Wait, is that why you look like Lady Gaga? Did you have another nightmare?"

A knot lodges in my throat. I nod.

"Oh, hon." Her arms wrap around me. Underneath a ton of cheap perfume, I can smell the pungent odor of vodka seeping from her pores. "Maybe you should go back on the sleeping pills."

"No way. And do *not* tell my mom I'm still having them next time she stops by," I threaten, pulling away from her. "She'll just make me go back to that shrink."

Smiling devilishly, she says, "If you let me do your hair for this date, I won't say a word."

I raise my eyebrows. "This is what our friendship has come to? Blackmail?" I throw my hands in the air and stand. "And here I considered asking you to be one of my bridesmaids."

"See? You're totally back to your old self. Hop in the shower and let Momma Kelly fix you up. This Adam guy is going to see you for the first time by the light of day. You don't want him to think you're a vampire."

I gather my shower supplies in my arms. "You know *exactly* what to say to make a girl feel better."

She slaps me on the ass, making me squawk. "Just *go* already. We've got major work to do. Your eyebrows are a mess and I think I see the start of a zit under your chin. It's going to take nothing short of sacrificing a virgin to save you."

"At least we know your life won't be at risk!" I yell over my shoulder.

MY CO-WORKERS THROW ME FUNNY glances during my shift at the library. Kelly went a little overboard on the shimmering eyeshadow and revealing outfit. When she left our room, I grabbed a bright chevron scarf to wear over her low-cut shirt. I feel more at home in one of my favorite concert t-shirts, a pair of worn jeans, and my Vans. At least I was able to talk her into braiding my hair off to the side so I feel somewhat normal.

It's nearly five when my gut goes wild. I have no idea how much Adam had to drink when we met. Maybe he's actually one of those who can be loaded and hide it really well. Maybe he'll change his mind and decide he's not interested in seeing me again.

My supervisor, Felicia, watches me from behind the front desk as I sort through returned books. She rests her chin on her hand, pointing a pencil my way. "You're awfully chipper for once, and you're dressed like one of those preppy assholes. Should I be researching signs of alien abductions?"

"Can't a girl just be filled with unbridled bliss by her thankless job?"

"No. Either you're fearful that you're going to turn into a fairy with all that junk on your eyes, or you're just incredibly eager for *something*." She lowers her dark framed glasses to the bridge of her crooked nose like an old librarian, even though she's just a year older than me. "Which is it?"

"I'm just *meeting* someone," I say, feeling a wide grin creep across my lips. "It's no big deal." I grab a tissue from the counter and blot lightly at my eyes, hoping to lessen the look without completely ruining it. Kelly's skilled at using makeup, but sometimes she likes a little too much flash for anything that doesn't involve a Broadway production.

"No big deal," Felicia repeats, snorting. "I wish someone would get that excited about meeting with *me*. You should smile like that more often. It makes you *really* hot."

"You know I don't swing that way. Women are too complicated."

"Maybe you don't swing my way, but I'm guessing that guy watching you from the reading section will follow whichever way it is you're going." Pushing her glasses back up to her face, she continues typing, her straight brown hair blocking what I'm sure is a smart-assed grin. "You should go over and tell him about our 'no lewd glances at hot librarians' rule."

I spin around to the area designated for casual reading. Adam's gray eyes light up when our gazes meet and his dimples slowly deepen. Meeting his smile, my spirits soar. He's just as gorgeous as I remember, and just as easy-going.

"Hole. E. Shit," I whisper without moving my lips.

Felicia grumbles something about ditzy blondes under her breath.

I lower the books from my arms to the portable cart and calmly cross over to where he sits at a table by himself, wearing loose cargo pants and a white button down with thin gray stripes that make his eyes pop even more. He's freshly shaven, and even smells like expensive aftershave.

Dear Lord. By the light of day, he's even more amazing.

"So you've quit school, yet here you are in the campus library." I feel like my cheeks will split in half from smiling so broadly. "Can't seem to quiet your inner geek?"

Leaning back in the chair until the front feet are off the ground, he sets a book on the table in front of him. My stomach flutters excitedly when I realize there's a bookmark in the new Dean Koontz novel, like it's something he's actually reading. I've never really known a guy who reads for *fun*. The types of guys I've dated are more into ESPN and Hooters.

Like he really needed another thing to make him even hotter.

"Couldn't help myself," he says with a maddening grin. "I wanted to see you in your element." He motions to my hair. "The braid totally completes the whole librarian image."

Lightly patting my hair, I giggle. "It's not too Katniss Everdeen?"

"Not at all." He sets the chair legs back down and rests a hand under his chin, studying me closely. After checking me out from head to toe, he meets my gaze, smirking. "You look incredible."

A lump rises in my throat with his compliment. I want to tell him this isn't what I would normally wear, but I take the compliment as is. "And you could pass for someone with an invigorating future."

His eyes flicker to the dotted ceiling. "If only my parents could see me now." Heavy sarcasm weighs in his words like they wouldn't approve of him, no matter what he did. Are they disappointed that he quit school? It's just one of the many things I'm dying to know about him.

I glance at the clock, willing it to speed ahead. "You're early. And you said you were picking me up at my *dorm*."

"Afraid to duck out a few minutes early and see what it's like to live life on the edge?"

I can't remember the last time I smiled as much as I have in the past twelve hours. *Especially* not with Levi. A twinge of guilt twists in my stomach when I realize just how often I've been comparing the two guys since I met Adam. It's not fair to either one of them. My heart isn't in this relationship with Levi, so why drag it out any longer?

"Just let me do the responsible thing and check out with my supervisor."

I barely hear Adam say something in response as I all but stumble away. I have to get a grip if I'm going to make it through this date. There's no way I can enjoy Adam's company with thoughts of Levi in the mix.

"I'll be right back," I tell Felicia as I pass her desk.

I break into the quiet hallway, gulping in deep breaths, talking myself through what I'm about to do. My hand shakes as I pull my phone from my back pocket. I'm about to lose my nerve and end the call when Levi answers among the sounds of a rowdy bar.

"Hey, babe, what's up?"

It's so typical that he doesn't even ask how I'm feeling. I lick my lips, taking a moment to gather my courage. "Hey, Lee. I didn't want to do this over the phone, but there's something I need to tell you." Part of me feels heartless for not doing this earlier when we were face to face. But then I remember how he acted like a horny dog, and I'm over it. "I wanted to tell you this earlier, but then Kel showed up, and...I think we should spend some time apart. Maybe see other people."

"Where'd this come from?" He sighs in his irritated way. "I guess if that's what you really want...*whatever*."

His words are an unexpected jab. I've heard him get more upset about backordered motorcycle parts. He doesn't even care, so why should I? I clutch my phone tightly, anger washing over me. "What I want is for you to show a little goddamn emotion every now and then. Act like you give a shit."

I take a deep, calming breath. I'm met with silence, as expected. We haven't engaged in any heart-to-heart revelations in the short time we've been together, and I probably blew him away with my unexpected outburst.

"What's with all the drama?" he finally asks. "I already told you I'm not looking for anything serious. I thought the sex was good enough."

"Goodbye, Levi." I end the call, slipping my phone back into my pocket.

I'm not upset about breaking it off with someone who wasn't good for me. Levi was nothing more than an anchor, considering there wasn't an emotional bond between us. I *know* I did the right thing. Instead of congratulating myself, however, there's a vast emptiness where I should be feeling relief. What if I've become unable to feel anything for anyone? What if this numbness never goes away?

When I walk back through the doors of the library to where Adam waits, I have all I can do not to break down.

Four

IN THE LIGHT OF DAY I DISCOVER ADAM'S wheels are more than just a "sleek" car. It's actually a brand new Dodge Challenger painted a smoky gray with a sporty black stripe down the center. Either Adam's spoiled or he saved up a lot of dough for this beauty. I pat the dashboard, smirking. "Sweet ride for a homeless guy."

"This?" He smirks over at me. "It's just a commuter. The Bentley stays in the five-stall garage during the week."

I let out a humorless laugh, not sure if I'm supposed to take him seriously or not, and still unable to shake the uneasy feeling I've had since telling Levi we're through.

Downtown is fairly quiet as usual on a Sunday evening, except for the restaurants just beginning to fill. Adam parks in front of a meter before turning to me, his eyebrows raised. "Everything good?"

"Damn dewy decimal system had me perplexed at work today."

"Sorry," he tells me in a clear display of sympathy.

I stare at him, a warmth tingling through me. I was expecting him to make some kind of joke about the stress of working at the library, or even to tell me it was time to get over it. Could he possibly be any nicer?

"I ordered Kate's for carryout," he says, tilting his head to the building beside us. "I ordered half cheese, half pepperoni. I figured it's a relatively safe topping if you're not a vegetarian."

"Pepperoni's my favorite," I admit. "We're eating in the car? Are you afraid to be seen with me in public?"

"I thought maybe we'd go hang out by the bluffs. Are you okay with that?"

I nod, unable to remember the last time I did anything outside other than run with Kelly early mornings. I've been so caught up in studying and work that I haven't had much of a life. The thought of going somewhere outdoors just to hang is kind of nice. The sun's still a few hours from setting, and everything's finally green after the unusually long, harsh winter.

He turns the car off. "Sit tight, I'll be right back." When he climbs out of the car onto the sidewalk, I can't help but check out his backside. Some guys have virtually no hind end, but Adam's is perfectly firm, matching the rest of his nicely built frame.

My phone buzzes in my purse, as if busting me for being so shallow. Flustered, I pull it out to see a text from Kelly.

How's the non-date?

So far so good. And btw I broke it off with Levi.

Hardly a second passes after I hit send that Kelly sends another text.

WTF????? CALL ME ASAP!

Adam bursts through the restaurant's door, a square box in hand. I quickly text, *GOTTA RUN!* before jamming my phone back in my purse. A second later I hear the buzz of another text, but ignore it, instead reaching across the driver's seat to open Adam's door.

The heavenly aroma of marinara sauce and cheese follow him inside.

As he pulls back onto Main Street, I glance at the radio. "Mind if I turn on some music?"

His dimples materialize. "Go for it."

I fumble with the dial until finding my favorite rock station. I turn it up a little more when I realize it's Queens of the Stone Age, one of the many awesome bands I had a chance to see live at Lollapalooza.

Adam glances between me and the road. "What *is* this? Your kind of music?"

Shrugging, I say, "Depends on what kind of mood I'm in."

"Are you in the mood to smash something?" He watches me carefully with a growing smirk as Josh Homme shouts through the speakers.

"Just give it a chance," I plead, giggling. "Let yourself listen without judgment. These guys are pretty stellar. The lead singer was in a band with Dave Grohl from the Foo Fighters...you know, the drummer from Nirvana. You should see Josh play the guitar and piano. The guy was in a band when he was *twelve.* He's collaborated with dozens of bands. He's even produced some records. He's crazy talented."

Adam's eyes twinkle as he studies me, their intensity making my hormones go wild. I don't think he has a clue what I'm talking about, but he seems fairly amused. "You're *really* into music, huh?"

"Yeah, I am," I say proudly, lifting my chin. "And I'm totally going to make you a playlist. One to go along with your other list. It's time to culture you on good music. Now shush it, and listen carefully to these guys. Your lesson starts now."

I crank the volume so it's just one decimal below shattering our ear drums. Adam's eyes grow wide, but his lips curl at the edges when he sees me bouncing around to the beat. After the second time through the chorus, Adam taps his thumb against the steering wheel. I can't stop myself from beaming at him.

ADAM MOTIONS FOR ME TO JOIN HIM from the edge of the bluff. "C'mon."

A family with two young children sits at a picnic table a few feet away. Two attractive high schoolers with matching knit beanie hats stand near the edge, clinging to each other like they couldn't breathe if they were to part.

From the protection of the parking lot's edge, the view of the Mississippi River stretched out in front of downtown La Crosse is breathtaking. The water's a murky shade of deep blue, and the bright greenery against the clear sky makes me wish I had my little Canon along, even though we're a good hundred feet in the air.

Holding on to the hood of the Challenger, I feel my heart racing. "I'm good right here. I can still see everything just fine."

His expression falls. He curses under his breath as he starts toward me. "Shit. I forgot you're afraid of heights. That was an asshole move to bring you up here."

"Pulling out the asshole card is a bit harsh," I say, laughing brightly. "I *did* tell you I went zip-lining."

Setting the pizza bag down in front of the car, he pulls the blanket he grabbed from the trunk out from underneath his arm. The fleece blanket is worn thin, the ends tied together with knots, the pattern of dinosaurs. It's quite obviously a treasure from when he was a little boy. I cover my mouth so he won't see me grinning.

Adam catches my expression. "Yeah, I know. It's all I have."

"I think it's sweet that you kept it all these years," I insist, trying not to laugh. "Really."

When he looks down to straighten the blanket on the ground, his cheeks grow red. He sits with his legs crossed and opens a paper bag filled with plastic silverware and paper plates. I sit across from him, most of the view safely obscured behind me.

"Would you rather go somewhere else?" Adam asks, handing me a plate filled with gooey goodness. He plucks bottled water from the paper bag and hands it to me.

"Thanks. I'm fine, I swear." My stomach growls eagerly, so I waste no time in taking my first bite. "Omigod, this stuff is *amazing*. It's like there's a little Mariachi band playing on my taste buds."

Adam chuckles, watching me thoughtfully with one of his knee-weakening grins. I'm glad when the little kids from the picnic table begin running around us, screaming, because this is feeling way too much like a date, and I'm still feeling pretty raw from my unplanned breakup with Levi.

Adam watches the little boys, laughing, even reaching out to play with them a little when they dare to get close. After finishing his first piece he offers me another, even though I'm only halfway done. We both finish our second pieces, then begin dumping everything back into the empty paper bag.

Wiping his hands on a napkin, he reaches into his pocket. "I brought you something."

He hands me a piece of folded up notebook paper. I wipe my hands before taking it from him, and laugh. "Oooh, are we going to play m.a.s.h.?" But I unfold it to see "*Adam's List*" written in pencil with the neatest handwriting I've ever seen from a guy. Underneath he's written:

1. fly in an airplane
2. watch a concert from the front row but avoid the mosh pit
3. catch a jazz band in New Orleans
4. zip-line and other life threatening things in Arizona
5. paddle board in Hawaii and save turtles

"You act like you're taking this seriously," I say, looking up at him. When he nods, my mouth hangs open. "I thought we were just goofing around. You *can't* be serious. You're really going to *do* these things? No bullshit?"

He flashes me one of those amazing smiles that I'm sure could cure all diseases if properly channeled. "I've been thinking about what you said at the party, and decided it could be fun. I could turn my free time into something productive and join the Peace Corps or go on some kind of mission trip, but those things take too much time to set up." He wraps his arms around his knees, looking past me to the

Mississippi in the distance. "If I'm going to do something, I have to do it *now*. You know, while I'm unattached to any real responsibilities."

"Wow," I say quietly, glancing back down at the list. "It's definitely not my business, but are you planning on washing windshields along the way? Flying to Hawaii isn't exactly cheap."

He hums a quiet laugh under his breath, his gaze swinging back to catch mine. "Ever heard of Ausgez beer? My grandfather was the founder. Money isn't a problem."

"That explains the car," I say, trying to imagine just how wealthy his family must be. Everyone's heard of Ausgez beer. I stare at him, my eyes narrowed. "You haven't told me anything about yourself. Do you have any brothers or sisters?"

"One younger brother. You?"

I feign surprise. "You mean I don't scream *only child*? Tell me more about this brother."

"Erik is...*Erik*. He's the golden child in the family, and he knows it. I do everything I can to avoid being in the same room with him."

"Sounds charming. How old is he?"

"Nineteen." He rubs the back of his neck while scowling at the ground, signaling that there won't be any more talk of his brother. "What side of town do your parents live?"

"Would you quit? I'm trying to get to know *you*, but you keep throwing it back on me. You already know what my parents do, and that I travel a lot. I want to know more about *you*. Where did *you* grow up? Tell me more about your childhood."

"I was raised in Milwaukee. My parents still live there. It's like I said, I lived a pretty sheltered life. I spent a lot of time in my room, to myself, usually with a stack of Legos."

I recline back on my arms, letting the remaining sun soak into me. In another month it'll be time to break out my bikini, and work on a real tan. "You'd think with all that money your parents would've taken you on vacations."

"They were always busy. My life story is pretty boring." He raises one of his eyebrows. "I brought that list because I was hoping you'd help me add to it."

"You're *seriously* planning to do whatever I suggest? Like, you're literally going to buy a plane ticket and just take off? Are you certifiable by chance?"

He chuckles in the deep, rolling sound I've decided I adore. "Within reason. I'm not going to climb Mount Kilimanjaro or anything that extreme. You've been to a lot of places. I'm curious where you'd tell someone like me who hasn't been outside of the state to visit. I have no idea where to start."

For the smallest second I'm extremely jealous. If I had that kind of time and money, I probably wouldn't hesitate executing my own bucket list. Still. Who *does* this kind of thing? What if he's actually a complete nut job?

"Wow, this is a lot of pressure," I tease, playing with the tip of my braid as I think.

A list of my favorite family trips rolls through my head. Ever since I was little, I've been the type who appreciates a trip anywhere. Anything outside of Wisconsin feels like an adventure. But my favorite trip of all-time was with my parents the summer right after I graduated high school, when things weren't so complicated.

"What about New York? Everything in that city is so iconic. You wouldn't *believe* all the buildings in Manhattan. You can walk for hours without leaving the city. It makes Milwaukee look like a skating rink. When they say that the city never sleeps, they're not being facetious. There's literally something fun to do any time of the night. There was this little bodega that we would visit every night before checking into our hotel, they had the most amazing pastries..." When I realize I'm babbling and he's watching me closely, I blush. "I mean, it's cool, if you like that kind of thing."

He licks his lips and nods. I swear he's taunting me to kiss him.

"Maybe. It sounds like a pretty big place."

"Well, New York would probably have to have a list all on its own. For sure the nine eleven memorial. The Brooklyn Bridge and skyline are a must see. And for sure the top deck of the Empire State Building. The view at night is spectacular."

Laughing, he says, "For someone afraid of heights, you really seem to like high places. So New York is a definite. What else?"

Folding the list back up, I hold it out for him. "It was fun when we were just talking about this hypothetically. Now that I know you're serious, I think you should hire a real travel agent. What if I choose things that you find incredibly lame? I can't be responsible for a bad trip."

He pushes the note back at me. "I get the feeling you're not capable of that. And I think instead of telling me about all these places, you should be my tour guide." His eyes hold the intensity that drives me wild as he beams back at me. "Jewels, I want you to come with me."

Staring back at this handsome stranger I've known for less than twenty-four hours, I giggle. Any girl would probably jump at the chance to travel with him as he's suggesting, if he was actually serious about it. He's like one of those shirtless models they put on the bags of trendy clothing stores, and seems impossibly sweet.

"Yeah, right. Maybe if I won the lottery."

Adam's intense gaze doesn't break. "You can get cheap flights through your dad, right? I can take care of the rest. I plan to hit the road for most of the places. It wouldn't have to cost a lot if we camped some of the time and rented timeshares."

A burst of intense feelings races through me. Ever since I first met Adam, I've become a new version of my old self. Not only am I completely charmed by him, but I'm thrilled by his proposal.

Still.

"*Dude.* I can't just up and leave on the kind of trip you're talking about."

"Why not?" The right side of his mouth turns up. "Is it because of this non-committed guy you're seeing?"

"No. It's because I have school, and my parents would never agree to it!"

With the elevation of my voice, the parents of the two little boys both glance our way. I pull at my braid, completely flustered. A million more reasons pass through my mind before the biggest reason that *should've* popped into my mind first hits me.

"I don't even *know* you, Adam," I tell him, trying to calm myself. "We *just* met."

My heart races at the thought of actually doing what he's suggesting. Of course, it would be exciting, and probably the trip of a lifetime, but I...can't go. I just can't. This is ridiculous.

He holds his hand up, obviously seeing how worked up I've become. "Just hear me out. It's less than a month until the end of the semester, right? You can finish your classes for the year, and we can get to know each other in the meantime. If you decide I'm not the kind of guy you want to spend your summer with, I'll just go alone. There wouldn't be any pressure."

My mom already lined up a summer job for me in one of the clothing stores she manages downtown. I worked in a different store for her last year after high school, making pretty decent money, and saved half of it hoping to rent an apartment with Kelly next year. It wouldn't be enough to live off for an entire summer, but—

I rise to my feet like a Jack-in-the-box when I realize I'm seriously considering his offer. "You're crazy. This is crazy!"

"Can we calmly talk about it?" He gently pulls on my hand. "I think those people over there are *this* close to calling the cops."

When I look back to the parents of the young boys they're staring our way with matching frowns. I wave awkwardly. "It's all good," I yell to them. "We're just having an intense debate on the tragedies of Shakespeare. You know, the creepy thing with Romeo and Juliet being so *young* and all."

The man looks at me like I'm completely crazy, but the woman smirks like she knows I'm full of shit. She calls out to her boys, and the four of them head back to their minivan.

"Shakespeare?" Adam snickers behind me.

I turn back to him. His face is all lit up like he's the happiest he's ever been. "Would you quit looking at me like that? It's not helping the crazy thing. At all."

Wiping at his face, he chuckles quietly. "Sorry. I've just never met anyone like you before."

I lower myself back to the ground beside him. "It's safe to say I've never met anyone like you, either. You're asking a stranger to go on a really big trip. If you're serious about this list, why not take one of your buddies, or someone you actually *know*?"

"Because the few people I know are so damn boring." He rolls to his back, folding his hands behind his head, grinning, even though I told him to stop. "I don't know, I guess you seem fun. You're into music, and traveling, and probably a handful of other interesting things."

"If you think I'm interesting, then you really *must* hang out with some boring people." I sigh loudly. "You can't ask a girl you've just met to travel across the country with you."

"Why not?" He looks up into the blue sky and laces his hands over his chest before closing his eyes. "Have you ever been close to someone who died way before it was their time?"

My breath catches in my throat, and my hands begin to tremble. "Yeah," I whisper. "I have."

"My best friend died last fall."

My eyes burn with phantom tears that won't come. I know exactly how the pain of losing a loved one festers over time, relentless. I squeeze my legs to steady my hands. "God, that really sucks. I'm sorry."

"He was one of the funniest guys I've ever known, even when he was lying in the hospital bed, dying. He was sick most of his life, so he never got the chance to travel either. He would pick movies for us to watch in his room based on where they took place just so he could pretend he had been there. When he found out his heart wouldn't hold out much longer, he made me promise that I would quit putting things off for another day, and do something unexpected, something I've always wanted to do. It's part of the reason I dropped out of school."

His watering eyes meet mine. "I know it probably sounds lame, but everyone I know is guilty of taking advantage of life when there's no guarantee that we'll be here another day, or even another hour. I've watched my dad bust his ass all my life. He worked insane hours and hardly ever came to see anything I did at school. I don't understand why there's this pressure to work ourselves to death if we can't even stop to enjoy life. Why should we have to work five or six days a week, and leave the fun for a few hours at night, maybe a day or two on the weekend? We're beings with complex emotions. We should be able to enjoy ourselves. *Experience* things.

"Zach taught me life's not supposed to be about just trying to survive, it's meant for *living*. We're young. We should be allowed to see what's out there before we decide exactly what we want to do for the rest of our lives. I mean, we have *years* to decide that kind of thing. *That's* why I think we should go on this trip together. Why *not* throw caution to the wind? Why not see what else is out there? I'm just asking you to give me a few weeks of your life."

My heart thrums wildly in my chest when he's done talking. There's a feeling in the pit of my stomach whenever I'm around Adam. I know it's ridiculous considering we *just* met, but he makes me feel all kinds of things that I thought were deadened from my medication. The intense energy between us can't just be my imagination, can it?

Neither one of us mentions the list or his unclaimed offer as we walk down an easygoing trail in the park that weaves through the thick forest of tall oaks that have become gnarly and twisted with time. Adam has a million questions for me, yet he still seems unwilling to share anything about himself. I end up telling him stories of concerts Kelly and I caught in the past year, probably boring him to tears considering he knows so little about music.

By the time we return to his Challenger, the sun's just beginning to set below the horizon, making a stunning display of soft colors reflecting off the river below. A few more couples have gathered around the couple in beanies to witness the spectacular sight. Sunsets are *definitely* something reserved for romance, and I'm not having any of that.

I try to summon the courage to ask Adam to take me home, even though the last hour has been so awesome that I'm already dreading telling him goodbye. I should just walk away before things get complicated, before the tangle of complex emotions becomes uncontrollable, and I'm back in a situation where I've lost all control.

Adam's eyes snap onto mine as he runs a hand through his hair. So much expression lingers in his gaze, the loudest being hope. "I know you said you have to study, but it's still early and my friend's playing in a band at the Starlite. If you're up for it, I could have you back by eight."

Ugh, the dreaded promise of *a* live band. It's as if he already knows exactly what it takes to entice me. I tell myself it's just *music*. I'll go, hear this band with him, and we don't ever have to see each other again.

I roll my eyes as if it's a ridiculous question. "I'm *always* up for music."

With a tilt of his head, we meet up at the passenger's side where he opens my door. I flip through the radio stations as soon as we leave the park, taking care to play a good variety so I can culture him on more of my favorite tunes.

Adam parks in front of Buzzard Billy's, and leads me up a steep set of stairs inside. I've been to Billy's a few times with Kelly and other friends, but never upstairs to the lounge. The place is totally retro, reminding me of the Rat Pack days with its paneled walls and bright colors. Cocktail tables with high-backed turquoise chairs and a various styles of couches look inviting under the dim lights.

There's a small crowd gathered. Adam seems to know a group of guys at the bar as one of them waves, raising his eyebrows upon seeing me. Adam lifts his hand in a quick greeting before steering me to an open red velvet couch. I sit, but he stands over me, looking paranoid.

"The band won't be out for another half hour. You interested in sharing a slice of key lime pie?"

"Sure," I say, even though I've never tried the stuff.

"I'll be right back." He's off to the bar before I can say anything else. I watch as he pumps fists with the guy who waved earlier, and they become engaged in a lively conversation. Yeah, so this isn't supposed to be an "official date," but I'm still a little hurt that he doesn't bring me over to meet his friends. It just creates a host of more questions. What *are* we doing together? Why would he invite me on this trip, then choose not to introduce me to his friends?

I dig in my purse for my phone, finding a number of missed calls and texts from Kelly. As the last all but threatens my actual life, I quickly type out a message to her.

Tell u everything later. At Starlite 4 a band. Will b late.

Adam's still busy chatting it up with his buddies, so I check my social apps for anything interesting. I snort under my breath when I see a Facebook message from Levi.

I want my helmut back.

He didn't even bother to ask nicely. And he can't spell.

A month ago he gave me his spare helmet so he could pick me up on a whim. At first I was jealous of all the girls who probably wore it before me, and was thrilled when he asked if I wanted to hold on to it. I took it as a sign that he was ready to commit to me, and stop seeing other women.

"Everything good?" Adam asks, making me jump. I look up to see him standing over me, his hands stuffed in his pockets.

"Yeah, it's good," I say, closing the app and stashing my phone. "Kelly's just being...Kelly."

When he settles within a touching distance from me on the couch, I catch the guys from the bar sneaking glances over at us. "Friends of yours?"

Resting his ankle on his knee, he huffs loudly when he looks back at them. "Kind of. They're my old fraternity brothers."

"*You* were in a fraternity?"

"I was a totally different person back then." His eyes are hard when his gaze flickers back to me. "It was a lapse in judgment."

"Hey, we all make stupid mistakes." After all, I stayed with Levi this long.

A tall, thin waitress with shiny black hair sets a slice of pie in front of us with two forks. When she sees Adam, a flirtatious smile curls at her lips. "Hey, Adam. Haven't seen you around in a while."

"Hey, Bets," he replies. "How've you been?"

She giggles in a harmonic melody. "You know. Same old work, no time for a social life, blah blah." Jealousy lights up my insides. With a porcelain complexion, cool eyes under dark eyelashes, and bright red lipstick, she's a knockout. Like a pin-up girl you'd see in a 40s magazine.

Adam sets his arm behind me on the couch. "Betsy, this is Jewels."

Betsy looks me up and down before grinning. It's the way you assess someone you think will eventually become a friend. Cordial, not judging. "Hey. Always good to meet a friend of Adam's." She turns back to Adam. "Let me know if I can get you guys anything else." She winks his way before walking away.

"She seems cool," I say. And she does, except I still can't shake the feeling that she wants something more from Adam. It makes me feel strangely territorial.

With his arm still draped behind me, he turns so close that the warmth of his breath spills across my face. "I used to hang out here a lot."

My throat becomes incredibly tight. It would only take a little nudge for our lips to touch. It's one of those magical moments when you can feel your first kiss with someone coming. Our eyes lock. He rubs his lips together. As we stare at each other, I notice he isn't breathing either.

I spring back to study the glowing green and white desert. "That looks...good."

Adam reaches for the plate. "Get ready for the best key lime you'll ever taste."

I take a small, cautious bite, waiting for the flavor to hit my taste buds. The bitterness of the lime mixed with the sweet of the whipped cream is like a little party in my mouth. Puckering my lips, I close my eyes and hum. "Considering this is my first time trying it, this is like *really* good. Delicious."

"You're kidding." He sets his fork down. "You've never tried key lime pie?"

Shrugging, I cut myself a much bigger bite. "I used to be a picky eater." A full moment passes before I realize I'm talking with my mouth stuffed full. Turning red, I press a few fingers over my lips.

Adam doesn't seem to notice as he takes a similarly large forkful. "Maybe while *you* work on *my* list of things to do, *I* should be working on one for *you*."

After swallowing the pie I stuffed in my mouth, I snort. "Except I'm the one who's actually *gone* places, remember?"

"But no key lime pie? I'll bet there are a ton of things you haven't experienced. I'd venture to guess you'll learn just about as much from me as I will when we execute your list."

I'm filled with warm chills. I love the way he assumes we have a future together. The way he assumes I'll say yes to his crazy idea. The thought of us being alone. On the road. "Oh, yeah? Try me."

Setting his fork down on the suddenly empty plate, he raises his eyebrows. "Ever gone snowmobiling?"

"No way," I answer rather forcefully. "Anything that has to do with the cold, you can count me out. I become a hermit once the first snow hits."

When I realize I ate most of the pie without even asking if he wanted the last bite, I'm mortified. I've never wolfed anything down in front of a guy like that before. It seems I'm so at ease with Adam that I don't even think about sitting straight, adjusting my hair, or making sure my lipgloss is well applied. It's like hanging out with Kelly if she opted for a sex change.

"It's not cold if you have the right gear."

"Yeah, well, the only *gear* I have is a down coat and cotton mittens. I can barely cross campus without worrying about frost bite."

Adam chuckles under his breath. "You can rent those kinds of things, you know. I'll bet you haven't been downhill skiing, either."

"Heights, remember?"

"Says the girl who has been zip-lining and on the observation deck of one of the world's tallest buildings." His arm returns to the couch behind me once again. He looks down at me, his dimples flaring beside his wide grin. "Maybe we can make a stop in Colorado so you can try one or both."

Licking the last traces of pie off my fork, I huff. "Slow down there, big guy. You're acting like I've already accepted your proposition."

He smirks, confident. "You haven't turned me down."

Then it hits me out of nowhere. I'm damaged goods. This guy is way too good for me. I should tell him I can't go, and it's best if we don't see each other again.

I open my mouth to speak up when his friend's band takes the stage. After a round of quiet applause, the foursome of hipsters start in on a kind of souped up blues rock. While they play, I'm conscious of every move Adam makes beside me. His hand grazes across my shoulders when he rests his arm behind me. His breath tickles my ear whenever he leans in to yell something over the music. It takes everything I have not to bolt from the bar and call a taxi. It takes everything I have not to lean in and kiss him. So many contradictory feelings rage through me that my head spins.

I *just* broke things off with Levi a few hours ago. And I've heard so many stories about rebound relationships, even though we weren't officially dating. Still, I don't want that to be the case with Adam. Although sometimes a bit on the somber side, he's kind, and sweet, and funny. I don't want to ruin things by rushing them. And I don't want him to think I'm just looking for something physical, although I wouldn't necessarily be opposed to the idea.

By the time the band is done, it's late and I have to finish reading two chapters by morning, so Adam drives me back to the dorms. There's a moment of awkwardness as we sit in the dark, the question of a kiss weighing heavily on my mind.

Finally, Adam twists around to look at me. "I hope you had a good time."

After being with Levi the past few months, it's so odd to hear someone ask me that after a date that I almost laugh. "Are you kidding? The death-defying view, the pizza, the pie, Martin's band? For someone who's musically deprived, you hang out with some pretty stellar folks."

"You want to do it again?" His smile suddenly matches mine. "I mean, not the *exact* same things, but—"

"Yeah," I interrupt, nodding. "I do." The answer surprises me so much that I pull in a sharp breath. Didn't I just resolve never to see him again? I consider telling him the truth; that I can't handle a serious relationship, if that's where he's heading. I should at least take time to think, maybe clear my head.

"How's tomorrow?"

I let out a deep sigh and smile. "I'm at the library again until five."

Adam's eyes dip to the corner. "That should work. I think my schedule's pretty wide open. Same time, same place?"

Nodding, I clutch the door handle, ready to bolt. Our eyes catch in the glow of the dashboard. For a painfully long moment, I'm breathless.

"Thanks," he tells me. "For tonight."

"Thank *you* for the pie and pizza. You're the one who showed me a good time."

He shrugs. "Anytime."

The lights are off when I slip inside our room. Kelly stirs on her bed with the sound of my keys hitting the desk. "How was the date?" she asks groggily.

"It wasn't a *date*."

Kelly's giggles fill the small room. "That good, huh?"

I lean back on my bed, sighing. "He seems like a great guy."

"Then what's the problem?"

"I don't think I'm emotionally ready for someone like him. I don't think I'm emotionally ready for *anyone*. I'm not even sure *why* I broke it off with Levi. I don't think I can do the whole boyfriend thing again. Not without fucking it up."

"Listen. There must be something about Adam that made you wake up and realize you were headed nowhere with Levi, *fast*. I know you're afraid of letting yourself fall for someone again, Jewels, but at some point you have to forgive yourself for breaking it off with Jason. Don't check yourself out because you're afraid of feeling something for this guy. *Please,* give this thing with Adam a chance before you totally write him off."

I'm rendered speechless by Kelly's ability to see exactly what's going on. I finish my homework and turn off the lights, but my emotions and feelings for Adam keep me up much later than I intend.

Five

I DRAG MYSELF TO CLASS IN THE morning with thoughts of Adam and our night still replaying in my head. Though I normally can get lost in my interest of Musical Cultures, today I'm busy typing a list on my laptop of the pros and cons involved with Adam's trip, and can't answer the professor's question when she calls on me. The disappointed gaze she throws me before continuing on to someone else doesn't escape me.

The last year has been a roller coaster of bad grades and missed classes. I've finally gotten to a lull where I at least make Cs and Bs, which has appeased my parents so far, but if I'm going to even consider going with Adam, I'm going to have to buckle down and prove to them I've changed. I snap out of it and listen intently the rest of the hour, but every few minutes I catch myself smiling.

Exactly ten minutes to five, Adam walks into the library wearing a retro Nirvana t-shirt. I hide a giant grin behind the book in my hands so my supervisor doesn't start in on me again.

"Go, be gone," Felicia tells me, waving a hand through the air without even looking up. "I don't want to spend the next ten minutes cleaning up your drool."

I nudge her playfully before leaving to join Adam, my expression somber. "What's this?" I point to his obviously new purchase.

"I was out grabbing a few groceries and it just kind of called to me. I figured you'd appreciate it. Too obvious?"

I cross my arms, pretending to be annoyed. "Name *one* of their songs."

"It's not like I've lived in a cave all my life. My buddies listened to them all the time. I remember a lot of screaming. I could pick them out on the radio."

"Wrong answer," I say. "You better go turn it inside out. You can't be one of those posers who wears a band shirt just because they're in fashion. I refuse to hang out with someone like that."

His grin falters. "You're serious?"

"The alternative is for you to immediately start listening to all their albums until you can appreciate why Dave Grohl is so epic, and why Kurt Cobain's death was so tragic." I hook my arm through his when he doesn't say anything more. "Don't worry, they only recorded four albums. And you're in luck, I just happen to have them all."

Dumbfounded, he exits the library at my side. "This is your big plan for the night?"

"About that..." I look down at my feet before meeting his gaze again. "I think I'm gonna have to cancel. With finals coming up, I need to cram in some major studying. This has been a crappy semester."

He raises his eyebrows. "What are your classes?"

"Um, Musical Cultures, Cross-Cultural Psych, and History of Jazz, and English Lit."

"I'm sensing a theme here. Are you sure you aren't on track to become a music teacher?"

"I think it's more my advisor's way of telling me I'm lacking in culture because first off, I'm afraid of children. I once saw a *toddler* show her mom *how to run her iPad.* I'm telling you, their advanced intelligence is abnormal. And I'm pretty sure you have to be able to sing or play some kind of instrument to teach music.

Trust me, you don't want to hear me try either. I'm just trying to fill my generals until I find what it is I want to be when I grow up. *If* that ever happens."

Adam runs a hand across the back of his neck, smirking. "I definitely don't know anything about *those* classes except maybe English Lit, but is there any way I can help you study?"

PARKED IN A GRASSY LOT ON THE EDGE of town, we alternate between Adam quizzing me on the relevant chapters, and me reading my latest assignment while he listens to Nirvana. At first I feared there'd be too much pressure parked together in a deserted place in the dark, but the time flies by. Before I know it, it's nearly midnight and we've completed the final album.

"Well?" I ask, unplugging my phone. "What's the verdict?"

Adam rubs at his chin. "The guy has a really interesting voice, and I can see why you think the drummer is so amazing." He beams back at me against the dashboard's glow. "Do I get to wear this shirt again?"

"Not so fast. Which song was your favorite?"

He taps his fingers on the steering wheel for a moment. "The one where he sang about having a new complaint, I guess. It had a wicked melody."

I sigh, pretending it pains me to grant him the permission. "Okay, you're allowed to wear the shirt now. Just don't let me catch you again buying one from a band you know nothing about. Next time I won't be quite as lenient."

OVER THE NEXT WEEK, WE FALL INTO A familiar routine. Adam picks me up either at my dorm or the library. Most nights we grab supper on campus before going somewhere quiet where he helps me cram for finals. By our fourth night out, I ditch Kelly's fashionable clothes for my comfy band t-shirts with hole-covered capris, cuff bracelets and favorite Vans. Adam's eyes turn bright when he first sees me in my natural state, making my heart flutter even faster.

From our deep conversations between studying, I'm finally able to get a better overall sense of Adam. He tells me he was never overly athletic, though he does love a good game of ping pong or bowling. He knows movies the way I know music, and can quote a line from just about any one when challenged. He's read as many books as I probably have over the years, preferring horror to any other genre. He sometimes volunteers at the Make a

Wish Foundation in memory of his friend Zach, and he donates blood when Red Cross sponsors drives. He has a gaggle of little cousins he loves to watch play sports, though they live four hours away so it's hard for him to catch their games. He's always felt like he's living in his brother's shadow, even though he's the oldest. He thinks his mom is incredibly shallow, and his dad is a big pushover.

By the time Friday rolls around, I'm either doodling Adam's name like a love-struck high school girl, or secretly planning out places we could hit on our epic trip across the country. That afternoon I'm so lost in daydreams as I walk across campus to my last class that I hardly notice when my phone vibrates in my hand. I look down to find my first text from Adam.

Hate to do this, but have to take a raincheck for tonight. I'll call u tomorrow.

We had reservations for a comedy club in Rochester as a way to reward ourselves for all the studying we've crammed in. My heart sinks as the voice of self-doubt immediately takes over, storming in like an uninvited guest. He didn't give any explanation for why he's canceling. Although things have been going so well between us, what if he changed his mind about me altogether, and this is the official blow-off? For the rest of the day, it's as if a storm cloud hangs over every move I make, dark and cold, sucking every bit of joy from me that's built up in the time I spent with Adam.

Since I asked for the night off from the library, there's nothing to stop me from obsessing over our canceled plans. I waste a couple hours completing assignments, flipping through the boring channels on TV, and even trying to read a book before getting incredibly frustrated. Even my favorite playlist of songs fails to calm me down.

I resort to pacing the room, my irrational fears nearly crippling. Why would he cancel without giving any kind of reason? What if he randomly tells me the trip is off, and just disappears from my life as quickly as he came in?

This is exactly why I can't let myself get involved with someone again. I've become emotionally unhinged.

When Kelly comes breezing in from work, I heave in great relief. "Thank god. We need to go somewhere. Do something. Get me the *hell* out of here."

She peels her sweatshirt off, giving me a wild look. "What's with you? You out of crack or something?"

"No. I just...I don't know. I'm on edge, I guess." I take a long, slow breath, gathering my hair into a ponytail behind my head. "Adam and I had plans tonight, and he just randomly canceled. No excuse, nothing."

"Ah." As she quickly strips out of her uniform on the way to our shared closet, she's giggling. "It's only been a week since you dumped the anchor, and you're all hyped up over this new guy. Codependent much?"

Irritated, I rub at my face. "Can we just forget it and go out? I need to go...somewhere. I can't stay in this stupid room any longer."

"Whatever you say." She emerges from the closet, already wearing skinny jeans and my favorite turquoise blouse. "Get dressed. We're going to Matt's."

GOING TO A FRAT HOUSE WASN'T WHAT I had in mind when I told Kelly I wanted to get out, especially after nearly losing her last time we went out together. But a much smaller crowd gathers at the old two-story house our friend shares with twelve others. Most of the brothers have some level of a girlfriend, and I get along with most of them. Nights like this I feel awkward, however, like the proverbial third wheel on a big rig. Still, I'm thankful for the distraction, and glad that Kelly is willing to humor me.

Kelly and Matt have a hot and cold relationship that I quit trying to understand long ago. She sits on his lap while sipping on her drink, his long fingers comfortably resting at the top of her thighs. He's a decent guy with boyish looks and bedroom eyes that sometimes make me flush, plus, he always makes the Dean's List. I guess he's just not interested in dating anyone at this point in life, and Kelly's okay with the occasional hook up.

The guys mostly talk about sports, so I find myself playing with my phone half the night, pinning cute outfits and trolling on irritating videos. I nearly jump out of my seat when my phone suddenly rings, a selfie of Levi and I from one drunken night filling the screen. I pull in a long, stuttering breath. Even if Adam doesn't ever call me again after today, it was still a wise decision to cut loose from Levi.

"I'll be right back," I tell Kelly, slipping into the hallway. The smell of old house mixed in with what I think to be stale beer and sweaty feet about makes me gag. My heartbeat rakes my chest when I accept the call, bracing myself for the sound of Levi's sexy voice.

"Jewels?" his speech is drawn out, although not quite slurred. "Baby, where are you? I want to see you."

I let out a low laugh under my breath. There's nothing about these drunken booty calls from him that I could ever possibly miss. Since I couldn't get into the bars, most nights he was out I'd stay home to watch movies. He'd come looking for me after closing to have sex before passing out.

My hand tightens around the phone. "I'm at school. And you're drunk."

"I'm standing outside your room. Your light's not on."

"You're at my house?" When I picture my dad finding Levi in our yard, drunk, my pulse quickens. They've never even met him, and my dad owns several guns. I haven't bothered to tell my parents that we're over. If Levi tells them in this state of mind, it would give my dad an excuse to call the cops without worrying about how it would affect me. Just because I don't want to be with Levi anymore doesn't mean I want to see him thrown in jail.

"No. I'm outside your dorm."

"*What*? Levi, tell me you're joking." I picture him driving his Harley across town, swerving over lines and cutting off traffic.

"Why did you leave me?" There's an angry nip to his words. "We had a good thing going, baby. Come down. I wanna see you."

Different scenarios race through my mind. I could bring Kelly and Matt with me, but they're having a good time, and I don't want to ruin her night, too. Plus, I'm sure she'd try to talk me into leaving Levi to pass out on the campus lawn, but I can't do that to him. I could bring him back here to crash for the night, but he'd be livid to wake up surrounded by the type of guys he loathes. Maybe it'd be best to tuck him in my bed and take the couch at Matt's.

For a sliver of a second, I consider asking for Adam's help. But I don't want to get him involved in this, and I don't want him to see Levi pawing me in his drunken stupor. And I don't want to have to explain to him that Levi's upset because I dumped him in anticipation of something happening between us. Besides, it's not the *sole* reason I rid myself of him.

"*Stay there*," I command, as if he's a puppy. When he gets this loaded, there isn't much of a difference. "I'll be there in ten minutes."

I shove my phone back into my pocket and run into the other room. Kelly's completely entangled in Matt's arms now, her head resting on his shoulder. A crooked smile passes her lips as he tells a story that has everyone rolling in laughter.

"Kel, can I borrow your car?" I ask, hoping she won't see the anxiety in my eyes. "I told Sierra I'd give her the notes from class today before she leaves for the weekend." Lying to my best friend feels like I've reached a new low, but I don't want her to worry. Levi isn't her problem. "I'll come get you whenever you're ready."

She tosses me the keys without any question.

"I'll give you a ride when you're ready," Matt offers, rubbing his hand slowly up and down her arm. His brown eyes, two shades lighter than Kelly's but still giving off the same warmth, twinkle with mischief.

"Thanks," I say, flashing him a nervous smile. The way things are going between them, Kelly won't be coming home tonight. And that means I'll be stuck all alone with Levi. A ball of dread stirs in my chest.

ONCE I'VE WOUND MY WAY THROUGH the far end of visitor parking, the headlights finally stumble across Levi's Harley parked in the section reserved for motorcycles, his helmet resting on the handlebars. *Shit.* Guilty pangs hit me like a punch to the gut. He never drives his Harley when he's been drinking. He cares more about his bike than he does about his own life. Is it possible that I somehow broke him?

I continue on to student parking and hurry across the road to the dorms. Levi sits alone on a bench underneath the yard light in the grassy knoll, head bent with his hair falling around his face, elbows resting on his knees, hands folded in front of him. For a fleeting moment I'm reminded of the day he was told his mom had breast cancer. He was so devastated, and it was the only time I ever saw him cry.

"Lee?" I call out softly, surprised to hear my pet name for him resurface.

His head slowly tilts up and he pushes his hair behind his ear to meet my gaze. The glowing whites of his eyes penetrate the darkness, igniting something deep inside me. "Jewels. I figured you wouldn't come."

Suppressed affection pushes at my chest, pulls at my heartstrings. He may not have his shit together, but there was a short time I was falling head over heels for this beautiful man. Or maybe it was just the idea of him. "Did you drive your bike like this?"

He stands, running a nervous hand through his dirty blond hair. A fire burns inside me as his muscular torso twists underneath his snug shirt and Harley jacket. No matter how much I want to despise what he's done to me, a part of me will always be attracted to him. "I only had one drink. I came to apologize."

Resolving to hold my ground, I cross my arms, frowning. "For what?"

"Being an ass." He lifts his hands out at his sides before shoving them in his jeans pockets. "I mean, look at you. Any guy would kill for a chance to be yours, and I threw it down the shitter. You deserve better. I don't want to lose you, Jewels. I shouldn't have been such a dick when you called."

Still not convinced, I shake my head. He was the first guy I wanted to date in a long time. I couldn't believe it when he wanted to be with *me* and thought I was *so* lucky when he agreed to go out a second time. But it just goes to show how naive I've been. "I was never yours, Levi. I was just there to fulfill your sexual needs. I don't need that kind of a codependent relationship. It isn't healthy."

He bursts forward, stopping just a foot away. I recoil a bit when the scent of leather and Axe deodorant appease my senses, reminding me of all our past intimate encounters. Reminding me of the way his hard body feels pressed against mine.

"You're wrong," he says in a low voice. His eyes are rimmed with a puffy redness, as if he's actually been crying. "I mean, yeah, at first I was amped at the thought of having sex with you. Who wouldn't be? But I never should've said those things about not wanting anything serious with you. My head was a mess all day when I realized I may never see you again. I know I can be a real asshole sometimes, but I'm begging you to give me another chance."

He reaches out suddenly, pulling me up against him. My body vibrates with the familiar feel of his hands against the small of my back, the way our hips fit together. "I think I might love you, Jewels."

I balk. All thoughts of Levi being crude, immature, and heartless fade away with the three little words I thought he wasn't capable of feeling. My lips part with a small gasp. Levi misunderstands the act, seeing it as an opportunity to kiss me. His mouth feels uncharacteristically gentle against mine as his warm tongue nudges its way inside, filling my taste buds with a hint of mouthwash. One of his hands reaches up to cradle my face as the kiss intensifies.

I stand with my arms stiff at my sides, still engaged in an internal battle, even though my mouth and the rest of my body respond to him on their own. A few weeks ago, this would've been exactly what I wanted, for Levi to actually *want* to be with me. But in just a couple of days, it feels like everything has changed.

Adam has reminded me there can be so much more to a relationship than two good looking people hooking up and having hot sex. Levi and I have so little in common, and he almost never showed interest in me beyond the bedroom. I don't want to end up stuck in La Crosse, spending nights alone as Levi puts in late hours at his shop. As much as I want him to have a relationship with his son, I don't want to deal with his crazy baby momma, either. Levi's a dead end. It was right to break things off with him.

Yet, I intertwine myself with him, my body aching for him to touch me the intimate way he does when we're hot for each other. A low moan rumbles in his throat when my hands climb up underneath his shirt, exploring the ridges and smooth muscles I know by heart. He suddenly breaks the seal between our lips, lowering his mouth to my ear.

"Let's go upstairs," he whispers, trailing a line of hot kisses down my neck.

"Lee," I protest, trying to separate my sensible thoughts from my raw desire. "It's not a good idea."

"We'll just talk," he promises, still nibbling at the skin on my collarbone. "I just want to hold you. Please, let me hold you."

His promise of being together without sex seems genuine, yet is so unexpected that I nod, pulling him along to the entrance. One of my hall-mates holds the door open as she leaves the building, grinning at me and Levi knowingly.

Levi's hands are all over me as we climb up to my room. After I flip on the light, he pushes me back up against the door, pinning my hands above my head. His kisses go from innocent and meaningful to hungry and wildly passionate. His tongue is relentless inside of my mouth, licking, probing, tasting.

My nagging doubts and building resistance are overtaken by my hormones as I get caught up in him, basking in the familiarity of it all. I push him off me to help peel his jacket from his arms and throw it to the floor, then his shirt. In return, he slips my shirt off so fast that my head spins. His fingers slip underneath my bra, unclasping it to massage my breasts with raw need. My body aches for him, wanting him to appease the sudden throbbing between my thighs. When his lips enclose around a nipple, sucking and tugging, a million shivers rip down my spine. He unzips my pants, playfully running a finger up and down my pelvic bone without going down to touch the part of me that wants him the most.

My panties grow wet as desire envelops me. I feel his full excitement push up against my thigh and reach into his pants for it, wanting to please him. He's rock hard, shaking with the blood forcefully pumping through him. I wrap my hand around him and tug gently as our mouths return to eager kisses. He finally slips his fingers inside of me, and I cry out into his mouth, my body on fire.

The reality of what I'm doing doesn't kick in until he whispers, "You like that? You want more?"

I twist from his hold, shocked by how easy it was to get carried away. "Wait." He looks up, the hunger in his eyes pulsating. Normally, I would find it to be a major turn-on, but now it just reminds me of the one track his mind seems to be forever on. "I thought we were going to 'just talk'."

With a resigned sigh, he dips his head, taking a step back. "Right." I collapse next to him on the bed. His hardness presses against the part of me that still pangs for him when he pulls me into his strong arms. "God, I've missed you this week." A little grin transforms the light in his eyes, and he buries his face into my neck, breathing me in.

Licking my lips, tender from his wiry goatee, I try to decide how to tell him what I'm feeling. If I tell him I miss him, too, it would be a straight out lie. And I can't tell him I love him, either. Because I'm 100% positive I don't. I have no idea how I let myself get into this situation.

"I'm not taking you back. I've already decided to move on," I finally say. I push on his chest, wishing I could just yell at him to let go. "Even if I *did* decide to give you another chance—"

"Move in with me." He leans back, catching my gaze. His eyes are dull. "After you're done with the semester."

Heat rushes through me as my breathing becomes tight. I suddenly feel rooted in place, wanting to either scream or hit something until I collapse. "*What?*"

He shrugs. "I want to prove to you that I can do this, Jewels. I want this thing with us to work." His fingers swipe away a strand of hair that falls in my face.

I scramble to my feet, feeling as if the walls have closed in with the bomb that came out of nowhere. I wrote Levi off, and he hasn't crossed my mind in all the time I've spent with

Adam. "I broke up with you for a reason. What makes you think I want to take this to another level? You've never even called me your *girlfriend*."

He reaches out to hook his finger in the loop of my jeans, pulling me back down to him. "I meant what I said. I want you around and think whatever this is, it could grow into love." His lips brush softly against mine, filled with promise, and his hands get lost in the thick of my hair.

Then it happens. His words trigger something deep down. I lose all inhibitions, and get lost in the strong arms of Levi Travis. My brain screams out to *stop*, that I'm taking things too far and Levi isn't the one I want, but my body refuses to obey its commands. It's been like this since we first got together. His touches stir something within me that's been bruised and broken since I broke up with Jason. They make me feel alive, and remind me that I'm wanted. That I'm still worthy of being loved.

Our breaths become quick and labored as we toss our jeans to the floor. He flips me on my back, rocking above me as we devour each other. Everything about his hard body feels so familiar, from the warmness of his skin to the sharp ridges of his biceps and chest. As always, when his mouth falls down to my breasts and his warm hand travels down between my legs, I become insane with desire for him. I grip his jaw, pulling his mouth back up to mine. His hand drops to the side of the bed as he fishes around for his jeans and the condom he always keeps in his back pocket.

I've wiggled out of my panties before Levi's finished rolling the rubber on. He pushes inside of me with one healthy thrust, his face alight with pleasure. I dig my fingernails into his back and whimper when I realize I'm letting this happen. I want to tell him to stop instead of pushing my hips against him, matching his rhythmic thrusts. His hands wrap around my bottom, squeezing, as his tongue barges halfway down my throat.

Tears spring to my eyes. I meant to break up with him, not have a last romp. I have no idea if I still feel anything for him, or if I'm just caught up in the hot sex so I *will* feel something. My stomach roils with regret.

I open my mouth to yell out "stop", but there's a sudden sharp rap on the door. Relieved by the perfect timing, I begin to wiggle out from underneath him. "It's probably Kel," I whisper.

"She can wait," he mutters in a throaty voice, drawing his mouth back to mine.

I push him with enough force that he glares back angrily. "It's her room, too. We can't just lock her out all night." I throw on my jeans and shirt, braless. As I pad over to the door, I twist my hair off to the side, hoping it doesn't look too wild after Levi messed it up. At least her melted candle masks the smell of sex. Glad for the interruption, I open the door, beaming. "Hey —"

Only all excitement plummets when I'm met with Adam's dimples.

Six

DEEP WITHIN, I CELEBRATE THE pleasurable sight of a freshly shaved Adam in my doorway, wearing a cobalt zip-up sweatshirt, his steel blue eyes alive. His excitement dwindles, however, when he gets a good look at me. "Is this a bad time?"

I hear Levi slip into his jeans behind me and suddenly forget how to swallow. I squeeze the doorknob with such force that I half expect it to shatter into a million pieces.

"Who are *you*?" Levi asks, appearing shirtless at my side. His arm slips around my waist, as if making it clear that I belong to him. I swear I can feel my heart drop into my stomach. On one hand, this may be the first time I've seen Levi jealous. On the other, it really pisses me off. I already broke up with him, so he has no right to play alpha male.

Adam offers his hand to Levi. "Adam Murphy."

I almost laugh when I realize I didn't know his last name before now and had actually considered running off with him. Maybe I *do* need to slow everything down to get my head on straight. I can't even properly dump Levi at this point.

Levi refuses Adam's hand as he looks him over, lip curled. "It's late. Why are you here?"

"He's a friend," I snap, wiggling away. "I told him to stop by so I could give him notes for Econ." The lie falls from my lips so effortlessly, just as it had with Kelly.

"It can wait until tomorrow," Adam retorts, his hard gaze unrelenting.

"No, it's okay." I touch Levi's chest. "I left the notes in Kel's car. I'll be right back."

As I reach for the keys on the desk, Levi spins me around, pulling me in for an embarrassingly long, deep kiss. I break away from him, my face red. He hits me on the ass, hard. "Don't be too long. We need to finish where we left off."

Adam stands in the hallway, his eyes drawn to the side. I slam the door behind me and lead him to the safety of the stairway. "I'm sorry. I *really* wish you hadn't seen that."

He looks down the stairway, as if looking for someone to interrupt us, saving him from the torture. "You don't have to apologize." He tilts his head up to look at me, his plastic smile saying everything I need to know. The artificial nicety feels like a personal blow. Adam's one of the most sincere guys I've ever known, and I've already forced him to fake it. "I knew you were seeing someone when we first met."

"But I'm not." With my heart racing in my chest, I shake my head. "I mean, I was, but I broke it off with him. It's like I told you, it wasn't anything serious."

"Then who was that?"

"That was him, the guy I broke it off with. I didn't know he was coming over tonight. It's complicated." I rub at my face. "Can we meet up tomorrow so I can explain everything? I don't want to leave things like this."

He shuffles a small distance away from me, his palms held up. He's difficult to read as if he's deliberately shutting down. "It's okay. Really. I didn't expect this to become anything more than a friendship."

His words bring my world crashing down in a heaping blaze. I'm such an idiot to assume he wanted to be anything beyond friends. I look down at my fingers, picking at a stubborn hangnail.

"I'll still meet you tomorrow, but you don't have to explain yourself," he tells me in a soft voice. "I don't want things to be weird between us. I don't want to ruin what we started this week."

Looking up to catch his gaze, desperation fills me. I don't want to just be *friends*. I want us to fulfill his list, exploring new places and trying new things, and end the day settled in each other's arms. "I have to work tomorrow. Can you meet me for breakfast, or does that mess with your busy schedule?"

The hint of a smirk graces his lips. "I can probably pencil you in. I'll pick you up. Does seven work?"

"That's awfully early for a slacker."

The dimples pop back into his cheeks. "I'm a people pleaser."

I try to play it cool, but my pulse races. "So I've noticed."

"See you tomorrow." He starts down the stairway, one hand in his pocket and the other on the railing. I have to stop myself from following after him and telling him how I really feel, and that I don't want to see him go. But a small, unsure voice reminds me once again that I may not be capable of pulling off a meaningful relationship with Adam. Or with anyone.

"THIS IS BULLSHIT," LEVI HISSES, collecting his jacket from the floor. "I drove over here to tell you I have these feelings for you, and you're kicking me out? What the fuck?"

With my hands on my hips, I sigh. "I'm sorry, but I didn't ask for this. In fact *I broke up with you*. Nothing about that gives you an open invitation to randomly show up and expect to spend the night with me. You still haven't done anything to prove that you're in this for anything more than sex. Telling me you *may* love me just sounded like another way to get me to fuck you."

His cold, hard eyes lock with mine, making a trail of dread blaze down to my gut. "Does this have something to do with that guy who was just here? Is that why you said you wanted to see other people? Are you *fucking him*?"

He stands rigid, waiting for me to answer, veins straining against his neck, anger radiating from him in waves. Although I've seen him get in a few fights—one resulting in the other guy walking away with a broken nose— none of them have ever been over me. He's pushed me around a few times when he was drinking and upset, but he never meant it, and

I've never been fearful that he would hit me. Until now.

Shying away, I shake my head vigorously. "No. Adam has nothing to do with this," I say gently, hoping I can talk him down. "It's about you and me, Levi. And we're done."

The tension in his neck falters, but anger still clouds his vision. "We're *done*? You just decided this *now*?" Spittle flies with his words. "You want something serious, I asked you to move in with me! Now you're telling me I can't even spend the night in your dorm? What's this all about?"

"Maybe I'm finally growing up." When my words seem to anger him even more, I step forward to touch his arm, my eyes gentle. "Hey, you tried. It might just be too late for us. We don't have that much in common. I don't think there's anything left here that we can save."

Jerking his arm from my hold, he stares down on me with what looks like total hatred. "If I find out all of this is because of that asshole, he's dead." With that he storms from the room, slamming the door so hard a bunch of our pictures jump off the wall, crashing to the floor.

WHEN THE BLACK CHALLENGER COMES into view, I pull out my compact one more time to check on the braid Kelly insisted on giving me. This time she wove my blond hair across the side of my head and pinned it in a sloppy bun at my neck. Adam seemed to like the last braid I wore, so I hope he approves of this as well. Despite her expert makeup job, my eyes are still a bit puffy from nightmares filled with Jason and Levi, each of them angry, each of them yelling at me for being such a bitch and overall disappointment.

Kelly was livid when Matt dropped her off, not that Levi broke our pictures, but that he had threatened Adam and frightened me. While braiding my hair, she tried to convince me to file a restraining order in case his anger flares and he actually follows through with his threat. But knowing Levi, he's likely angry enough that I won't have to worry about seeing him ever again.

Watching Adam maneuver through the parking lot, I'm extra fidgety, checking to be sure my leggings are tucked neatly into my riding boots, my minty green shirt positioned just right around my collarbone without showing my bra straps. It's been a while since I've been this concerned about my looks. Most days I roll out of bed and throw on sweats for class. But after Adam said he didn't expect anything more than friendship, I feel like I have to know if it's because he's not attracted to me, or because he thinks I'm really still involved with Levi and he doesn't want to interfere.

As soon as the car's parked at the curb in front of me, I hop in. "Hey!"

"Hey. You look great." While Adam pauses a millisecond to take me in, smiling, I do the same. In a black button down and dark blue jeans, he looks dressier than I'm used to seeing him, and there's a slight shadow dusting his jaw. "Any special requests?"

"Surprise me," I say, shrugging.

He takes me to the small diner downtown where my parents used to take my grandma when she came to visit. A tall, young waitress with bright red hair leads us to a small booth in the back, leaving us alone with plastic menus and the smell of bacon thick in the air. A few older couples litter the quaint diner, most of them sipping on coffee and glancing at us with curiosity. Two girls my age sit in old-fashioned red stools near the front counter, one chatting animatedly with her hands, the other nodding while staring down on her cell phone. When done skimming through the breakfast selections, I set the menu on the table and watch Adam.

After taking a moment to summon enough courage, I clear my throat so he'll look up. "I know you didn't want me to explain, but it's something I have to do if we're going to keep hanging out."

He settles back in the short bench with his arm stretched over the plastic material, one eyebrow raised. "Fine. Let's hear it."

After a calming breath, I lay my hands down on the table as if bracing myself as the truth spills out. My eyes fall steadily on Adam's. "I decided Levi and I don't work together. He's in a different place in his life. He works all the time at his motorcycle shop and hangs at the bars. He even has a two-year-old son he never sees or makes an effort to see. We really don't even have much in common." *Other than sex.* But I spare him that cruel detail. "What you saw last night was him trying to weasel his way back into my life. But I kicked him out after you left. I probably shouldn't have hooked up with the guy in the first place. Last night you saw the real asshole side of him."

Adam shrugs, glancing down at his menu. "He was just being protective." He's quiet for a moment before his attention returns to me. "Why *did* you hook up with a guy like that in the first place? Is he your type?"

Face flushing, I say, "I've been asking myself the same thing lately. I guess I was attracted to him. You know, older guy, motorcycle, the kind your parents wouldn't necessarily approve of." When Adam looks confused, I shrug. "I was almost always drunk whenever we got together. Before him, I only saw guys a few times before becoming bored and moving on. But then I met Levi, and thought I was ready for a *grownup* relationship." I hook air quotes with the word "grownup", feeling ridiculous for having thought such a thing.

Adam straightens with a gruff chuckle. "That guy didn't seem like the *grownup* type."

"Yeah, I'm not really sure what I was thinking and I don't know why I let it drag on as long as it did, but that's over now. I'm ready to start a new chapter in my life." Our eyes catch as a look of surprise crosses his face.

"Are you ready to order?" the waitress asks, suddenly at our side. She places two glasses of water on the table before pulling a pen and pad of paper from her apron.

Adam turns to her. "I'll take the strawberry crepe, no whipped cream."

I've never had a crepe, but decide it sounds good. "What he said."

We hand her the menus, and she's gone again, leaving the two of us in an awkward state of silence. I shift in my seat and play with a packet of sugar. Just being in Adam's presence lifts my spirits to a higher level than they've been in too long of a time. And I'm locked in a perpetual state of excitement that pinches at my chest.

"So you haven't told me why you had to cancel on our plans last night. I figured you had probably changed your mind about me."

When I glance up, he's swirling the glass of water around, staring at its clear contents. "Family emergency. Nothing bad." His eyes skate up to meet mine. "You really thought I was ditching you?"

"It was the first time you sent a text instead of calling. It wouldn't be the first time a guy used that trick."

Adam sighs, rubbing at the back of his neck. His eyebrows draw down in sternness. "Jewels, please tell me you didn't dump this guy just because of me."

For a moment, I'm speechless, my lips flopping open soundlessly. I look back down at the sugar packet, squeezing the grain between my fingers. Swallowing with difficulty, I'm finally able to say, "I told you—"

"That you kicked him out last night after you saw me, yeah, I got that part." He leans back into the bench. "Listen, I know it was incredibly impulsive and probably odd to ask a complete stranger to go on this trip with me. But you're nothing like most girls I've met, and to be honest, I really don't know what the hell I'd be doing if I went on my own. I like hanging out with you. It's just...I'm probably not in the best place to start any kind of a relationship. I'm sorry, I probably should've made that clear right away. It wasn't my goal to steal you away from your boyfriend."

My face burns hot with embarrassment. I continue to focus on the sugar packet, my fingernails digging into the paper.

"Hey." Adam reaches across the table to stop my hands from fidgeting. "Look at me." His eyes are soft, filled with a gleam that twists at my gut. "You're gorgeous. I'd be an idiot not to recognize that. And I *really* like spending time with you. But I'm headed nowhere, fast. I dropped out of college. I live on a buddy's couch with no long term or even *immediate* goals. If you think that Levi guy wasn't good for you, I can promise you that I'm not any better."

Did he really ask me to go on this trip strictly as friends? It seems impossible that I could keep things platonic, denying these feelings that keep growing stronger each day I get to know him better. "Why would you say that about yourself? There's still time for you to do something meaningful with your life." I lift my chin higher. "And I think it's up to me to decide if you're right for me or not."

"You don't want to get involved with me," he tells me in the gruffest voice I've heard all week. Leaning over the table, he closes his stormy eyes for a moment. "Trust me. My family's a nightmare. My life's a mess."

His argument only frustrates me further. I can handle difficult parents. It's one of my specialties. I've been able to charm the pants off some of the crankiest people. But it's starting to feel like he's trying to find any excuse to reject me. Paranoia invades my every thought, spreading like poison.

"I still don't get it. If you just want us to be friends, why *didn't* you ask one of your buddies?"

"I already told you. My friends are boring."

I look down to the sugar packet still in my fingers and grimace. "But what if I were to actually like you as something more than a friend?" I surprise even myself by saying it out loud, and don't dare glance up to see what kind of expression Adam has because of my confession. Do I sound desperate? My cheeks flush.

I hear Adam pull in a slow breath. "Considering you *just* broke up with someone a few days ago, I'd say I wouldn't want to be *that* guy." He mutters something under his breath as he shifts around. "It's like I said, I have a lot of fun when I'm with you. Is there any way we can keep going on like this, or are things going to get too weird between us now?"

What he's saying sounds like an ultimatum: either I drop my little crush on him, or we can't be friends. I realize we've only known each other a little less than a week, but every minute I've spent away from him has felt like a lifetime. And I'd rather try this friendship thing than never get to see him again. Pulling myself together, my eyes snap back to his.

"That was hypothetical. Besides, you're way too nice for me to get involved with you. Bad guys are kind of my thing."

Relief settles in his expression, and he smirks. "I guess that explains the biker."

The waitress appears again, setting identical plates in front of us. "Anything else I can get you?"

Adam raises his eyebrows at me, silently asking if I need anything more. I tip my head at the waitress. "Thanks, I think we're good." As she spins around, Adam watches me dig into my crepe with a flittering smile that doesn't quite transform the worry in his eyes. "Are *we*? Good, I mean?"

By now I'm used to stuffing my face in front of Adam, and don't hold back with a heaping forkful. The mix of strawberries, cream cheese and chocolate syrup stuffed inside the crepe is like a piece of heaven. I moan, pointing at my plate with my dirty fork. "We're definitely not as good as this. Does the rest of the world know about these things?"

"I'm pretty sure, yeah." He chuckles, cutting his first bite. "You've never had a crepe before?" When I shake my head, he laughs even louder, the sound of his voice cutting through the quiet lull of the diner. "Days like this I'm not sure which of us is more deprived."

Our conversation leads far away from my confession, leaving me a little sad and confused, although still glad Adam wants to see me again all the same.

WHEN I RETURN TO THE DORMS AFTER work, Kelly gasps dramatically from the couch. In a pair of spandex capris and a mesh athletic tank top, her brown hair pulled into a high ponytail, it's safe to guess she just returned from another run without me. I've always considered it gross that she doesn't shower as soon as she gets back. She usually eats an ice cream bar and watches smut TV first. The empty wrapper rests on the floor next to her running shoes.

Her eyebrows raise. "Wow, what gives me the honor of your presence today, after I *just* put in an application for a new roommate? Why aren't you attached to Adam's hip?"

"Very funny," I answer, flopping down beside her. "He said he'd pick me up later at the library. I just have to decide if I'm going with him or not."

"Ooooh, trouble in paradise? *Already*?" she teases, nudging me.

I grunt. "There's no *paradise*. He made it clear this morning that he only wants to be friends."

Kelly's eyes pop wide as she whips her ponytail over her shoulder. "Wait. Is he gay?"

"No way!" Then, for a fraction of a second, I consider his sex appeal going to waste on me and shake my head. "Doubtful anyway. He said something about not wanting to be the rebound guy. He made it sound like his family is pretty intense."

"Sounds like a load of shit to me. Maybe he's just a total player." Kelly glances down at her chipped pink nails before deciding which one to chew on. "When are you going to introduce me to this guy? I'm starting to feel like the secret friend not suitable for public viewing."

"Give yourself a *little* credit. I at least take you out for walks." I giggle when she feigns insult. "It'd be way too awkward to officially introduce you if we're not actually dating. You'll just have to conveniently run into us one of these times." I breathe out a long, slow breath, resting my hands on my stomach. "If there *is* a next time."

Her eyes glower with suspicion. Times like this she's more like the overbearing big sister I never had than my best friend, but I appreciate how much she cares. Since I lost most of my high school friends and my parents are so skeptical of my ability to independently function as a human, she's kind of the only person of value left in my life. "Does he still want you to go on his little trip?"

"I think so." I shrug, crossing my legs then uncrossing them again. "I don't know. I'm not sure if I can act normal around him for that long anyway. I mean if he just wants to be friends, I may have to invest in physical restraints."

Could I really pretend I'm not majorly attracted to him for that long? I have a hard enough time when we're alone for just a few hours. No matter how much I try to avoid it, my mind wanders to places that would definitely violate any kind of platonic friendship.

Kelly chews on her nail a little longer before springing from the couch. "Well, if you're not going with him tonight, then you have no excuse to get out of going to the first end of the year mixer at Matt's sisters' house."

The thought of teetering around all night in heels and a cocktail dress makes me want to roll my eyes. It's one of the many reasons I purposely chose *not* to join a sorority. Kelly gets all hyped up over that kind of thing, but I'd rather hang on the couch in a pair of sweats and watch horror movies where no one will bother me.

"Thanks for the invite, but I think I'll pass."

"*C'mon*, Jewels," she pleads, patting my calf with her foot. "For the first time in months, you're *officially single*. I could name off a dozen guys who would foam at the mouth if they heard this. Let's get dressed up and show you off."

Adam's rejection still weighs heavy on my shoulders. I *do* feel like blowing off a little steam. Going to a semi-formal dance isn't my idea of fun, but a night here by myself doesn't sound that inviting, either. "*Fine*," I grumble in resignation. "As long as you let me dress like something *other* than a lady of the night."

USING ADAM'S AVOIDANCE TRICK, I SEND him a text rather than calling, saying I'm too tired for a night out (just as Kelly's pulling me through the sorority house door in the 3-inch, red-soled designer heels she got as a hand-me-down from her millionaire aunt).

I tug at the hem of the little black dress I bought for my high school graduation, not too surprised that it's suddenly tight around my toned thighs. I haven't worn a dress since attending my one and only mixer last fall, and I quite honestly feel more naked than dressed. Kelly curled my hair into loose waves that cascade over my bare shoulders dusted in shimmer.

Kelly's cobalt blue dress covers a bit less than mine, its thin straps skimping across the sides of her shoulders and the hem stopping above her knees. I watched her twist and pin her brown locks for all of ten minutes before I was baffled by her mad hair skills. She looks amazing, like some kind of freaking supermodel.

We pass a cluster of girls near the entrance dressed in leggings and cowgirl boots. Not the usual fare for these kinds of parties.

I stare after them. "This is a semi formal, right? Are you sure we shouldn't be wearing ten gallon hats and stick grass between our teeth?"

Kelly huffs while pushing her way through more of the same redneck attire. "Who gives a shit? You're a total knockout in that dress!" A few guys in sports jackets follow us with their eyes as we pass by, one of them giving a low wolf-whistle. Kelly nudges me. "See? It's irrelevant."

As Kelly has a thing for being fashionably late, the house is already packed shoulder-to-shoulder. A DJ with a pretty complex lighting system heads up the far end of the party room, blasting Jay-Z through a collection of tall speakers as bright lights flash everywhere. Some of the crowd jumps up and down to the beat, creating a lazy wave of heads in front of him. A pathetic display of bright streamers and balloons drape from the ceiling as the house's sole decoration.

We push our way through the warm bodies until reaching the bar where Matt and his fraternity brothers huddle. Matt greets us with a, "Well, *hellooo*, ladies!" and extra drinks already in hand. Kelly rests her hand over the buttons on Matt's dress shirt as she leans in to whisper something in his ear. His free hand rubs the lower half of her exposed back as a longing grin pulls at his lips. I shuffle away into the crowd with my drink in hand, feeling like I just caught them making out. Which they'll probably do shortly.

I recognize a few faces from other parties we've been to, as well as seeing a few fellow students. The overall chatter is a low murmur against the thumping music, but filling up into the high-ceilings just the same. The only thing I like anymore about these parties is the architecture inside the old homes. The complex oak woodwork with circled patterns and deep grooves reminds me of going to see my grandparents in their big farm home when I was little.

Thankfully, the sorority sisters are much more strict on the no smoking rule. The only smells tonight are that of spilled drinks, an atrocious blend of perfumes and colognes meant to seduce, a bit of ripe body odor, and the musk that comes with old houses. It's a medley of stenches that can only be experienced with the thousands of dollars that are dropped into a college experience. I almost prefer the smoke.

Sipping on the clear liquid from Matt, I grimace. It's vodka and lemon-lime soda, probably my least favorite drink after gin. One of Matt's brothers, I think his name is Dean, appears at my side. Built like Matt, he's tall and well-toned with dark hair styled into a neat faux-hawk. He wears a tan jacket over a white button down and khakis. He's just like the other brothers, prim and proper, yet pretty full of himself and an innovative leader in the partying department.

"*That* looks appetizing. Here, try this." He hands me a dark brown liquid.

I take a sip. It tastes like Captain and diet. "Thanks. I think I'm going to get a beer. One can never have too many carbs!"

Grinning, he takes the drink Matt gave me. "Keep it. You look like you could loosen up a little. It's Julia, right?"

"*Jewels*. My parents cut to the chase of using a nickname."

I stare down at the drink. I don't want to go through the usual routine of getting plastered and worrying about losing Kelly, especially now that I'm interested in Adam and don't want to blow my chances of being with him. But then I remember the way he looked at me when he said he just wanted to be friends, and I decide something to numb the hurt is exactly what I need.

Dean starts in on small-talk, asking questions about my classes and my major. It's the same unimportant conversation I've had with a hundred guys—nothing but a bunch of artificial niceties when he'd much rather skip to the chase and ask permission to jump into my pants. I can see it in his eyes, the way he lightly touches my bare arm.

I'm only half there for the conversation, answering whatever I can when all I want to do is skip out and find Adam.

After nearly downing the whole drink, I'm amazed how I suddenly feel close to hammered. With an extensive track record like mine, one does *not* get intoxicated from a single drink, but I guess it could be due to the fact that I haven't drank again since hanging out with Adam. Or maybe Dean poured a double.

The wristlet Kelly loaned me buzzes. Holding the cup in the crook of my arm, I fish out my phone to find a text from Adam.

Thought u said things between us were good

I pull in a stuttering breath. What would make him say that?

My eyes feel heavy. The letters on my phone become a jumbled mess. Drawing my eyebrows down, I type.

They r

A few seconds later he responds.

Stopped by to make sure u r not mad

"Shit," I mutter. I should've just flat out told him that I was going out with my roommate instead of making up a lame lie. But apparently I've become an expert at avoiding the truth this past week.

Kel dragged me 2 spring mixer

Pushing the send button becomes a chore when all at once my head feels extremely heavy. I feel a sudden urge to just lie down.

I feel a vibration with another message from Adam, but my eyes won't focus long enough to make out the words. Random letters blur in and out, making no sense. I slowly bring my head up to watch the people dancing nearby. The room takes on a carnival-quality depth, making them look like they're a hundred feet off in the distance. I feel like I'm floating, even though my feet are still grounded.

Suddenly feeling dizzy, I stagger.

"Everything okay?" Dean asks.

"It must be these damn heels," I think I say. Everything takes on a dream-like quality as I look up at Dean, his handsome face swaying in front of me. The music becomes hallow like it's being played in a garbage can in a garage a block down. I bring a hand up to my head. "Something's wrong."

Strong arms wrap around me. "Whoa, take it easy."

My eyes roll shut. I feel weightless.

I LOOK UP AT A DIMLY LIT CEILING IN A quiet room. Trying to roll to my side, I realize I'm in a bed and give in to the softness of it. Another wave of unconsciousness follows.

SOMEONE TOUCHES MY FACE. I struggle to open my eyes again.

Adam eventually comes into focus. He stands over me, his handsome features marred with worry.

"Am I dreaming?" I ask sleepily, reaching up to touch him.

His face feels warm. Real.

"*Fuck*," he mutters under his breath before looking over his shoulder. "I think she was drugged."

Shadows farther back in the room shift. Suddenly, Matt and Kelly stand at his side, as if appearing by magic. My best friend's eyes are fearful, her cheeks smeared with mascara.

Fear pinches my chest. I choke on a sob. "What?"

She leans down, stroking my forehead. "It's okay, sweetie. We're taking you to the hospital."

Panic makes me more lucid. "*What*?"

If my parents find out, they'll make me quit school and move home. They'd think I was too weak to be on my own. A raging burn fills me when I think of my entire life being ripped out from underneath me. I can't go back to living under their constant supervision. My fingers clasp tightly around Kelly's wrist, using the leverage to sit up.

"No! Just take me home! *Please*! I'm begging you, Kel! Don't do this to me!"

Adam gently pries my fingers off Kelly and gathers me in his arms. "Everything's going to be okay, Jewels."

I snuggle into his chest, breathing in deeply, wishing I had the courage to tell him exactly how I feel. That he's all I think about anymore, and I can't ever get enough of him. That I don't just want to be friends, because just the thought of kissing him makes me feel alive. Like I have something to look forward to again.

"Please, my parents would make me move home if they found out," I say quietly. "I can't do it. I can't go back there."

REALITY WEAVES IN AND OUT.

Flashes of people appear then disappear.

Warm, brawny arms slip behind my legs and back, carrying me.

Muffled conversations trail after me.

Then, the appeasing smell of leather.

I'm in Adam's Challenger.

Everything goes dark.

Seven

MY SKULL SWARMS VIOLENTLY WHEN I sit up, like I'm plagued with the worst hangover of my life. The sun blasts through our dorm room windows, showing Kelly's empty bed, her turquoise sheets a mess like they always are whether she's slept in them or not. Somehow I ended up in my favorite cotton shorts and pink tank top that I usually wear to bed. Considering my bra is still on, I wonder if Kelly had to help me get undressed.

My eyes fall to the couch. Adam's sprawled on top, my leopard print blanket from high school draped over his legs. How did he get here? Did I let him in? When I try to remember what I had to drink at the mixer, I vaguely remember talking to Dean, and realize my memories of the party have vanished with the daylight. Fear sinks in. I've had plenty of drunken nights where I couldn't remember vague details, but I've never completely blacked it all out.

In addition to having a killer headache, my stomach feels completely out of sorts. It reminds me of the time in elementary school when my parents made me go on an old people's cruise with them to the Virgin Islands. We took pills that were supposed to help with motion sickness, but they counteracted with my system and I walked around the ship with my hands out at my sides, thinking I was going to crash into the walls. Not only was it the most boring time I'd ever had on a vacation, but I spent half of it in our closet-sized bathroom, puking my guts out. My equilibrium was still messed up for days after we disembarked.

Only now, the feeling is amplified.

"Adam." I reach for my bone-dry throat. When he doesn't answer, I try clearing my throat and saying his name louder.

He finally stirs, then bolts upright. "Hey," he greets me softly with one of his sad, plastic smiles. "How do you feel?"

My head spins like I've spent an hour on the world's most maniacal merry-go-round.

Worse yet, bitter saliva rushes to my mouth with lightning speed. "I think I'm gonna hurl."

Adam darts across the room to grab the trash can, holding it out next to me just as I hurl. He gathers my hair behind my head as I cradle the garbage between my legs. My body heaves as my stomach continues to empty its contents. I cough and gag, tears of pain burning down my cheeks as Adam rubs my back. It's bad enough to get sick, but I'm mortified that he's witnessing me at my absolute worst.

Once I've settled and my stomach has calmed, he leaves my side to return with my bath towel from the closet door and a bottle of water from the fridge. "Small sips."

I wipe my mouth with the towel and take one small pull of the water, shutting my eyes when the cool liquid calms my burning throat. Although I feel like death and must look horrendous, I'm excited to have Adam beside me. I fuss with my hair, hoping to at least tame any flyaway chunks. "What are you doing here? What happened?"

His jaw flexes, almost manically. "Do you remember anything?"

"Not really." I shake my head with ease so as not to upset my stomach again. "I just remember going to the party with Kel."

Rubbing at his neck, he glances down before his eyes return to mine. "Jewels, you were drugged last night."

A trickle of ice cold fear washes over me. I pull my knees up against myself, dragging my sheet up with them. "Was I...I mean, was there sex involved?" My face burns hot as I swallow the giant sob rising in my chest.

"No. At least we're pretty sure nothing happened." His nostrils flare. His gaze hops around the room, as if it's too painful to look directly at me. "The asshole who roofied you swore up and down nothing happened after we said we were calling the cops. You begged us not to take you to the hospital, but we called the ER. They said to keep an eye on your breathing and fill you with liquids. And they said if there's any reason you think he's lying...I mean, if you think he did anything to you...that you need to check into the ER right away for a rape kit."

I lost my virginity almost three years ago and know far too well what it feels like the morning after having sex. The dull aches and tenderness, the swelling. Shifting my weight, I'm positive nothing happened. The only things out of sorts are my head and stomach.

"I don't need to go," I say, my face burning. The last thing I need is for my parents to decide I can't handle college after all, and force me to move home. I don't have it in me to go back there.

Adam's body remains tense, on edge. "You sure?" When I really look at him, I notice his lips seem a bit puffier than usual, and there's a small cut in the corner of them. My gaze travels up to his eyes, finding a bit of discoloration around his left. Frowning, I reach out to brush my fingers against his temple.

"How did this happen?"

He winces a little under my touch, and pulls my hand down. "Don't worry about it. I'm just glad I got there when I did."

I skim over the hard edges of his facial features, wondering if he threw any punches back. The Adam I've grown comfortable with doesn't seem to have a mean bone in his body, but I suppose everyone has a breaking point. "You're the one who found me?"

"You didn't answer my last text. I was worried you were upset with me because of what I said at the diner." His expression softens. "I knew about the party you mentioned, and I only live a few blocks down so I went over there to talk to you in person."

I take another half-sip of the water and lick my dry lips. "Where'd you find me?"

The pained way he looks back at me makes my breathing shallow. Whatever he saw obviously upset him. Badly. "He took you up to one of the bedrooms."

"You just happened to guess I'd be up there?" My hands tremble underneath the sheet as my stomach roils. Does he think I'm a slut? Still, if he hadn't found me when he did, I could've been raped. Was Dean the one who slipped me the roofie?

Adam sees the sheet quivering and sets his hand over mine, calming my nerves. "One of my old fraternity brothers saw that asshole helping you up the stairs. He thought the two of you were together."

Tears burn behind my eyes and snot trickles down my nose. I quickly wipe it with the back of my arm with a hallow laugh and rake my fingers through my hair. "Shit. I must look hideous."

Adam's dimples I adore pop into their rightful place. "Actually, I was just thinking I didn't know it was possible for someone to still look incredible after barfing like that."

Burying my face behind my knees, I laugh gently into the sheet, trying not to jar my stomach. "*Liar.*"

He laughs along with me for a minute before squeezing my hands. "Can I get you something?"

I shake my forehead against my knees, still humiliated that he's seeing me this way and wishing my stomach would stop quaking all over the place. Every movement I make seems to make the pounding of my head worse. I just want to ball up in the fetal position and disappear.

"What time is it, anyway?" I ask, slowly tilting my head back up.

Adam drops his hand from mine to wipe at his tired face. "Just a little after noon. Kelly already left for work. She didn't want to go, but I told her I'd stay with you."

"You didn't have to, but...thanks." Sighing, I push my hair away from my face. "It's freaking hot in here. And I just want to go back to sleep."

"The ER nurse said you'll feel exhausted for the next few days. The hot flashes and throwing up are normal, too."

When I reach behind me for my pillow, Adam dashes to my side, pulling it underneath my neck and supporting my head as I set it down. "Sleep as much as you want." Smiling, he adds, "I think I can clear my schedule for the next few days to keep an eye on you."

More tears spill from the corner of my eyes, dropping down on my pillow. I wipe my face. "God, this is embarrassing. I guess I owe you my life, or at least my eternal gratification in a poem, or well thought out soliloquy," I whisper in a hoarse voice. I reach for his arm. "Thank you."

THE NEXT TIME I BECOME FULLY conscious, Adam's huddled underneath my reading light next to me on the bed, engrossed in a hardcover book resting against his legs. When I look closer, I see it's my beloved copy of *Full Dark, No Stars*. A fan blasts cool air on top of the desk, spreading Adam's musky scent with it. I snuggle under the blanket a little more, moaning. My breath's probably atrocious considering I haven't brushed my teeth since throwing up. "What day is it?"

Amid his deep chuckle, Adam whispers, "Still Sunday. But it's late. Kelly's sleeping." He bends the corner of the page he's on and tosses the book aside. "Are you ready for some water and ice chips?"

Although I'm not as hot as I was before, my throat is as dry as the Arabian desert, so I nod. "That sounds great, thanks."

He slips off the bed to quietly rummage through the tiny freezer inside our fridge. I'm about to tell him we don't have ice when he brings me a small baggie and a bottle of water. "I asked Kelly to bring some back from work," he explains.

I scoot up to my elbows and reach for the water. I feel a charge from our fingers touching and look up at him for a reaction. His eyes freeze on mine, giving me chills. The shadows from the reading light only exaggerate the black eye he's working on and all at once I feel guilty for everything I've put him through.

"You don't have to stay. I'm sure you've got other things you want to do, like sleep in your own bed. Maybe even eat." I take a long swig of the water and then dig into the bag for a small handful. As the cold soothes my throat, I hum happily.

Adam sits on the edge of the bed, shrugging. "It's the couch here, or the couch at my buddy's place, and Kelly's been bringing me food. But I can leave if you want privacy."

"*No*," I answer a little too rambunctiously, happy it's too dark for him to see me blush. "I mean, I like having you here. It makes this whole thing a little less scary." I motion to the book. "But you don't have to be on guard all night. You *can* sleep."

"I don't always sleep well at night. If the light's bothering you—"

"No, it's good," I say, shaking my head. "Really. I'm not always the best sleeper either." Sadly enough, there's a bright side to this whole experience. If I had any nightmares since being roofied, I definitely don't remember them for once.

His eyebrows draw down. "Your stomach feeling any better?"

"Maybe." I push on it tentatively. There's even a small ache of hunger deeper within, so I find myself wondering just how far I can push it. Feeling hung over without being drunk to cause it in the first place feels like the most backwards of logic.

"Are you ready to try some food, or do you want to go back to sleep?"

I stare at him, amazed that I found such an awesome guy who's willing to dote on me. We haven't talked about either of our past relationships other than my confessions about Levi. I don't even know if Adam's *had* a girlfriend. Then again, maybe the fact that he's so kind and patient with me means he was in a serious relationship at one point. There has to have been at least *one* lucky girl along the way who stole his heart.

I imagine giving your heart to Adam Murphy is an experience unlike any other, but I can't let it happen to me. Mine's far too fragile to mess with.

"*What?*" he asks, chuckling.

Flustered by my runaway thoughts, I point across the room. "There's a box of Captain Crunch in the cupboard above my desk. Could you maybe grab it?"

When he turns away, I watch the muscles in his back contort underneath his gray t-shirt, and feel a sudden impulse to reach out and touch him. Then I remember I probably look like hell, and have something even more dreadful than dragon breath.

My throat's so tight when he returns with the box that my "thanks" comes out in a squeak. Captain Crunch is probably one of the last things you want to eat with someone sleeping a mere twenty feet away, so I pull my blanket up over my head, moving my jaw in slow, precise bites.

"*What* are you doing?" Adam asks, peering under the blanket with a grin.

"I don't want to wake Kel!" I whisper loudly, my heart fluttering at the sight of him looking back at me underneath the sheets. I now have a complete vision of what it would be like to wake up with Adam after a night of what I'm sure would be great sex. Finding a way to control myself around him is becoming impossible.

Still smiling back at me underneath the blanket, he asks, "You want me to find you something quieter?"

"This is good," I say with a shake of my head. When he drops the blanket, I take one more bite before coming up for air. I'm met with Adam's soft laughter.

"You're incredibly weird sometimes."

"I'll take that as a compliment, because I'm not sure what else to do with it." A big yawn pulls at my jaw. I quickly slap a hand over it before he catches a whiff of my raunchy breath.

A crooked, sweet grin drags one side of his mouth up. "You can take it however you want."

I set the cereal on the other side of my bed, and snuggle back into my pillow, staring up at him. "I'm going to take another little nap. When you finally get tired, you can lie here if you want. I mean on the bed." My lips curl up to show my teeth in a goofy grin. The idea of lying next to him in the night makes my pulse race. "Just keep your hands to yourself. I hear guys like you are no good for me."

His eyes dance in amusement. "Fair enough."

I'm out almost instantly.

SOMEWHERE NEARBY, A DOOR CREAKS. My eyes burst open. When I discover Adam's t-shirt twisted inside my fist, I release my hand with an internal gasp and cover my mouth. He lays mere inches away, his lips slightly parted, his dark eyelashes nearly brushing his cheeks. The shadow dusting his unshaved jaw has grown thicker, making him look older. The bruising around his eye has darkened with the light of day, but at least the swelling on his lips seems to have subsided.

I look past him just in time to see Kelly sneaking out the door, apparently headed for class. Once she's gone a moment later, I look out the window and see nothing but blue skies and a few clouds drifting along lazily. Skipping class seems like a terrible idea, but I'm still majorly groggy, staying in bed like this with Adam all day is probably the biggest temptation I've ever faced. I turn back to enjoy the guilty pleasure of staring at him without his knowledge, breathing in his delightful scent.

And then it strikes me—I'm going to tell him yes. I'll do whatever it takes for my parents to let me take off for the summer with him, even if I have to sneak around to do it. I can't think of anything I'd rather do than wake up with him like this every day for almost two solid months.

Using the skills it took to sneak out of my parents' house for parties when I was in high school, I slip from the bed without waking Adam to gather everything I'll need to take a shower, get dressed, brush my teeth, and most importantly, gargle. I'm still feeling groggy as I head for the hallway, but if I'm going to continue hanging out this close to Adam, cleaning up is my number one priority.

SHOWERING AND GETTING DRESSED into yoga pants and a t-shirt completely drains me, as if I just ran one of Kelly's insane mini-marathons. All I want is to sink back into my bed next to Adam. But when I open the door to the room, he's sitting on the edge of the couch. His beautiful eyes brighten when I step in. "*Hey.*"

"Hey," I return, setting my shower caddy on the desk. With my wet hair twisted over my shoulder, and not a stitch of makeup, I feel self-conscious. With past boyfriends I would go to sleep with makeup still on so I wouldn't scare them away by the light of day. Few people have seen me this bare. I laugh under my breath, pulling at a strand of wet hair. At least I'm no longer barfing.

He stands suddenly, expressionless. "You showered." Before I have time to respond, he's taking long strides toward me, his face still void of any emotion. "Good," he says in a tight voice. He folds me in his arms with an intensity to his gaze that makes me breathless. Then, without hesitation, he presses his lips to mine.

I melt underneath his amazing kiss. The way his soft lips move against mine is so gentle and tender, it's as if he's afraid he'll hurt me with anything more. As his eager hands move up to my jaw, my heart flip-flops with his touch. I lean into him, holding onto the back of his neck and pressing my body to his. Every part of me tingles in anticipation.

The kiss becomes blazing hot, filled with the kind of longing that can drive a person insane. His tongue brushes with mine, over and over, as if tasting my essence. I whimper into his mouth, one hand grabbing what I can get of his short hair, the other pressing to his chest that's just as hard and taut as I had imagined. We become a tangled mess of limbs, eager to drink one another in. I could disappear forever in this moment, in the comfort of his burly arms, and not even care.

Before long, however, my knees literally grow weak. I clutch his arm, desperate to stay upright, desperate to continue on, regardless.

All at once his lips break away, and his eyebrows furrow in worry. "You okay?" he asks in a husky tone.

"Wow." I gasp, grabbing onto his strong shoulder to steady myself. I'm not so sure I won't pass out. I can't decide if I'm still dizzy from the roofie, or if it's because of the earth-shattering kiss. One thing's for sure though—I want to kiss him again. As many times as humanly possible before daunting things like food and water become necessary.

Adam's hands slip down from my face to my hips. "You need to sit down." He steers me over to the couch, both of us lowering down at the same time, sitting with our knees touching. He brushes a strand of my wet hair from my face, grinning. "You okay?"

Technically, I'm not. I'm weightless, floating above the clouds with no plans to come back down. The kiss was unlike anything I've ever felt before, unlike anything I could even *dream* about. Kelly once told me the best kisses are always from someone either really experienced, or someone you've developed really deep feelings for. It always made me question why make-out sessions with Levi never knocked my socks off.

I reach up to touch my throbbing lips, gaping over at him. I'll be feeling the power of this kiss for days to come. "What happened to you not being good for me?"

"I'm still not," he answers gruffly, his grin fading. He pulls my hand down to lace his fingers with mine. Although it reminds me of the night we met and searched for Kelly together, this time it feels *real*. Because now I finally know he wants to be with me the way I had hoped. "It's just...the other night when I realized what could've happened to you if I'd been too late...it almost killed me."

"But you weren't too late," I remind him quickly, locking eyes with him and squeezing his fingers.

"Damn it." He rubs at his neck with his free hand, looking away. "I promised myself I wouldn't let this happen."

Rejection teeters on the edge of my mind, threatening to destroy me. "You mean the kiss?" I manage to ask. Does he already regret it?

"This," he says, holding our hands up. "*Us.* I was under the delusion that we could take this trip together and just be friends. I didn't want to fuck things up."

My brain fogs over, reminding me why I'm sitting in my room and not in class. I lean my head against the couch, studying him. "I don't see us being together as a *fuck-up*. And there's nothing wrong with us being more than friends."

He rubs the palm of his free hand against his jeans. I realize for the first time he hasn't changed since Saturday night either, but I don't even care. It's not like he smells bad or anything. But even if he did, I'll take him any way I can. "That's not what I meant. Not exactly." He displays another half-assed smile. "But I should've known better."

Biting down on my lip, I try to hide my over-the-top excitement. "You should know, I've decided I'm going with you."

His eyes pop wide as he inhales deeply. In this moment he looks so adorable, and happy, and lovable that I spring forward, kissing him before he can say anything. He's quick to respond, putting his arms around my waist, and nudging my mouth open to slip his tongue in once again. Warm aches consume me as he arches against me. The kiss intensifies.

I could easily shut out the rest of the world and stay in the comfort of his arms forever. Our teeth click at one point as we eagerly devour each other, but neither one of us backs down. I straddle him and let my sexual urges take over. Even though I worry there's still the slightest taste or smell of puke somewhere on me. Even though I won't have sex with him right now because I don't want him to see me as easy. Even though I'm afraid of letting myself fall for someone again.

His unshaven face is prickly, and I'm worried I'm being too rough with his lips until he moans when I nibble at them. My body throbs, wanting him to touch me. I grind against him as we kiss, unable to back down. I've waited so long for this moment. I slip my hand under his shirt, shivering with the feel of his tight stomach.

He recoils with a deep breath, disentangling himself from me.

"Shit. We can't do this." Gathering my wandering hands, he nudges me off of him and stands. Guilt ridden, his eyes dart past me. "I have to go."

A vice grip twists at my chest. This is definitely the ugly face of rejection. I fight back the surprising need to cry, even though it's been so long since my meds would allow me the luxury. *He's* the one who approached me at the party. *He's* the one who asked me to go on this trip with him. *He's* the one who kissed *me*. Why is he doing this to me now?

"Is it because I threw up?" I ask quietly, wishing he'd look at me. "Did I do something wrong?"

"You didn't do anything, Jewels. I just need some time to clear my head." He turns his back to me, starting for the door. "Go back to bed and rest up. I'll come check on you again later. Call if you need me sooner."

For a drawn-out moment, he pauses at the door, and I think he's going to turn around and tell me he's sorry. But he turns the handle and disappears.

After the door closes behind him, I collapse in a heaping sob.

Eight

MY JUNIOR YEAR OF HIGH SCHOOL, I made football cheerleading captain. This made the senior girls on the squad incredibly jealous. A few of them even quit. The ones who stayed in secretly plotted to get even, dropping me from the top of the pyramid during the halftime show on Homecoming night. Not only did I fracture my arm and have to wear a cast for the rest of the season, but I was completely mortified and figured it would be the catalyst for a downfall in popularity. At the time I didn't know it would create an anti-bullying campaign among the seniors.

Jason and I had been dating for a few months before it happened. He was *livid* when he got wind that the "accident" was planned out ahead of time. Later that night after my trip to the ER, we went to his house instead of the school dance as it was my favorite place to escape everything, that night especially. His family had updated a really old house with a massive wrap-around porch where we'd sit on the swinging bench for hours, talking and kissing until my curfew. In those beginning days, we could never get enough of each other. Jason was a touchy-feely guy who always felt the need to hold me and stroke my arms, face, whatever was closest. He was still like that even after we had been dating for two years.

"They should all be kicked off the squad," he told me, running his fingers above the bright pink cast on my arm. "Your coach should demand that they get OSS for a few days, too."

"I get it, they're jealous," I said as I wiped fresh tears from my face. "If I was a senior I probably wouldn't like someone younger telling me what to do, either. I should withdraw as captain and let one of them have it. Not like I'm going to be able to do as much with this dumb thing on my arm anyway."

Jason gently turned me around so I'd be forced to see the concern washing over his dark eyes that were made even darker by his thick eyebrows and full lashes. He was boyishly cute with shaggy brown hair, a somewhat crookedly sloped nose, and a bright smile that was contagious. He was the type who could charm even the grumpiest of people with his upbeat attitude.

"Would you stop being so damn compliant? You worked hard for this, Jewels. You deserve it. Don't let anyone make you think any differently. And whatever you do, don't let them see you crying over what happened. I mean, it's okay to cry, just save your tears for the really big stuff. There will be far worse things to come."

It's ironic how at the time, I couldn't imagine there being anything worse.

DAYLIGHT EVAPORATES AS I WAKE sporadically, still sprawled out on the couch. Kelly comes in after class to ask how I'm feeling, or maybe I just imagine it. I don't bother checking my phone for texts or missed calls until the room becomes pitch black again, bringing on another restless night.

Adam bows out just as I had expected, sending a message telling me it sounds like Kelly has things under control, and that he'll stop by in the morning.

I must've missed a dozen calls from my mom that continue to go unreturned. While I can't tell her what happened, I also know that if I keep avoiding her she'll become upset to the point she may come over to check on me. But I don't really care. I'm so hollow and empty that I feel like a cracked shell. The darkness consumes me over and over, bringing more nightmares.

Another morning comes, or at least I assume by the daylight trying to rip me from my cave. Time slips into a black hole. I only get up once or twice to pee. Kelly tries to wake me a few times. I hear the low tone of her voice as she talks to someone on the phone. Later on, after I hear her say she's leaving for classes, there's a burst of knocks on the door. I stay curled up in a ball on the couch, imagining myself disappearing, physically becoming the nothing I feel inside.

I WAKE TO FIND MY MOM LOOMING OVER me, her features pinched, her voice agitated. I don't understand her words as they spurt from her. Kelly stands a few feet behind, anxiously chewing on her fingernails. Something small and light is pressed into my hands, and I'm given a glass of water.

I don't think, I just swallow it down.

MY MOM'S SIGNATURE FLORAL PERFUME invades my nostrils before I even open my eyes. "Jewels?"

She pulls the blanket away from my head, forcing me to shield my eyes from the intrusion of a harsh light. Whether it's the start of another day or just the light turned on in our room, I don't know. I remove my hand, groaning.

My mom stands over me in high boots and skinny jeans with a dainty pink scarf draped over an ivory blouse. It's something *I* would wear. Even her blond hair, one shade lighter than my own, is curled in the same twisted waves Kelly likes to give me for special occasions. I'm surprised she hasn't had any plastic surgery yet to hide her crow's feet, and attempt to be my *exact* twin.

"Jewels, what happened to you?"

My stomach twists. Kelly is no longer in the room. Just how much did she tell my mom? "I haven't been feeling well," I mutter, wiping at my face, and slowly dragging my feet to the ground. I don't feel like functioning quite yet, but I need to put on a good show if I expect my mom to leave me alone ever again.

She reaches down to touch my forehead, her collection of sparkling bangles clinking against her wrist. "Why didn't you call? You know the agreement. I had to take time off work to come check on you. Have you been taking your medication?"

"Sorry," I say, although I don't really mean it. "I've been sick. I guess I forgot to take it the last couple of days because I wasn't feeling well."

"You're not running a temperature." She sits on the edge of the couch where my legs were two seconds ago. "Is there something you need to tell me?"

I bristle. This is the part where she tells me I'm not ready to be on my own, where she informs me she's arranged for my things to be sent back home. She knows something's off, and I have to provide her with a reasonable explanation to appease her worry. To keep her from thinking I'm so far gone that I need to spend a few days in the hospital again.

"I broke up with Levi."

"For god's sake, Jewels. *That's* what all of this is about? Do you need to see Doctor Klein again?" She fusses with the blanket, her lips pulled down in a disapproving frown.

I sit tall, subtly shrugging her hands off. "I'm fine. I'm over him. I'm serious, Mom. I got this nasty flu is all."

"Were you drinking?" she asks, her tone sharp. Her hazel eyes study me with a load of disappointment.

One of the conditions that my parents set for me to live in the dorms was that I can't drink while on my depression meds. If she knew the truth, she'd be stuffing my things into bags with the speed of a Tasmanian devil.

"God, Mom, *no*. Can't I get a normal cold like everyone else?" I lick my dry lips. "I'm going back to class today. I'm sorry you had to take off work. My phone died, and I was too sick to care."

There's another rapid knock at the door. I spring to my feet. My head still feels cloudy, but I'm focused on trying to look fine so my mom will just leave. I swing the door open to find Adam, looking like hell. Like someone ran him over. Twice.

He exhales deeply, his shoulders sinking. "You're up."

I pull the door up against my back. "My mom's here," I say before he starts in on what happened last time we saw each other. "I'll call you later."

"Who is it?" Mom calls from behind me. "Just because I'm here doesn't mean you can't have company."

I press on the bridge of my nose, feeling my life spiraling out of control. Adam's watching me with a concerned look, so I shake my head while opening the door farther. He steps into the room, resting his arm on the curve of my lower back. *What's with all the mixed signals?* I want to snap at him, but I've already done enough to make Mom suspicious.

Adam greets her with his charming smile. "Hi, Mrs. Peterson. You're just as beautiful as your daughter."

It's so obvious the way she looks back at him that he's instantly made the lasting impression on her as he did on me. "Why, thank you." She steps forward, her hand held out. "And who might *you* be?"

"Adam Murphy," he answers smoothly, taking her hand. His dimples flare, sealing the deal. My mom's a goner. I swallow down a groan.

"Funny, you haven't mentioned anyone named *Adam* before," Mom tells me as their hands separate. "In fact you haven't been calling me regularly."

My face turns hot. Will she launch into our agreement in front of Adam? "I've been busy."

"Studying," Adam adds. "Jewels and I have a few classes together. She's either working or studying with me at the library."

I eye him, shocked. He must sense that my parents have me on a short leash, even though I haven't alluded to it in our conversations. And he definitely knows how to properly work my mom.

My mom giggles like a teenager, grinning at Adam from ear-to-ear. "Well, at least I know my baby's in good hands." Ugh, she's actually flirting with him. She's seriously beautiful for her age, but does she always have to act like she's fifteen years younger around my friends? "What happened to your eye? That's quite the shiner."

I grow tense, silently begging Adam not to reveal the truth. But he's too busy cranking up the charm. "Got elbowed by one of the guys shooting hoops. I see it as a reminder why I never went out for any sports in high school."

Mom hisses through her teeth. "Ouch. Looks painful."

Adam glances down at my yoga pants, the edges of his mouth twitching in amusement. "Are you wearing that to class?"

"No," I answer quickly, running a hand over my hair. I must look atrocious once again after spending the last couple of days in a ball on the couch. "I have to shower."

Mom sighs, as if I'm too much trouble for her to deal with. "Then you better hurry."

"Go," Adam tells me, motioning back to the hallway. "I'll keep your mom company."

He's giving me an easy out. Adam knows that if the two of us act like we're on our way to class, she'll get out of my hair. I nod, darting around the room to gather my things. Just before I leave the room, I glance at Adam.

With his back to my mom, he offers me a warm, genuine smile. It's a peace offering.

"YOU DID NOT!" MY MOM YELLS AS I WALK back into the room. She stands *way* too close to Adam, laughing, one freshly manicured hand on his arm.

"What's going on?" I ask, setting my toiletries down.

Adam turns to me, all dimples. "You look great."

Affection pinches my throat. Although I didn't want to waste the extra time, I dried my hair and curled it the best I know how without Kelly's assistance. And I'm wearing makeup for the first time in *days*. The jeggings and loosely fitting top are Kelly's, but super comfortable, and so me. I actually feel better. Refreshed. Like myself again. "Thanks. Ready to go?"

"You have to leave?" Mom asks, looking back and forth between us. "Now?"

"Class starts at nine," I say, reaching for my bag and cell phone. Adam promptly takes my bag away, slinging it over his shoulder.

Mom glances at her watch. "Well, I suppose I can make it back to work before the mid-morning meeting." She holds her hands out to Adam, smiling. "It was certainly a pleasure meeting you, Adam." As she leans in for a hug, he gawks at me, helpless. I hide a fit of giggles behind my hand.

"You too, Mrs. Peterson," Adam tells her, patting her back.

She moves on to hug me. "Next time I expect more communication, young lady." She squeezes me so tightly, I can hardly breathe. I actually feel a little guilty for making her worry like that. When she pulls away, I nod.

"I'll call more," I promise.

A few feet from the door, she turns to point at Adam, her bracelets clanging together. "Take care of my baby."

"I will," he promises, glancing at me. Butterflies invade my stomach.

"Talk soon!" Mom calls to me, blowing a kiss.

The minute she closes the door, I fall to the couch with my hands over my eyes and blow out a long breath. "Oh my god, that was awkward. I hope she didn't try to grab your ass while I was in the shower."

Adam sets my bag down, chuckling. "She seems harmless." He sits down at my side. "Are you really doing better? You had me pretty freaked out when you wouldn't answer the door all day yesterday."

Suddenly, I remember his cold rejection, and freeze up. "I was sleeping. I'm fine."

His fingers touch my elbow. "Jewels, I want to explain why I acted that way."

"Don't worry about it," I insist, jerking away, looking past him. "I'm over it."

"No." He brushes my cheek with his thumb. My skin blazes from his touch, sending shivers down to my core. "I was a total ass to you, and you don't deserve that." He brings his hand back down to rest on his knee and bends down like he's trying to catch his breath. After a minute, both his hands brush over the back of his neck before he clasps them together on top of his head. "I've been trying to figure out the best way to do this without hurting you, but every scenario I come up with still ends badly."

"I'm confused. I thought we were having a good time hanging out, and you're already dooming whatever chances we may have together. Why are you so afraid of hurting me?

How do you know I'm not going to be the one to hurt *you*?"

His hands come down to rub at his face, carefully avoiding the black eye he got at my expense. "Remember when you said we don't have to tell each other everything right away, because we'll have time to get to know each other better on this trip, *if* you decide to go?"

A heavy pressure blankets my chest. Is he going to un-invite me after I accepted? I nod, knowing he's about to reveal something monumental. And I doubt from the look on his face that I'll like any part of it.

He licks his lips slowly, his eyes steady against mine. "There's something I should tell you, but I've been avoiding it because it will change everything between us. I don't want you to treat me any differently. And you *will*."

Dozens of different scenarios rush at me as I stare back at him. No matter how hard I try, I can't come up with anything that would make me run away and never want to see him again. He has to be one of the goddamned sweetest guys I've ever met. All the things I'm able to envision he probably wouldn't even be capable of. I bite down on my lip before building up enough courage to answer.

"What do you want me to say to that? Go ahead and tell me anyway? Don't tell me? For a dude you sure send out a lot of mixed signals."

A shy, modest smile twitches across his face. "I want you to say that you don't think I'm an asshole for wanting to keep things the way they are."

"Would you quit calling yourself an asshole? I don't think you truly comprehend what that word means!" I ache to reach out and loop my fingers with his again, to feel that familiar charge that will electrify me all the way down to my bones. But in this moment I'm worried he'll decide to bolt from the room again like he did the other day. "I don't understand why you're so sure this big secret of yours will come between us. Whatever it is, we can work around it."

"It's not as easy as that." His eyes flicker down to my hands, as if he's feeling the same pull to touch *me*. "Damn it, I wish it was."

We sit still for a moment, each of us being consumed by our thoughts. I'm too far invested in my feelings for him to just walk away, even though I should. He doesn't want things to change between us, so why should I push him into something he doesn't want to do? Whatever secret he's keeping may be dangerous enough to tear us apart. And above everything else, I don't want that.

"I trust you," I blurt. "Whatever it is, it's *your* secret to keep or share. I don't want things to change either. I don't want to lose you."

He lifts his chin, his steel blues hopeful. "Wait. Are you sure?"

"No, I'm not sure." I bounce from the couch, my anxiety levels through the roof. What if he just keeps changing his mind, and pushes me further and further away? "If it's the only way for us to go on this trip together, I'm willing to try. I can't promise anything, but *you* have to promise you won't hurt me again like that."

"You're really willing to try?" His eyebrows shoot up. "As *friends*?"

I balk, wondering if I'm truly capable of keeping things that way. He's everything a girl could ever want in a boyfriend—sweet, caring, funny, and a *phenomenal* kisser. The memory of his lips rests on the edge of this decision, tempting me to draw him in for another kiss. Making me want to pull his shirt off, and touch him, find out if he's just as good of a lover.

Pushing the thoughts back to the corner of my mind, I nod. "Okay, fine. As friends."

I'll do whatever it takes to appease him, because at this point, I can't stand the thought of letting him go.

THE NEXT WEEK WE FINALIZE PLANS FOR our trip whenever I'm not in class, at work, or studying for finals, which doesn't leave a whole lot of extra time. Still, we manage to map our route, create a loose schedule, and prepare a list of the supplies we'll need. Things are light and playful between us amid our building excitement. Most of the time we meet in the library after my shift, other times we hang at the dining hall on campus.

Even though I get the feeling Adam could afford for us to stay in hotels the entire summer, we agree to camp out in the back of his cousin's pickup for a few nights here and there, an idea I got from Pinterest when researching how to save money traveling. I've never really been the outdoorsy kind, and the thought of camping out on the actual ground makes me squeamish.

The promise of maintaining a strict friendship feels like a third person at times. After knowing what it feels like to kiss Adam, I have all I can do to remind myself not to touch him, not to let him see the ache in my gaze. I purposely avoid sitting too close, or letting my eyes stay on him for long. Kelly sees me struggling and volunteers to join us a few times, hoping to alleviate the sexual tension.

I steer him far away from my dorm room, knowing I probably can't trust myself to be alone with him unless Kelly happens to be around. One night we stop by the rundown house his buddy lives in so Adam can grab something from his belongings. I stand in the living room, careful not to touch the visibly dirty walls or cross the uneven floorboards. The sight of pathetic, worn-out couch he's been sleeping on makes me glad I let him crash in my bed after I was drugged. After I meet the owner of the house, a little guy with a bad complexion who laughs at everything, I develop a whole new level of sympathy for Adam. If his parents have so much money, why is he crashing with a friend and not renting an apartment?

All the time we spend learning about each other's lives—regrets, mannerisms, likes and dislikes—I'm positive I made the right choice in agreeing to this trip. Even the silence that sometimes passes between us is a thing of comfort. By the time the next weekend rolls around, however, I'm convinced I won't be able to continue on much longer without letting things go too far.

Friday night we grab pizza at Kate's. While waiting for our order, I tap my foot anxiously against my chair, twisting a straw rapper around my fingers.

"Hey." Adam touches my arm across the round table, electrifying me. It only proves how difficult it's going to be for us to sleep so close together every night. *Alone*. "You sure you don't want me to come along tomorrow?"

"My mom may have been charmed by you, but you haven't met my dad." I stop fidgeting to meet his gaze. "He's going to be a much harder sell." Going home to ask my parents to let me take this trip in person seems the only way to go. I should've asked weeks ago, considering classes will be over soon, but I've spent all this time working up the courage.

My dad thinks it's too soon for serious dating, and my mom most likely won't like the last minute notice that I'm not going to be working for her this summer. I don't think *either* of them will understand that Adam and I are doing this as friends. Especially when I'm not behind the idea myself.

"At least let me give you a ride. You just seem really...stressed."

It would come as a great relief to tell Adam exactly *why* I'm so stressed, that I feel like an alcoholic with a drink hanging over my head every time I see him. But as close as we are to leaving, I'm not ready to risk it. Having him drive me there sounds kind of nice, so I nod. "Okay, fine. But I get to control the radio."

"I wouldn't expect anything else."

If he only knew how wild it drives me every time he flashes his radiant smile, or stares back at me in a way that's so sexy it makes my toes curl. As our eyes meet, I shudder.

ADAM PARKS BY THE CURB, STARING AT the two-story monstrosity I called home for seven years. The light yellow house with stone accents and a sloped red roof suddenly looks cold and empty from outside. Maybe it's because I know despite having four bedrooms, only two people occupy it now. My mom was the brains behind the intricate Spanish design. For years she invested all her time and effort into the place, making meetings with the builders and subcontract workers a priority over my school events and family time. A part of me has always hated the house, mostly because it took up so much of her time that she could've spent with me.

Though it's just on the other side of the city, I haven't stopped by since Christmas. Sometimes it's too hard to be where memories of Jason by my side lurk in every room, making it impossible to breathe at times.

"Great place," Adam comments.

"The inside's just as obnoxious, I swear."

Adam lets out a small chuckle. "Remind me never to take you to my place."

Once again I'm perplexed by Adam's reluctance to let me anywhere near his family. I already know they're wealthy, so it wouldn't surprise me they own a sprawling estate. But the voice of reason returns, reminding me there are darker secrets that Adam's keeping from me. Maybe his home is a part of that.

I wrap my hand around the door handle. "I'll call you when I'm ready for a ride. It probably won't be until later tonight. My mom makes a big deal out of having a family dinner whenever I stop by."

"I'll be ready whenever you are." I turn to step out of the car. Adam reaches out to stop me. "Hey."

My heart races, thinking he's going to say "screw it" and kiss me. Or he's going to beg to come along so he can hold my hand as I break the news to my parents.

But his hand drops into his lap as he grins. "Good luck."

AS THE ROUTINE GOES ON MY DAD'S days off from flying, he's sitting at the marble island on one of the leather stools, reading the Saturday paper. His peppered blond hair looks like it's been recently trimmed, and a new pair of black glasses set off his bright blue eyes. On the outside he's your stereotypical handsome pilot who always looks serious and can't be cracked, but underneath the prim and proper look, he's an up and coming stand-up comedian. Plus, he babies me. A lot.

Mom slaves over the mixer across from him, wearing her frilly apron over a fashionable tunic and black leggings, chatting rapidly about someone I assume to be one of her new employees. From the sweet smell in the air, I'd guess she's cooking up her famous blueberry muffins, probably in preparation for tomorrow morning's weekly brunch with her friends. My dad hums in response, probably not hearing a word she says.

For a moment I stand in the kitchen entryway, wishing things could be like they were five years ago, before everything became so complicated. But my dad's newly sprouted gray hair and the hard lines of my mom's eyes are a reminder that my high school days are over, and I'm supposed to be a grown up now. Time has continued on despite my desire for it to stop.

"Hey," I say quietly, stepping into the room.

They both gape back at me, like they've been slapped.

"Jewels!" Dad folds the paper down, his expression bright. "What brings you here?"

"Sweetheart," Mom chimes in, stepping away from the mixer. Her arms wrap around me carefully like she's afraid I'll break if she gives me a genuine hug. "Everything okay?" All at once I'm reminded of the worried glances she gave me after I was drugged. She steps back, giving me the same distraught look.

"I'm good," I promise, setting my purse on the island to give my dad a hug. "Can't I just come home for a day without there being something wrong?"

Dad kisses me on the cheek before pulling me in for a much stronger hug. "We're just surprised is all." When I pull back from him, I catch him giving Mom a stern look.

Mom returns to my side, running her hands through my loose hair. Her lips turn down in a scowl. "You should've called. We have a gala tonight."

I try not to let her see me take a deep breath. All week I've been dreading spending an entire day alone with my parents, knowing the questions they'd have, the deep conversations that would ensue once I told them the real reason for stopping by. And my fears were for nothing.

"That's okay. I have plans tonight anyway," I lie. I already told Kelly I wouldn't go to the house party she's planning to hit, but maybe Adam's free. All I know is I won't be hanging out in this big place by myself, surrounded by the ghosts of my last two years with Jason.

"We'll take you out for a late lunch," Dad offers, reaching for his cell phone in his pocket. "I'll make reservations downtown."

I shake my head. "Actually, I was kind of hoping we could stay home. I have to talk to you guys about something."

"You're pregnant," Mom assumes, her eyes as large as saucers. Dad sets his phone on the counter, his expression first turning shocked then livid.

"*What?*" I press at the bridge of my nose, realizing how difficult this is going to be. "Jesus! No! I told you I broke up with Levi. *Seriously.* Give me some credit!"

Mom crosses her arms, pressing her lips together. "What about that Adam boy?"

"Mom, he's a friend."

My dad sits taller, his shoulders terse. "Should we be concerned?"

"No!" I say, holding my hands out. "God, you guys always assume the worst!"

"So this *doesn't* have anything to do with a boy?" Mom asks, raising her eyebrows.

They're both watching me closely, waiting for a nervous tick or guilty expression to give me away. And just like that, I know there's no way they'll agree to this trip with someone my dad hasn't even met. Not after my breakdown. Not after my mom found me the other day at my worst, and discovered that I hadn't been taking my pills. I'm just lucky they're letting me continue living on the other side of town and not locking me away like I'm too fragile to share with the world.

A heavy stone drops into my stomach.

My parents have been overprotective for as long as I can remember, walking me down the block to meet the bus up until I was twelve, calling the parents of kids who bullied me in middle school, refusing to buy me a car because I didn't get a perfect score on my driver's test, making me wear a helmet in my early teens whenever I rode my mountain bike. I was surprised when they dropped their guard to let me date Jason for so long. The chance of them agreeing to let me go on a trip with a total stranger is non-existent.

I slump into the empty chair next to my dad, feeling like I'm ten years old. "I just want to talk to you guys about this summer. Mom, I know you already have a job waiting for me, but Kelly offered me a job working at her family's camp up north. My advisor said it would be an excellent addition to my resume if I decide to go into childhood education."

The lie summons a million pins and needles of guilt, but it's the only way.

Nine

AS I FIRST BATTLED MY DEPRESSION, I had the emotional equivalency of a melted M&M. I was hard on the outside, and a gooey mess underneath. I crawled into bed with no intention of getting back out. My mom worked the first couple of days, thinking I had the flu and calling to check on me every couple of hours. When I stopped answering her calls and refused to get out of bed, or eat, or do virtually *anything*, she took off from work and put all her energy into making me function again. But it didn't work. By the fourth day, she called Dr. Klein and he recommended an emergency commitment.

Things happened during my stay in the hospital that I wasn't prepared for. I don't know that anyone could prepare for their sanity to quite suddenly fall under constant scrutiny. I had to strip down in front of a female nurse and let her search me for hidden weapons. I was placed in a locked ward with people who ranged from psychotic to completely withdrawn. An old man who looked perfectly sane snapped during lunch and lunged at me with a plastic butter knife. A young woman with shifty eyes ran around during group time screaming, "*Give me back my baby! Who took my goddamned baby?*" My assigned roommate, a middle aged woman who tried to overdose on aspirin, constantly stared at me in my sleep. I nearly had a heart attack the first morning when I flipped my eyes open to find her two feet away, crouched beside my bed.

The reality that I was being treated as one of those crazy people I was surrounded by was enough for me to snap out of my funk and prove to the hospital's psychiatrist that I was functioning enough to be back on my own. By the end of the third day, I was released back to my parents.

My mom insisted that I commute to school from home for two solid months after I returned. Word must've gotten out that I was committed as people I knew at school seemed to go out of their way to avoid interacting with me. Kelly and my roommate Sarah were the only two who treated me the same, as if nothing had happened. Kelly's the only one who never asked how I was feeling, or if I was okay. She knew I wasn't, and she knew I had to deal with it on my own terms.

Preparing to go somewhere without my bestie at my side really begins to sink in as I organize for the trip. Our dorm room resembles the aftermath of a tornado since we've started packing. It takes hours of swearing and tossing things aside to pick my things out from the remains. It's a relief to box my textbooks up, knowing finals are behind me and that I did fairly well after studying with Adam. I assured my parents that I did well enough to warrant a nice-sized bonus check for what they called my "summer adventures." If they only knew.

Minutes before Adam is scheduled to arrive, Kelly helps me drag my stuff down to the curb. The smell of freshly cut grass mixed with the warm sun outside makes me giddy with promises of what's to come. Campus has become a flurry of students ready to get the hell out of town and start summer. If I weren't going on this trip, I'd most likely be avoiding all the madness with Kelly somewhere far off campus. We weave our way through disgruntled parents obviously helping their freshmen move back home for the first time.

Kelly whines as she plops my bright pink duffle bag on the sidewalk outside, tossing my pillow on top with a grunt, as if they were *that* heavy. Dressed in her favorite yoga capris and a bright PINK t-shirt, her hair piled in a sloppy bun on top of her head, she looks nearly identical to the Kelly I met last year. Our friendship has changed tremendously in that time, practically solidifying her as the sister I always wanted.

There isn't anything I wouldn't do for her, and she obviously feels the same since she's covering for me, feeding into the lie that I'm spending my summer working alongside her and all her sisters at her grandparents' summer camp. I realize with a pang of sadness that I'm not going to see her in person for *weeks*.

"You're *sure* you have everything?" she asks for what I'm sure must be the fifth time. "I'm not going to drive across the country to bring you your toothbrush unless you *really* beg. I'm talking down on your knees, real tears flowing."

I wheel my carry-on suitcase over to the duffle bag, setting my cross body purse and computer bag next to them. "Everything I could fit into these bags. I don't need a new outfit for every single day like *you*. I plan to use a washing machine at least once a week."

"Make sure Adam doesn't make you wash his clothes." Her face scrunches up. "If you start doing his laundry, it will definitely violate the friendship line he's so adamant on drawing. Friends don't wash other friends' underwear."

"You've washed mine."

Crossing her arms, she shrugs. "That's different. I don't secretly want *in* your underwear."

"Seriously?" I click my tongue, pretending to be offended. "But you're always telling me I'm so *hot*."

"Sorry, Peterson. You just don't have the necessary parts to rock my world."

A bright blue pickup, shiny despite looking at least a decade old, pulls up to the curb. Stickers of various bands decorate the back window. Adam honks wildly, pumping his fist into the air and grinning at us before hopping out the door.

"God, he's weird, but still crazy ass hot," Kelly says with a small smirk. "Are you sure you want to be alone with this guy the new few months? How are you going to keep your hands off him?"

"No talking her out of it now, Kel," Adam cuts in, appearing beside me. "She's mine."

Once I realize there's no way he heard what Kelly just said, I internally relish the sight of him in a faded Badgers t-shirt and cargo shorts. His brown hair has grown out since we met, curling ever so slightly around his ears.

I nudge him gently in the side. "Besides, we made a blood pact."

Kelly gapes at us, eyes wide, mouth making a near perfect "O."

"What?" Adam asks, playing into the lie. "It's not like we shared dirty needles."

Kelly rolls her eyes and squirms like she's grossed out. "You two freaks of nature deserve each other. I mean, *really*."

With a deep chuckle, Adam grabs my duffle bag, throwing it in the backseat of the crew cab where there seems to be ample room for all our luggage. A large, black duffle bag rests in a heaping pile beside two sleeping bags and a blow-up mattress—all still brand new and in their packages.

I eye the back-end of the pickup. The bed's a bit wider than I pictured, although still small enough to make our planned sleeping arrangements make me flush with anticipation. It will be nearly impossible to be that close to Adam if he expects us to stick to his plans for a platonic friendship.

Adam closes the back door, then opens mine, waiting as I slide in before shutting it. I rest my arms over the open window frame as Kelly steps over.

"Always the freaking gentleman, isn't he?" She rolls her eyes as if she thinks he's gross, but I know she's crazy about him, too. "You seriously need to send me pictures every single day, lady. In fact, you better send some that look like you're camping out in the woods so you can show your parents what 'camp' looks like." She sighs dramatically. "This is going to be like the *longest* summer *ever* without getting to hang out with my bestie."

Adam leans over my seat, grinning at Kelly. "There's always FaceTime. We'll take you up to the Empire State Building and shit."

Kelly huffs. "It may be as close as I ever get to going anywhere awesome. She leans in to kiss my cheek. "Love ya, girl. I'm so glad you've done away with your old self and decided to take this trip. Have a fabulous time for the both of us."

With my back to Adam, I bite my lip and widen my eyes in a silent, nervous plea. She knows holding back my feelings for Adam has been difficult. "Love you, too. *Don't* get too crazy this summer without me there to keep you in line."

"I'll be a perfect angel." She holds up her crossed fingers with a devilish grin as Adam pulls away from the curb.

I wave back at her through the window until she turns to leave. Then I slump into my seat. "I seriously worry about her."

"You said she has sisters who are counselors at the same camp, right? I'm sure they'll keep a close eye on her."

"You haven't met her sisters. They're just as bad."

We're still on campus when I pull out my phone and the auxiliary cable. My only request in whatever vehicle we used was that it had a place for me to plug in my tunes. "I have like five *thousand* songs on here. Are you ready for this, mister?"

Adam looks over at me, freaking *gleaming*. My heart takes a major dive before fluttering like a chimpanzee on crack. Face stern, I hold up my hand. "Okay, stop right there. We haven't even been on the road for ten minutes and already you're beaming at me. Seriously, Adam. If we're going to do this as *friends*, there will be no affectionate gazes, no hand-holding, none of this opening my fucking door business. *Friends* don't do that crap. If you don't plan on sticking to those rules, we'll just have to turn this truck right around so I can actually be the lousy camp counselor I claimed to be for my parents. Are we clear?"

The light turns red. We stop. Adam turns back to me, unsmiling. "Crystal."

"Okay, good. Now let's get this road trip off to a proper start. I spent *days* on this playlist. The songs are perfectly timed with our location."

Lucky for me, it's unusually warm for mid-May. I peel off my one-sleeved shirt to reveal the bikini top Kelly and I decided would be perfect for catching Adam's attention. White with black and gray leopard print, it dips low between my breasts with enough padding to make my perfect C cups look to be at least DD.

Adam looks between me and the traffic light, his eyes wide. It's exactly the kind of reaction I had been hoping for. "What in the *hell* are you doing?"

"Relax, it's just a swimsuit. I need to fix my ghost-like appearance before we make it to California. Those people are always beautifully tanned."

As soon as the light turns green, Adam pushes on the accelerator a bit harder than necessary. I start the song "Have Love Will Travel" by The Sonics. Leaning out the window, holding my hands in the air and yelling as the wind whips my hair into the sky, I'm confident that Adam won't be able to keep things platonic for too long.

In fact, I'm counting on it.

A MERE HOUR INTO OUR TRIP I FIND myself crossing and uncrossing my legs, tapping against the dashboard to the wicked beat of In This Moment. Adam hasn't said much of anything since I revealed my sexy swim top, and his eyes haven't left the road once. It definitely *was not* the effect I was aiming for. I slip my shirt back on before turning to face him.

"Okay, time to start some road games. Truth or Dare."

Adam finally glances over at me, his eyebrows drawn down. "Something else."

"O-kaaay...how about 'hot seat'? One of us sits in the hot seat and the other gets to ask five questions. You *have* to answer, but you get one veto."

Letting out a loud breath, Adam ruffles his hair. "Jewels, I get it. Do you want me to tell you the reason we can't be together so we can just forget this awkward business?"

"That's *not* what I'm hinting at. Seriously, we've only known each other a few weeks. The questions don't have to be personal. I just want to know more about you."

"Fine. I'll go first. You're in the hot seat."

I sit tall, clapping my hands excitedly. "Okay, this is good! Fire away!"

"Why did you have to lie to your parents about coming on this trip with me?"

I roll my eyes and look out the window. "By all means, don't hold back."

"This is *your* game. If you want rules—"

"Okay, fine. I lied because they're really protective. I knew they'd never go for it. And part of being an adult is getting to make your own decisions, right?"

He glances at me. "Why are they protective?"

"That's another question."

"Fine. Second question. Why are your parents so protective? Do they have a reason to be that way?"

Eyes narrowed, I wrinkle my nose back at him. "That's three questions."

His teeth flash with a wide grin and he chuckles. "It's *your* game. Answer the questions."

I ruffle my wild locks, wishing I had a ponytail holder. Wishing I had some excuse to keep my hands busy. I wasn't ready to tell him about my dark past this soon. I ball my hands into fists at my sides. "I had a hard time in school last year...I had a kind of mental breakdown."

He glances over his shoulder, his eyes worried. "I'm sorry. I had no idea."

I look away when our eyes meet. "How could you? I never told you about it until now. Anyway, I guess my parents are protective because they're worried it will happen again. But I swear to you, it won't. I'm okay now."

It's not the total truth, but I'm not lying either. If I tell Adam about my stay in the hospital, the drugs I have to take every day to keep from falling into a funk, the reason my mom wants me to check in with her every single day, he may have second thoughts about this trip. He may turn around before we've even left the state. And I'm starting to think checking off his list will be as therapeutic for me as it will be for Adam. I'll be proving not only to my parents but myself that I can function like anyone else.

"Are you hungry?" Adam motions to signs for restaurants as they pass. "I should've asked if you grabbed breakfast when I picked you up."

"I'm good, unless you want something. I brought a little cooler of water and snacks if you'd rather wait a little longer. And you still have two questions left."

"We don't have to play anymore."

I shake my head. "It's part of the game. Don't worry, I promise not to be as brutal."

"Okay. Dogs or cats?"

"Seriously? *That's* your question? My preference to four-legged, domesticated creatures?"

"It's not your turn to ask questions yet. Just tell me. I think it reveals a lot about a person."

"Well, that's easy. Dogs all the way. They're loyal and show their emotions on the outside. Cats stare at you with that creepy look, like they're constantly plotting against you. My family had a dog while I was growing up. A little white and chocolate cocker spaniel named Bailey. We had to put her down when she started walking in circles. My mom said she'd never have another dog because it was too hard to sit with Bailey while she died. Someday when I have my own house it's the first thing I'm getting, before furniture." I twist around to face Adam. "What did that reveal about me? You were a philosophy major, you must have *some* idea of why a person hates cats."

"You're not allowed to ask me any questions when it's my turn."

"I never said that."

"New rule." He gives me a triumphant look. "Last question. Why did you agree to go with me on this trip?"

I slip my legs underneath me, huffing. "I thought you said you were going to take it easy on me."

"Never said that either."

"Man, this is cruel." I watch the little yellow car pass us on the interstate, a mom driving with two little kids bouncing in their car seats in the back. "When we first met there was...something about you. The more I got to know you, the more I couldn't wait to see you again. At first I thought you were really crazy to ask me to go on this kind of a trip when I didn't even know your last name. Then I realized when we're together, it's effortless for both of us. We get along without it being forced, without there being any awkward moments. I wanted more of it. I'm not going to lie, a part of me really wanted to get away from my parents, too."

Adam clears his throat, looking over his shoulder before turning into the passing lane to clear a car that's half a mile away. "Okay, your turn."

I cross my arms, smirking. "You know you could've taken it easier on me, and maybe I would've been nice to you. Just remember you set yourself up."

He shrugs. "Do what you have to."

"Okay. How many girlfriends have you had?"

His head swings over to me. "Seriously?"

"You don't get to ask any questions when it's my turn," I remind him.

He looks back to the road, grumbling under his breath.

"What's that?" I ask, cupping my ear. "Didn't catch your answer."

"I'm counting," he snaps.

And suddenly I'm wishing I didn't ask. *How many girlfriends could he possibly have had that he needs to count?*

"I don't know. Maybe five?"

"Since high school?"

His eyes flicker to mine. "That's question number two. And no. Since middle school."

"So I'm not the first girl you've pushed away?"

"That's three. Why would you say that?"

I wag my finger at him. "Nuh-uh. No questions for you, remember? If that one counts, you still have to answer."

His gaze seems transfixed on the traffic. "Yeah, there were others. I've never had much time for dating."

I raise my eyebrows. "Too busy doing nothing?"

"That's four. And if you'll remember, I only recently quit school."

Knowing he's only giving me one more question, I pause to think about what I want to ask. A big part of his life still sits beneath a big question mark. But how much of it do I want to know? If I uncover one secret, will it all come unraveling around us? We've barely started this trip. I don't want to ruin the fun.

"Favorite actress?"

I see his shoulders drop a little when he smirks. "That's easy. Kristen Bell. Beautiful blonde, funny, smart, a ball of fun. She's the whole package. Everything I would want in a woman."

For a minute I can't swallow. From the tone of his voice, it's like he's referring to me rather than Kristen Bell. "Good answer," I finally say, reaching for a bottle of water.

A long silence follows the completion of our game.

WE PLANNED TO STAY IN A HOTEL THE first couple nights so we wouldn't have to worry about driving the pickup through Chicago after the concert. Adam insisted on making arrangements, so I'm both impressed and freaking out when we enter the extraordinary lobby of the Drake hotel. The giant chandeliers hanging from the metal ceiling make me feel small and insignificant.

"*I thought you said we were going to stay somewhere practical,*" I hiss under my breath. "*I can't imagine ceilings incrusted in gold really fit into anyone's budget unless you're Gatsby.*"

He chuckles as he hands me his bag. "You'd be surprised the kind of perks the son of a beer mogul can score. Stay here. I'll check us in."

Adam approaches the front desk flanked with curtains. I watch the middle-aged woman perk to life, her smile a mile wide as she pushes a strand of her dark hair over her shoulder. Rather than watch her flirt, I stroll away, taking the view of the lobby in further.

Although I've never been to this hotel, I've been to Chicago at least a dozen times with my parents and twice with Jason. My great aunt lived near downtown in a rather posh apartment, and she was exceptionally close with my mom. The last time I was here was for her funeral right before my high school graduation.

"We have connecting rooms," Adam tells me, suddenly back at my side. He hands me a card before we follow signs to the elevators.

We're alone in the elevator. I let my imagination grow wild with thoughts of hitting the emergency stop button. There's no way I can let this friendship thing continue on for much longer. He's the one who's so big on life being short, and I think it's definitely too short not to discover what it's like to have sex with Adam Murphy. I already know he kisses like a pro. I can't imagine what he's like in bed.

"This is our floor," he tells me, holding the door.

Snapping out of my fantasy, I step out ahead of him. My room's just four doors down. Adam stuffs his hands in his pockets, looking past me to the empty hallway. "We have a few hours before the concert. You want to grab a bite to eat first?" His eyes roll back onto mine, anxious, yet afraid. I swear he wants to come into my room and do things to me just as badly as I want him to. What's he so afraid of?

My eyes fall to his lips and I grow warm from head to toe. "Give me an hour to get ready. I'll meet you in the lobby." I snatch my bag from him and dart into my room before my willpower breaks.

THE OSTENTATIOUS LOBBY CLAMORS with the night crowd, many of them men and women in business suits, probably representatives from Fortune 500 companies checking in after a day of meetings. Considering the luxurious rooms Adam scored, I imagine anyone staying here makes a ton of money.

My stomach twists nervously as it takes a little longer to find Adam among the chaos. I pull at the hem of my short sequined skirt, feeling a little skeezy among the business attire the way my long legs covered in self-tanner are exposed. The soft, fluttery tank-top in my favorite shade of aqua blue was another purchase made on my shopping spree with Kelly. Though I didn't get something that dips down in front as she suggested, I think it does flattering things to my figure and looks great against my blond locks I spent an hour on to get the large, loose curls. A little makeup, dangling earrings, an arm full of bangles and I was ready.

Only not really. I sat in one of the leather chairs in my suite for a good twenty minutes trying to recover my breath. Concerts have been my favorite guilty pleasure ever since my dad took me to see his favorite 80s band when I was little. I get caught up in the pounding base, the explosive beats of the drums and guitars, the electric excitement of the large crowd. I've never gone to one with a guy I'm majorly attracted to. It's going to be harder than ever to keep my emotions in check and my hands off the guy I'm falling for like a lead ball.

I finally discover Adam leaning against one of the leather chairs, wearing something casual that's similar to the night we met. Arms crossed, he watches the people come and go, a curious expression lighting his eyes. Why would someone like him choose to stay single for so long? He obviously enjoys having a good time, although he has a habit of shutting down the minute any conversations turn serious. I'm swaying on my cork wedges, gaping at him, when his head turns around.

"*Jewels.*" He says my name in a mere whisper, his eyes spreading wide. It's way better than the annoyed look he gave me at the sight of my low-dipping bikini top, because I can see the heat of desire burning in his eyes. The way he adjusts his lips it's obvious that he wants me, regardless of whatever he keeps telling me. "You look..." He blinks in languid movements.

"Hey," I cut in, letting him off the hook. I finger the white wristlet containing my ID, phone and cash, trying to ground my thoughts. To forget the way he's leering at me. "Ready?"

His throat bobs as he swallows hard before nodding. "The woman at the desk said there's a great seafood place nearby. Want to check it out?"

"What about *you*? I thought you weren't a big fan of stuff that crawls on the ocean floor."

"If it's something that's been in the freezer for a few months, not so much. A high end restaurant with professional chefs, definitely." He tips his head to the doors. "You okay to walk a few blocks in those heels?"

I nod, stepping close and looping my arm through his. Because that's something I would've done before things became complicated. If nothing else, maybe I can curb my sexual appetite by allowing myself to touch him in some way.

We break out onto the sidewalk, finding the early night air pleasantly warm. Traffic looks to be a nightmare this time of day with everyone getting off work. Although the sidewalks in downtown Chicago aren't quite as busy as the streets of New York, our causal stroll is passed up every few seconds by someone appearing to be on a mission.

Adam's hands return to his pockets. "Are you going to at least give me some kind of hint of who we're seeing tonight?"

I giggle. "And spoil all the fun? I'd rather see you squirm. Just know it's going to knock your socks off."

"Then I'm buying your dinner. You did most of the planning for this trip. It's the least I could do. Unless, of course, you want to give in and tell me."

"Not a chance."

ADAM'S FACE LIGHTS UP WHEN THE members of Coldplay take the stage among the glowing props, blowing us away with their first song. So he *does* know good music when he hears it. We both gasp when the wrist bands they handed out at the entrance begin to glow in the dark. The LED lights in various colors blink to the beat along with the thousands of other fans in the audience, making for the most beautiful visual I've ever seen in my life. Everyone around us grows wild with applause, so we join in.

There's always been something magical about seeing my favorite bands in person that leaves me breathless, and even a little teary-eyed. Watching Chris Martin hop around the stage with infinite energy, I'm rendered speechless. The audio and visual displays are completely off the charts, trumping any concert I've attended in the past. I'm as still as a statue, watching the band with tears filling my eyes when Adam brushes my hair away from my face, smiling so widely it's as if his cheeks will split in two. Our eyes lock, and I feel something inside of me click.

My feelings for Adam have gone so far beyond friendship, it's terrifying.

"HOLY SHIT, THAT WAS *AMAZING!*" ADAM gushes as we wait in line for a taxi. He stands by my side, the most animated he's been since we met. "And I've never seen anyone play the piano or dance around with so much emotion. The confetti, the beach balls...god, it was brilliant! You really know how to pick 'em, Jewels."

"I knew it'd be good." I break into a wide grin. "I've always liked them, but that was probably my favorite concert. Like *ever.*" I look down and cough a little, fighting the overwhelming need to kiss him, to feel the result of the energy coursing through him. "What now? Are you ready to head back?"

"No. Not at all. I feel...*alive.*"

I giggle. He's so giddy it's *adorable*. "Me too. I know of a fun place we can stop."

A taxi pulls up and we slide in. Adam's delighted smile drops as he watches me instructing the driver where to take us. For a minute I think he's going to lean in for a kiss. Then he turns away to look out his window.

"I don't know how we could possibly top this night, Jewels. It's safe to say Coldplay is my new favorite band."

"Ah, welcome to the awesome side of life," I tell him. "You should get your ass off your friend's couch and come over more often."

The line for the club isn't too terrible by the time we arrive. I've never been here, only heard of the place through Jason's buddy in the Corps. We're on the rooftop bar within fifteen minutes. Loud music pulsates into the dark night air, the faces of all the people dancing illuminated by a sexy blue glow from the lights. The surreal feeling of the night just keeps improving, like I'm floating through the best dream ever.

We find a place to wriggle in at a high table. "Do you want a drink?" Adam asks.

In all the time we've spent together, I've never seen him drink booze, and I've decided the only way to keep my hormones in check is to stay sober. "A sparkling water would be nice. I think I may have busted a vocal chord at the concert."

Adam flags a waitress down, grinning. "When he touched your hand, I thought you were going to pass out. Either that, or I thought my ear drum would shatter."

"Sorry." A telling flush fills my neck. "I kind of have a thing for hot guys who can sing and play instruments. Chris Martin's probably at the top of the list."

The waitress appears in a dress so tight I'm surprised she can move. Adam orders us each a sparkling water, and the woman winks at him before leaving. We wander over to the edge where a sweeping view of the city leaves us both breathless.

He turns to me after a moment. "You okay?"

"Oddly enough, this thin sheet of glass makes me feel safe from plunging to my death. Besides, I'm the one who brought us here, remember?"

We stand shoulder-to-shoulder, taking in the twinkling lights and still busy traffic below. I've always pictured myself living in a city this size one day. Chicago, New York, Miami, San Diego, it doesn't really matter as long as there's always something new and exciting to explore, new restaurants and bars to discover. Weather isn't even a factor for me. It's moments like this that I'll always crave—being able to view the beauty of the city from above while taking in a hip dance club. At least until I'm too old to go clubbing.

"Where do you see yourself ending up one day?" I ask. "I mean if you ever venture outside of Wisconsin again."

Adam ruffles his hair as he always does when he's nervous or unsure. "I haven't given it much thought. I'm too far into this living for the moment thing. You?"

"It's gotta be somewhere big. I can't deal with small towns. I don't think I'll stay in Wisconsin either. Part of me hopes I'll fall in love with a city on this trip and decide it's where I want to be." I rest my hand against the glass, suddenly feeling brave. "I live for the idea of being surrounded by strangers. There's always someone new to meet. Always something thrilling to do to fill your time. Concerts, galas, art shows, it's the kind of thing I see myself doing to stay busy and happy. I'm not the type to sit still and do nothing, or keep going back to the same bars every weekend. Know what I mean?"

I turn to find Adam staring at me with the kind of gaze I can't handle. I grab his hand, pulling him away from the view. "C'mon, let's dance. If this place is going to close soon, we need to make the best of it."

Turns out Adam's a goofy dancer, but extremely confident in his moves. We get lost in the pulsating crowd, moving carelessly to the techno beat as if we belong. At one point Adam reaches out as if to grind with me, but I wag my finger at him and remind him of the no touching rule I implemented. By the time it's midnight and we're getting shooed out, my sides hurt from laughing at Adam's less than suave moves.

We ride another taxi down to the Crown Fountain and The Bean where I remember taking pictures into the mirrored art as a kid. Seeing these things so late at night is so relaxed compared to the usual hectic times I've visited in the daytime. The golden glow of the city lights reflect off the sculpture for a view nearly as stunning as the displays from the concert.

Adam steps in and out of view, his expression changing with every step. I laugh and pull out my phone. "Stand there a minute."

We had an agreement long before we left that there would be no grumbling when it was time for pictures as I'm a visual nut and love photography. Adam obligingly tilts his chin down, looking up at me through the sculpture with a serene expression.

After I click a few shots, he steps forward, reaching for my phone. "Okay, your turn."

"I have a better idea." I lay on my back, resting my feet on the bottom of the mirror surface. "C'mon."

Chuckling, Adam lays down just inches from me.

"Now look at the camera." We make a series of varied faces throughout the pictures. I knew Adam could be a lot of fun and not take himself so seriously, but I about bust a gut laughing at his outrageous gestures. Once I'm satisfied we have enough, I send one to Kelly.

Adam stands, reaching down to help me back to my feet. As I reach out to take it, he jerks his hand away. "Oops, no touching, remember?"

I stick out my lip in a pout, pretending to be offended even though I'm giggling. "So that's how it's going to be?" Popping back to my feet, I chase after him. "Since it was *my* rule, I'm going to be the one to break it!"

We run around like kindergarteners, laughing and screaming in a game of tag. A couple in their 30s walks past, gaping at our immaturity, but we don't stop. We've thrown all our worries and inhibitions out the window to enjoy the moment.

I've reached a level of happiness I didn't know existed before now.

I STIR WITH A LIGHT TAPPING ON THE door leading to Adam's room. "Jewels, you alive in there?" The clock on the nightstand reads 12:30.

I shoot out of bed, patting my wild hair down before opening the door between our rooms just a crack so he can see nothing more than my eyes. "Hey, yeah, just jumping in the shower."

The sexiest of grins ruptures his face. He looks freshly showered and dressed. "I tried to text you earlier this morning to see if you wanted to go down for something to eat. You must've been in a fun coma."

"Are you kidding me? After the amazing night we had? That level of excitement requires a minimum of twelve hours' rest. Mark my words, you'll be crashing later this afternoon."

His eyebrows raise. "So are you coming to the Navy Pier with me, or should I leave you for another twelve hours of sleep?"

I open the door wider, allowing him to see my mangled hair. "Ready to be seen in public with me looking like this, or do you want to give me a few minutes to get ready?"

"It doesn't matter. You always look great."

His words cut through the spirit of our playful banter like a samurai sword. The well-meaning look in his eyes doesn't help, either. Damn it, I'm really into this guy.

Backing away, I say, "Twenty minutes," and slam the door in his face.

I lean against the door, willing my heart to stop racing. I'm done caring about his secret. Whatever it may be, I'm sure I can handle it. Besides, nothing says I have to allow myself to actually *love* him. There are still a plethora of other enjoyable things we can do without bringing those complicated emotions into the picture.

Ten

IT'S A BRIGHT, SUNNY AFTERNOON IN Chicagoland. I stand at Adam's side near the front of the boat, trying to take in the skyline with a new set of eyes. The last time I was on one of these little cruises around the city, I was barely old enough to see over the railing, so it's sort of easy to do. Except I'm crazy aware every time Adam bumps into me, or breathes into my face, or taps on my shoulder to point something out in another direction.

Adam takes a deep breath beside me. "You're right, this is amazing."

I nod, trying to convince myself that a reenactment of *Titanic* would be completely inappropriate, although it would feel oh so good to be in his arms. The "no touching" rule was one of my least intelligent ideas.

Adam nudges me with his elbow. "Hey. I've been thinking. I want to ask you about something Kelly said the other day."

"I thought we agreed the whole hot seat scenario was not to be revisited."

"This is just a straight up question."

I feel his smoldering stare and decide not to face him.

"What is this burning question inquiring minds want to know?"

"What did she mean about seeing the 'old' you? What were you like before? What changed?"

"Those are *three* questions. You suck at math."

"Jewels, come on. What is it?"

I turn to lean against the railing, my eyes finally coming up to meet his. The only person I can think of who may have eyes that could compete are the beautiful orbs of Bradley Cooper.

"She was referring to my less than stellar days when I was in the habit of raining on her parade. Pooping on the party. You know, being a stick in the mud. Like I said before, I had a hard time last year. I did a good job of hiding it with sarcasm and booze. I was known to drink myself into a stupor."

His thumb grazes over my forearm, sending my hormones on a collision course with my willpower. "Why do I get the feeling there's something more to it that you aren't telling me?"

I turn away from him to watch the skyline of Chicago lazily drift past. My eyes fall on the Sears tower. Jason tried like hell to convince me to stand in the clear glass box at the top that overlooks the city. Just the thought of doing it, however, threw me into a panic attack. There was a terribly long line for the elevator to go back down, so we dashed down the emergency steps for a few floors until we collapsed against a wall, eventually laughing at how ridiculous we must've looked to the other tourists.

Whenever I have the worst nightmares involving Jason where I wake myself with wailing sobs or panicked screams, I try to lean on those kinds of memories. I try to recall the way his cheeks pushed up when he smiled, the way he held me on his parents' porch, or the way his lips felt when we kissed.

I'll do anything to avoid the memory of breaking up with him, or the devastating call I got three days later.

Adam touches my arm. "Would you look at me, please?"

Fluttering my lashes, I look down. "There was a guy I dated junior and senior year. His name was Jason. We were the kind of couple everyone thought would end up getting married and living happily ever after. I was the captain of the cheerleading squad, he was the quarterback. It was like we were living some kind of stereotype."

I wipe at a few stray tears. "Jason was a great guy. Everyone loved him. They all thought he was a hero when he signed up for the Marine Corps our senior year. You'd think I would've been proud of him, but I was secretly pissed that he did it. I went on this self-pity trip where I wondered how he could do such a thing to me. I was so worried what I would do while he was over in Afghanistan. I didn't understand how I was expected to just wait around for him for *five* years while he was off being a hero and I was stuck in the same spot, going to the local college and trying to figure out how to be my own person instead of being half of this amazing couple everyone held on a pedestal."

Adam's fingers trail up and down my arm. "You don't have to tell me this."

I shrug, still unable to look him in the eye. "You wanted to know. Anyway, while he was over there, I messed around with someone one night. It wasn't anything more than kissing, but I was mad, and lonely, and a little drunk, I guess. It doesn't excuse what I did to Jason. I was too much of a coward to tell him, so I told him we were finished. I was having fun in college, and didn't want to worry about my boyfriend on the other side of the world. It was selfish. He was off defending our country, and I was busy hitting keggers. You can't get any more shallow than that."

"You're being too hard on yourself."

I wipe at my face and shake my head. "Just wait, there's more. I got a call from his mom a few days later, saying there was an accident involving Jason and an IED. She was crying so hard I could barely understand her. At first I thought there must be some kind of mistake, or that they were joking around and Jason was coming home to surprise me because he was really upset when I broke up with him. He kept texting me and sending messages on Facebook, saying he didn't want it to be over between us. When I pulled up to their house and saw all the cars in the driveway, I knew it was real. I knew he was dead. I spent the night driving around. My parents had to find me using the GPS on my phone. I blacked out in a park downtown."

I tried everything I could after Jason's funeral to suppress the visions of him wearing his dress uniform inside his coffin, but I slipped into an arresting state of guilt that took over for *months* afterwards. Whenever I remember his mom's call, or how I broke up with him, I feel the dark tentacles of depression sinking into my brain, threatening to pull me back under.

Adam reaches up to pull stray hairs from my face, his expression tender. "Jewels..."

I spin away, letting his hand fall from my arm. "You don't understand. Right before he died for our country, *I kissed someone else*. I *dumped him* when he was on the other side of the world, homesick and dodging bullets. I should've been his emotional support. I should've been there whenever he needed me. Instead I told him I couldn't wait around for him. So now you know exactly what kind of a royal bitch you're galavanting around with. I won't blame you if you want nothing to do with me."

Adam wraps his arms wrap around my waist and rests his chin on my shoulder, his body pressed up against mine. "I'm sorry he died. But you didn't know when you broke up with him that it was going to happen. How could you? It was just shitty timing. You can't beat yourself up over it."

A fat tear slips down my cheek. "Yeah, I can. What kind of heartless person cheats on someone who's in the service?"

"You're allowed to make mistakes in life." He kisses the side of my head.

I lean into him as the boat circles back into the harbor, preparing to dock.

"You asked why Kelly said that, what's changed. If you really want to know, I'll show you." I grab my phone from my pocket and turn around to show him a picture of us from the night before, smiling like total goobers. "*Us.* This *thing* we have going on, whatever it is. You're the first reason I've had in a long time that has made me want to go out and do something that will make me feel alive. You're the reason I suddenly want to get up in the morning. *You've* changed me, Adam. When I'm around you, it's like I can barely breathe because I'm afraid I'll do something to screw up, and lose you, too. I don't think I'm worthy of being anyone's girlfriend after what I did."

"You can't let one mistake define you. You *are* worthy. I wish you could see yourself the way I do. You're amazing, Jewels."

Eyes locked, we grab each other's faces at the same exact moment our lips collide. I'm filled with the scent of him I've desperately missed, mixed with aftershave. All of me throbs in celebration of the kiss I've waited for so long to return. My head tips back as his mouth covers mine, urgently making up for lost time. His warm lips part, giving me access to his mint-flavored tongue, igniting sparks deep within me. I gasp against his lips, feeling like I'll dissolve into a puddle when his hands trail down to my waist, his fingers lifting under the back of my shirt, teasing the small bits of flesh exposed.

The undeniable need for him becomes more intense. I curve myself against him, clutching his shirt in my fists. My lips and tongue can only do so much to appease my appetite for him. I have to remind myself we're in public, on a boat. Still, I yearn to have his hands all over me, releasing the sexual tension building up inside. Heat fills me from head to toe, making my head spin. Adam's thumbs continue to stroke the skin above my shorts as his kisses become more intense.

Then there's a loud, brash cough behind us. We turn to see the young tour guide standing next to us, her hands clasped in front of her. "So...we've, like, docked."

AFTER LUNCH AT BUBBA GUMP, WE RIDE the infamous Ferris wheel. My fear of heights escalates when we're stopped at the top until Adam kisses me. It's a sweet and light kiss, but it makes me wild for him all over again. When we agree we've had enough sightseeing, we head back to the hotel to "freshen up" before going out for the night. We hold hands in the elevator, but don't speak of the kisses or what has changed between us.

Right outside my room, I lean up against the wall. Adam moves in front of me like there's a magnetic pull keeping us together. The heat from his body drives me insane with desire.

"So what time are we meeting up?" I trace the lines of his arm with my finger, grinning down at his perfect body. By the way his shorts have shifted off to the side, he's most *definitely* as turned on as I am. I bring my mouth up to his slowly, tauntingly.

"What happened to the no touching rule?" he asks, his breath tight.

"I never said anything about kissing, did I?"

I duck away from him and slide my card through the door, grabbing his arm to pull him along. We float across the room to the bed where I push him down and straddle over him, my hair falling across his face. We both laugh. Gathering my hair to the side, I bend down to take his lower lip between my teeth, giggling when he flips me around to my back. He removes my shirt before brushing my blond locks from my face.

His baby blues drink in my exposed breasts and stomach before coming back up to stare into my eyes long and hard, as if trying to mentally pass me a message. I've never felt so exposed and vulnerable as I do underneath his gaze. I'm suddenly electrified to a new level, ready to devour him.

But he won't kiss me. His lips trail across the curve of my neck, down the soft line of my shoulder and beyond before he uses his thumb to yank my bra cup aside. His tongue circles around my hardened nipple, teasing it before taking a soft nibble. Moaning, I reach out to pull his face back to mine.

Our lips mash and suck, trying to make up for lost time. Our mouths move with our staggered, eager breaths. His fingers are like searing fire against my skin, caressing and kneading and softly pinching.

"You're so damn beautiful," he whispers, holding his mouth right over mine. His lips drop down to my stomach where his nose brushes against my skin as soft as a whisper. Grabbing his head, I attempt to pull him up for another kiss, but he fights back. With one hand he cups my breast, his thumb tracing around my nipple, his other hand fumbling around at the back of my bra.

"Front clasp!" I gasp, helping him.

He slowly peels my shorts down my toned legs, letting his fingers brush against my skin the whole way. I shudder when his teeth tug down my recently purchased leopard panties. His fingers trail down to put light pressure on the part of me that throbs the most, softly patting and stroking until I become wet. His warm breath tickles the sensitive skin between my legs.

I see his excitement bulging against his shorts and reach for it, but he curves away. He kisses the skin between my thighs, sending me into a whirlwind of desire and passion. I'm breathless when his warm fingers slip inside, moving slow and gentle.

"Damn it, Adam," My voice sounds husky, older, like a woman on one of those dirty sex chats. "I want *you* inside of me already."

I pull at his shirt, wanting to feel his hard muscles, wanting our skin to touch. He fights against me, his steely eyes radiating with desire. "Lie back and relax. I want this to be about you."

I try to do as he says, but when his warm tongue enters me, massaging my pulsating bud, I nearly jump from the bed. I reach for the first thing I can—his thick hair—and pull on its roots, crying out in ecstasy. I've never had a guy go *there* before, and it feels fan-fucking-tastic. My lust for him overflows to the point I feel as if I'll explode. Adam continues on, his hands reaching up to caress my breasts and pinch my nipples. I flex my hips as waves of pleasure rip through me. "Oh...my...*god*...yes!"

It goes on and on, feeling like hours but probably only lasting a matter of minutes until I come to an overwhelming climax. It's unreal, unlike anything I could've ever imagined. My insides thrum delightfully, a kaleidoscope of exploding nerves. With the final release my legs lock, pressing Adam's head between my thighs. Arching my back, I scream something that probably sounds to anyone walking past our room like a woman being murdered.

Adam emerges to clamp a hand over my mouth, chuckling. His other hand strokes the tender skin between my thighs. "Someone's going to call security."

Shuddering with the last of the delightful explosion, I collapse against the bed and pry his wandering hand off me to kiss it. "Can I just say, you should hire out for whatever it is you just did. You'd be a billionaire. *Seriously*." I pull him up next to me and trail kisses up his neck.

"Your turn." My hands work their way to the button on his shorts.

He stops me, lacing his fingers with mine. "Not now. I want you to enjoy the moment. You deserve this."

I eye him suspiciously. What guy says *that*? Can he tell it was my first time? "Are you for real?"

He buries me in his arms, trailing his hand up the back of my neck and nestling in my hair. "Remind me to do that again real soon. Your face, the way you arched for me...Jesus, it was unreal." He presses soft kisses to my forehead.

"Are you referring to my awkward cries of passion?"

He chuckles softly. "We'll have to work on that."

I peer up at his face. "*Please* tell me this means we're done with the *I'm not good for you* and *no touching* bullshit. I just want to be with you. I don't care about this big secret of yours anymore, Adam. We don't have to be all serious, or whatever, but I *really* want this. It can just be about sex if that's what you want. And you can do it again as many *times* as you want. Whatever you did with your tongue just now—"

"Has anyone told you that you talk too much?" A teasing smile crosses his lips. "Do you think you could just shut up and let me hold you?"

Still in a daze from my mind-shattering first orgasm, my feet tingling from its aftereffects, I drift asleep in the comfort of Adam's arms, savoring the smell and feel of him against my face.

TRAVELING FROM CHICAGO TO TOLEDO is like an entirely different trip than the first leg. I sit wedged into Adam's side whenever we aren't stopping for tourist attractions. Sometimes he rests his arm around my shoulders and his fingers play with my hair. A few times he kisses my neck, allowing his tongue to lightly graze the patch of skin behind my ear, nearly making me wet myself with memories of just what that muscle can do.

One time his hand trails up my leg and into dangerous territory, prompting a pit stop to the woods behind a rest stop where we go at it hot and heavy, never removing our clothes, but easily setting some kind of record for best third base hit without scoring a home run. We emerge from behind the shelter with red faces, wild hair, and crumpled leaves in the folds of our clothing, generating a handful of knowing glances from other travelers we pass on the way back to the pickup.

When our exit into Toledo appears, I fake a cough. "We're running a bit behind schedule. I say let's forget supper and go straight to the camping site."

Adam's fingers lace through mine. "As much as I want to do things to your smokin' body again, we're not making this trip all about how often we can get down each other's pants." His eyes twinkle when he glances at me. "We're sticking to the schedule. We have a checklist, remember?"

I squeeze his fingers, letting out a dramatic sigh. "Yeah, buddy. Let me know how that denial thing's working out for you." I check my phones for notes I took before we left. "The cemetery here is haunted. Maybe there's a quiet spot everyone's too afraid to go where we can work on a different kind of list."

Adam chuckles, pretending to be irritated. "Dear god, I've awakened a monster."

"Wait, have you?" I tug at the zipper on his shorts. "Let me see." I've got two fingers inside his underwear and coiled around his now pulsating swell when the pickup swerves.

"*Shit*! Would you stop? You're going to run us off the road!"

"Then you better hurry and pull off somewhere before we have an accident!" I answer in the same exasperated tone.

I pull down the rest of the zipper and nudge open the convenient slit in his royal blue boxers, leaning down to swipe my tongue across his tip. He's sweet and dribbling, ready to go. Adam groans, then gasps when I take him inside my mouth. I curl my lips around him as much as I can, delighted to discover he's even bigger than the surge in his pants would suggest.

The pickup veers off the highway at accelerated speeds. I let my tongue and lips do the magic, bringing him to full attention as the tires screech against pavement before we're still. It's rather uncomfortable the way he fills my entire mouth, nearly choking me, but I sense his arousal growing with each of my movements and don't stop.

"Holy *fuck*." He groans, lacing his fingers through the thick of my hair. His breath stutters with the powerful suction of my lips. "*Jewels*."

I love the sound of my name falling from his lips in pleasure. It makes me want to please him even more. Low grumbles of ecstasy rumble through his throat when I speed up the rhythm. It's hardly five minutes later that I hear his other hand slam against the steering wheel, his breaths deepening. His entire body becomes stiff and he hums a deep, satisfied grunt under his breath before releasing into my mouth. He quivers underneath my hold. "*That*...was amazing."

Giggling, I clean him up as best I can before taking a deep breath. "Do I dare sit up?"

"I'd advise against it. The old lady in the car next to us is giving me a funny look. We better get out of here before the cops show up."

As we tear out of the supermarket parking lot, I sit up in time to catch the wide eyes of the white haired woman in the old sedan next to us.

THE STEAKHOUSE WE AGREE ON HAS AN old-world charm underneath ornate lighting and arched ceilings, and smells like my grandma's house on Thanksgiving. It's fairly busy for a weeknight, although there isn't a waiting line to get in. The hostess shows us to a small, round booth with a fair amount of privacy at the far end of the restaurant. The continuous bench allows us to nuzzle together the moment she's gone.

"Let's order some champagne," I whisper in his ear before sucking on his lobe. "Celebrate the fact that you're no longer just a prude who's only into me for my friendship."

His hand wraps around my thigh, leaving his fingers to dangle dangerously close to the part of me that can't seem to get enough of him. "I'm not really a drinker. I've watched my brother get hammered too many times and make a total ass of himself."

"Half a bottle isn't going to turn you into a raging alcoholic."

A high school girl with dopey glasses and a crooked smile approaches our table, setting large menus in front of us. Her brown eyes fall down to where Adam and I have become precariously intertwined, and her face flushes red. "Hi, I'm Cassandra. I'll be your server tonight. Can I get you started with something to drink?"

"Champagne. The cheapest stuff you have." I answer. Adam turns to me, opening his mouth. I press my finger to his lips. "*My* treat."

"Sure," the girl says, eyeing each of us like she's already too embarrassed to ask if we're old enough.

Once she turns her back, I nestle closer to Adam, tracing my index finger up and down his spine. "Wanna see what kind of bathrooms are in this place? I'll bet ten bucks they have one of those velvet couches."

"You're making it impossible to keep my hands off you," he whispers, shifting in his seat. I imagine my touches are bringing him back to life once again. I reach down to confirm it. He jumps with my touch, hitting the table with his knees. "*Jewels, c'mon.* Let's take a breather and eat something."

"I'm happy enough devouring you," I say in my sexiest voice, dragging my finger from his spine up to circle around his ear. I drag my nose across his neck, savoring the smell of his fragrant aftershave. "And I could do it right here, if you prefer."

Glancing around the restaurant, he pulls in a deep sigh and tugs on my hand. "C'mon."

We slide from the bench and half skip back to the entrance, hands locked together. Being with Adam this way is more of a thrill than I imagined. I've never felt so *freed.* As long as we continue to alleviate the sexual tension between us, I can protect my heart from harm. I can be his this way, regardless of his seemingly complicated life.

The single-stall women's bathroom is locked, and there's no way I'm messing around in a bathroom where there's more than likely pee on the floor. I drag Adam toward a hallway around the corner.

"Where are we going?" he asks in a throaty voice.

There's a doorway at the end of the hallway, leading to a dark and ominous alley surrounded by dumpsters. Adam begins to fall back the minute we step outside into the warm night air.

"*Jewels.*" His tone is meant to scold, but I can hear the passion still twisted in his throat. "We're not messing around back here."

"Who said anything about messing around?" Shaking my head, I tilt his face down to meet mine for a sultry kiss. He's quick to answer my sudden zeal, hoisting me up by my thighs to perch against his hips. I wrap my legs around his waist and deepen the kiss, holding onto his face with a longing so deep and powerful I feel as if I could cry. His warm tongue matches the soft touch of his wandering hands.

We drift across the alley to the other side until my back's against a brick wall. Adam's warm hands lift my billowing tank top, drifting up to cradle my breasts over my bra. I rock against him, caressing the top of his mouth with my tongue. He hums his approval, pushing back against me. I feel him harden against my leg and meet his low hums. He breaks the connection of our mouths to taste the light sweat of my neck and shoulders while his fingers reach for my underwear through the bottom of my shorts.

I close my eyes and lean my head against the brick wall as his fingers do their magic, stroking, petting, entering me, soft and slow. Throbbing so hard for him it's almost painful, I dig my fingernails into his back, and allow myself a satisfied groan. His mouth covers mine, swallowing up my eager cries.

After another long set of kisses, I open my eyes to find Adam watching me with an intensity that takes my breath away. He's so unbelievably gorgeous that I don't care if our first time is among the sour-smell of the dumpsters and steam of some kind coming from underneath the street. I've never been this uncontrollably hot for anyone. Unable to take the building anticipation anymore, I start for the button of his shorts.

Adam stops, panting. Small, glistening lines of sweat cover his hairline, and his face looks red under the street light. "Wait. We're *not* doing this here."

I move my lips to his neck, nipping at the skin underneath his jaw. "I'm going to explode all over this alley like a geyser if you stop now."

He carefully lowers me to the ground. "I don't want this thing between us to be cheap."

Rejected and angry, I step back, folding my arms with a glare. "It doesn't have to be *expensive*. It's just a sex thing, remember? That way we don't have to worry about feelings getting hurt, egos getting bruised, etcetera and so forth."

His sexy eyes search mine like he's looking for someone else. "That's what this is to you? Just a *sex thing*?"

"Ugh. Are we going to do this here? *Now*? We've got this crazy-hot attraction thing going. I'm sure four out of five doctors would recommend not fighting against it." I glance down the alley, wishing for someone to step in and interrupt this inevitable conversation. "If you tell me you're going back on the no touching rule, I swear to god I'll hijack that damn pickup back to Wisconsin and leave your ass here."

He takes my hands in his with a caring gaze that makes me breathless. His fingers wrap around mine, feeling as if there's nowhere else his hands belong. "I'm not saying I don't want to *touch* you. Because I do...as much as possible."

He nudges me up against the wall, brushing his lips over mine again and again. I wrap my arms around his neck and answer his playful kisses with my own, ready to pick up where we left off. His teeth graze across my bottom lip before he stops, resting his head against mine. The intensity of his eyes burn a hole right through me. "I just want to slow things down.

You're so amazing...I don't want this to just be some kind of fling between us. I want it to mean something."

I flex my jaw. The words *I love you* twist through my head with the force of a surprise hurricane, unwanted and utterly out of control. Panic consumes me. Even if I did tell him now, he'd just think it's a ploy so he'll agree to have sex with me. With his big secret looming over our heads, it's best to keep things casual. I can't do the long-term boyfriend thing. I can't go through the torture of losing him.

I snort and roll my eyes. "What, you mean like boyfriend-girlfriend crap? We're adults. Don't you think we can skip past that? Keep this on the down-low?"

He leans in for another kiss, this one soft and extra gentle. It leaves me secretly struggling for my next breath, imagining the way he would kiss me if we actually made love instead of fucking just for fun. And I'm starting to realize if we let things go all the way, there's a slim chance it wouldn't mean anything to either of us.

"I think we should talk about it first." he tells me. "I don't want to screw this up."

"Then *don't*," I warn, pressing my thumbs to the back of his neck. "Don't make this more complicated than it has to be. I've been waiting for this moment ever since the first time you kissed me in my dorm room. The only way you can screw this up is if you keep turning me down and go back to that load of crap about wanting to be nothing more than friends. I want this, Adam." I lick my lips and attempt to swallow. "I want *you*. *All* of you."

He continues to watch me, his sexy baby blues unblinking. They spark back to life just before he smiles. It's not one of his most genuine smiles, although the dimples do appear. "Let's get that bottle of champagne and blow out of here."

ONCE WE'VE SETTLED FOR THE NIGHT IN a reclusive spot in back end of a grassy field, the mood between us quickly fizzles with all the effect of a cold shower. Adam's words from the alley stir though my thoughts, threatening to latch onto the delusional part of me that still believes I could allow myself to be in love with him. *I don't want this thing between us to be cheap*.

As if we have any other option. Knowing there's a dark unknown he's holding back that will destroy everything, I can't afford to give him my already damaged heart. I don't *want* to feel a pang for him in places other than down below. I've been broken once before and can't afford to go through it again. Keeping this strictly about sex is the only option, considering I'm too far gone to turn back now.

We lay side by side on the air mattress in the back of the pickup bed, only our thighs touching as we finish up the last of the champagne. I wedge one arm beneath my sprawled out hair to get a better view of the stars twinkling above us. They shimmer and dance through the sky like something out of a fantasy-fueled flick.

"This trip has already been totally worth it," I say dreamily. "I mean the concert, the rooftop dancing, the Ferris wheel, the whole Navy Pier, now sleeping under this sky...everything about Chicago was a thousand times better with you instead of my parents."

"Sometimes it's still hard to believe you agreed to come along."

I slap his arm, but don't take my eyes off the stars. "Don't flatter yourself. You had good timing is all. This trip will be a good chance for me to sort things out. Decide what's important in my life. Maybe give me some kind of direction. You know, the kind of things *you're* supposed to be doing."

"I have direction."

I glance at him. "Oh, really? Let's hear it."

"The list *is* my direction. I'm doing all the things Zach asked."

"Even if we keep on doing...*whatever it is* we're doing together, you still need some kind of plan for when we get back home." I turn my head to my side, staring him down. "I get that you want to explore your options and whatever, but if you're not going to go to school, then maybe you need to get a job. You plan on crashing at Calvin's for the rest of your life?"

Adam snatches my phone off my stomach.

"Hey!" I protest, reaching for it.

He holds it over his head, out of my range. "It's not like I'm going to look through your texts. Give me some credit."

I rest my other hand behind my head and huff. He holds the phone out, snapping my picture. I fumble to cover my eyes just as the flash flares in my face. "*Stop*," I whine.

"Why can't I take your picture? You know you're beautiful." He fumbles with my phone, warding off my grabby hands.

"*Now* what are you doing?"

"Sending myself this picture in case you delete it. And..." he concentrates a bit longer before Coldplay's "Yellow" begins to play, "...getting some appropriate music going."

Chris Martin launches into his old line about stars shining "just for you." I grab my phone, desperate for him to stop. This thing *can't* be about romance. Doesn't he understand by now he can destroy me with just one of his sexy looks?

I flip through my playlist until I come across Nine Inch Nails's "Closer."

"Hey. Go back." Adam eyes me with suspicion. "New favorite band, remember?"

"Trust me, this song is more fitting." I flip over to lay above him with one hand holding me up and the other trailing down his stomach, headed for his pants. I dance around on top of him, mouthing the words to the song. Adam's eyes grow wider when the song breaks into the chorus.

"Whoa!" he yells, nearly shoving me over. "I thought we agreed to take this *slow*." He springs for my phone, eagerly stopping the song like it's making his ears bleed. After a few clicks, the members of Typhoon are crooning into the night, discussing the perils of *love* of all goddamned things.

I brush off the relevant fact that he chose to play the mix I named "romance," and frown. "*I* thought we agreed we were coming back to drink champagne and get it on. You're becoming the reversed version of a cock block."

"Come here." He pulls on my hips, his expression suddenly serious.

And, *holy shit,* now they're singing about *strangers in the dark...and stars...*I should stop this right now. The music, the relationship, whatever game we're playing. But one look into Adam's eyes, and I'm a total goner.

I dip my head down, reluctant and cautious. He kisses me with a fire unmatched by anything, hints of champagne and the cheese balls we broke out for our makeshift dinner on his tongue. I breathe deeply through my nose, catching his musky scent mixed in with the outdoors. His lips, both benevolent and eager, stroke and brush around mine, giving room for his tongue to press its way in.

When I reach down to tug at his shirt, wanting to finally feel the muscles of his stomach without fabric getting in the way, his hand wraps around my fingers. He looks up, his eyes filled with so much emotion, it's as if he's about to cry. "Just kiss me, Jewels," he whispers. "Nothing else."

I fall back into him, wrapping my lips with his, not dwelling on reasons why he'd be upset, not caring that I promised myself I wouldn't get emotionally attached. I take his probing tongue between my lips and suck hard, rubbing my body against his in sync with our kisses. Adam backs down, pulling away just enough to reclaim his tongue and lightly suck on my bottom lip. Every time I try to kick it up a notch, he's quick to slow it back down.

I finally give in to his sweet gestures and marginal PG rated intentions. We continue kissing forever and ever under the bright stars, burning through the playlist I created with high hopes for such an occasion. The only stroking and touching of any kind involves heads and faces, and it's filled with compassion, tenderness. Although I'm still burning for him from head to toe, there's an intense need to match his pace and prove to him I *want* this. I want *him.*

Every time we stop to catch our breaths, Adam studies me closely, as if waiting for me to profess my love for him. As if wanting to tell *me* he's in love and doesn't ever want to let me go.

We've entered dangerous territory. You can't kiss someone with so much emotion if you're preparing to walk away. Alarms ring through my head, too loud and too obvious to be ignored. There are *way* too many complex emotions being passed between us.

I already know he's going to shatter my heart.

Eleven

TOURING THE BEAUTIFUL OLD cemetery in Toledo doesn't do much for either one of us. Though we hold hands, and have fallen back into our playful banter, there's an emotional wall that I strategically placed between us, setting us both to teeter on edge. When I woke in Adam's arms, I sprung free to clear my head with an early morning walk before he was awake. I've purposely avoided letting him get too close ever since.

Last night was far too comfortable. The only way to survive this is if I keep it casual and light.

After we grab a light breakfast, an unsure quiet settles between us in the parking lot. This slow-paced action the Midwest offers leaves us too much time to reflect on what we're doing and what will happen next. His thoughts and paranoia have rubbed off on me, making me question every little action between us. We need to get the hell out of Ohio. I need non-stop activities that will get Adam back in the mood to try crazy, reckless things.

"Here's an idea." I turn to him, my eyes bright. "Let's blow off the other stops and drive straight through to New York!"

His lips curve with an amused smirk. "What about Cleveland and Buffalo?"

"We'll spend the extra two days in New York. I seriously doubt we can ever get enough of the city anyway. We'll crash in a cheap hotel near Times Square until the brownstone in Murray Hill is ready. Maybe the owner would even let us in early. I know it will be a little more expensive, but YOLO, am I right?"

Adam shakes his head, laughing in a deep tone. "You're the last person I'd ever expect to use YOLO. That's something one of my brother's dimwitted flings would say." He steps in close to run his fingers up my forearm until my skin pricks with goosebumps. "Hey. Are you okay? Do you want to talk about last night?"

"Are you kidding?" I hook my finger through his belt loop and drag him closer. "I can't stop thinking about last night and what I'm going to do to you the minute we hit the big city."

Standing on my tip-toes, I press my lips to his mouth, cupping his backside in my hands and squeezing. I suck on his bottom lip for a minute before releasing it. His tongue tries to barge its way in, but I back away, giggling. "Consider that a preview of what's to come when we see the city lights, big boy. Now let's hit the road."

THE FREEWAYS ALL SEEM TO BE WIDE open under the clear blue skies, encouraging us to reach our destination in record time. To keep things from getting too serious, I focus on upbeat songs and initiate the dumbest games I can think of. We spend close to an hour with Kelly on my phone, talking about anything and everything that doesn't have to do with our complicated relationship and how we've let things progress. She's too busy telling us horror stories of campers wetting their beds and getting their first periods to realize I'm avoiding specific subjects.

Somewhere between Cleveland and New York, the next shift of the drive is turned over to me. As Adam snoozes against the side of the truck, I have to bite down on my lip to keep from pulling over to wake him, because *damn it* he looks crazy hot with his eyelashes brushing against his cheeks, and the way his fingers rest against my thigh and occasionally twitch...forget about it.

Curiosity won't let me allow his unknown secret to rest. I haven't heard him call *anyone* since we hit the road. Even I've talked to my parents every day, though not really by choice. Does he get along with his parents? What could he be hiding? Am I ready to deal with whatever it is, or do I just ride this affair out until the trip is over? What lies has he told in order to protect the truth? How do I know where the lies stop and the truth begins?

When the end of my three hour shift ends, Adam's still sound asleep, but I don't wake him. I'm too caught up in my growing fears that something big is going to tear our happy road trip apart.

"ADAM!" I YELL, NUDGING HIM IN THE RIBS. "C'mon, I need a copilot right about now!"

"Turn left," my phone commands. I jerk the car into the only open slot available. The Mercedes behind me lays on his horn.

Adam perks to life in the passenger's seat. As he scrambles to sit tall, his eyes grow wide. "Shit! Is this New York already? Why'd you let me sleep so long?"

"Apparently it's because I have a death wish. Will you please help me navigate through this nightmare? You already missed the Holland Tunnel. Statistically speaking, we're *not* in the worst city to drive in, but if we make it through this in one piece, you'll understand why I'm close to hyperventilation over here."

Adam rubs his eyes before grabbing my phone. "Where do you need to go next?"

"Technically, it's a straight shot up Sixth Avenue to Times Square, but I need you to help me watch for Kamikaze taxi drivers."

"Pull over so I can drive."

"And miss the rights to brag that I may or may not have survived driving through downtown Manhattan? Just please, tell me whenever you see your life flash before your eyes."

What could easily be nothing more than five miles takes us almost an hour, three middle fingers, and two near-crashes. I'm so eager to get off the main roads that I duck into the first parking garage we come across without caring if there's an available hotel nearby.

Once parked, I rest my head against the steering wheel. "So *that* was fun. Tomorrow we should sign up for skydiving lessons."

Adam pulls on my hand. "Hey, come here." He plants a drawn-out kiss on my lips before pulling back and resting his forehead to mine. "You were amazing. I doubt I could've gotten us through there in one piece."

"You are kind of a pansy," I agree, giggling. I break away from him and hop down from the pickup, stretching among the smells of gasoline and urine. The rather small parking ramp feels damp with humidity. "Welcome to New York."

Adam grabs our bags from the backseat before coming to my side, his nose wrinkled. "Hmmm. Smells wonderful."

"Some parts of the city aren't so bad. Although I did see my first rat a few blocks off Broadway in the subway station. It was trying to pull a half full latte down the tracks. Killed my taste for the stuff. Lattes, I mean, not rats. I haven't formed an opinion on the vermin yet."

Chuckling, he gathers our bags over one shoulder and drops his free arm around my back. "Let's go find a place to unwind." He leans in to kiss me, letting his lips linger. "Maybe take a shower before we go out."

"Ooo, I like the sound of that," I tease, wiggling my eyebrows and nipping my teeth over his bottom lip.

TWO HOTELS LATER, WE'RE STILL homeless and Adam has yet to see the jumbotron or the main walk into the bright lights and giant billboards of Times Square. By the time we walk into the fourth hotel, bustling with patrons, I nudge him and whisper, "Follow my lead."

Hands held, we weave our way through the crowd and toward the elevators like we're headed to our room. We're able to snag the second elevator headed up. And we're alone.

Adam watches me press the button for the top floor. "Where are we going?"

The minute the doors close I slam him into the metal wall. He lets out a pleasurable groan as I push my pelvis up against him, pinning him with my arms and trailing my lips up his neck. When our mouths meet, his fingers press to my bare back and he draws me tight against him. I part my lips and inhale deeply, literally stealing his breath before breaking away, grinning.

"That's all you're going to give me?" he asks, clearly turned on. He tugs at my belt loop, trying to bring me back. It's great to see him as the horny guy rather than the emotional mess who just wanted to lovingly nuzzle me the night before. I can do horny. The sweet spot between my legs throbs happily with thoughts of having my way with him. I can do horny just fine.

I turn back to the elevator doors, smirking. "For now."

"You're killing me."

Adam watches me as the elevator climbs. We reach the top floor and I slip out without waiting for him. I hear him fumbling to catch up with my fast pace. "What are we doing, exactly?"

"I stayed here with my parents when I was fourteen. One of the only pools in all of Manhattan is on this roof. We can take a quick dip to...ah...*cool down* and shower in the bathrooms before grabbing something to eat. Let's worry about finding a place later. If nothing else, there was a flat overnight rate in the parking ramp. We could always crash there."

"I'm not really up for swimming. You go, I'll nap."

"You're gonna miss out, buddy." Before stepping out onto the roof, I whip my shirt off and throw it at him, revealing the small bikini top I slipped into at the last rest stop.

Adam's eyes bulge. "How am I supposed to sleep with you dressed like that?"

I lean in to catch his lower lip with my teeth, sucking on it hard before releasing it. "That's the point. You're not."

The late afternoon crowd is so big that we're able to slip in without anyone stopping us to see if we're guests of the hotel. As much as I beg and plead, Adam refuses to join me for a swim. I stand at his side for a while as he gapes down at the city before I jump into the water and tread water for a spell.

After a quick shower in the lavish bathroom, I use their blow-dryer to scrunch my hair into sexy waves before putting on a sultry little pink dress that doesn't go past my fingertips. Kelly picked out the matching pink polka dotted thong. A few dabs of mascara over fake eyelashes, a trick with white eyeliner Kelly taught me that makes my eyes pop, just the right amount of bronzer, and I'm ready to rock and roll.

Adam's leaning against a wall across from the bathrooms in a white button down and tan cargo shorts. I lose my breath for a minute at the sight of his sharply cut jaw, steel blue eyes, and toned forearms that look darker in contrast to his shirt.

The most gorgeous guy in all of New York is waiting just for me.

The way his face transforms when he spots me and smiles, the way the light in his eyes turns into a living thing all on its own, I know he's falling for me. And it terrifies me.

He meets me in the middle to wrap his arm around my waist. "*You* look amazing. Edible, even."

A coy smile crosses my lips. I play with the top button of his shirt. "It's necessary if I'm going to be seen on your arm all night. I'm not up for any competition with these big city girls."

He leans in, brushing his bottom lip up my jaw line. "There's no competition." His warm breath huffs inside my ear, curling my toes.

We return our bags to the pickup and stuff ourselves with giant burgers just a few blocks down. Afterward, we wander beyond the restaurant, enjoying the warm night air. The city's just as alive with traffic and people as I remember it from all my other trips. There's never a dull moment in New York, never a time long enough for you to possibly ever grow bored. It's a city that's constantly in motion, constantly making way for change.

Adam remains light and playful. He holds my hand, laughing and pointing out everything unusual we come across, sometimes whispering into my ear to tease me about the way I get excited by little things, or the way I hide behind my hair when he makes me laugh.

Near the edge of Midtown, we come upon a large crowd spilling into the street from an Irish pub. Over fifty people form a line to a large coach bus parked on the curb. They laugh and talk in loud voices like they've been at this all night.

I tilt my head at the bus. "Let's go."

He resists me with a chuckle. "On *that*? We don't even know where it's going. And it's probably something you have to pre-pay for."

"Do we *care* where it's going?" I throw my hands up in the air. "This is *New fucking York*! Wherever it ends up is guaranteed to be somewhere amazing! Seriously, it'll be fun!" I shuffle closer to run my finger across his beautiful bottom lip. "Buddy. If you're on this trip for an adventure, you're going to have to start taking risks."

His eyes flicker from me to the people in line. Most of them seem to be just a little older than us, and incredibly intoxicated. Blending in shouldn't be a problem.

Adam gives in with a low moan. "At least by morning we should have free accommodations. In *jail*."

"Three hots and a cot? How could you turn a deal that good down?"

I yank on his arm and break into a jog. Like a couple of professional con artists, we slide between two couples talking in animation near the back. After a few minutes I swipe the bright pink sticker from a man's shirt at our side when he isn't looking, and slap it onto Adam's chest before making a show of tangling my arms around his waist and reaching for his mouth, slipping my tongue inside. Adam responds right away, pushing his tongue past my teeth and running his hands across my back. The couples behind us hoot and applaud their approval.

"Alright, you two," a woman says from inside the bus. "Let's get this show on the road."

Giggling, I lead Adam up the steps of the bus. A blue glowing light illuminates the long aisle up the middle. Everyone has claimed their spots near the front of the fairly new bus, probably for first dibs at the next stop. I lead Adam to the last row of chairs in the back and let him sit first, then slip onto his lap.

"Exciting enough for ya..." I look at the pink sticker and giggle, "*Roger*?"

Adam slips his hand underneath my hair, cupping my neck as if it's made of precious gemstones. "I'm starting to think you're kind of crazy, once I really get to know you."

I grin wickedly. "If you think I'm crazy now, check this out."

Among the boisterous noise of the other passengers and the radio blasting some kind of dance mix, I part my lips and press them to

Adam's mouth, sticking out only the tip of my tongue, gentle, teasing against his lips. My right hand runs down the center of his chest, slipping underneath his shorts and dipping into his underwear.

He flinches with wide eyes, reaching for my hand. I carefully push him away with my other hand. "Trust me," I whisper. "You're going to dig this."

I unbutton his shorts and release him through the slit in his boxer shorts. Titling my head to the side, I allow my long hair to make a veil between us and the rest of the bus, taking my time to suck and pull at his bottom lip, letting my other hand stroke his growing excitement. He moans soft and low in my mouth, letting his hand nearest the window creep up the bottom of my dress to my bare butt. A thousand nerves burst at the touch of his fingers against my skin.

"Raise your hand if your buddy isn't on the bus!" the woman at the front of the bus announces.

"My buddy's *definitely* on the bus," I whisper in Adam's ear, tugging him carefully. "And he's a *big* guy."

I kiss him again, stronger, more urgent as his fingers trail their way to the spot that's already wet and pounding, begging him to enter. His thumb swipes up and down at the edge of my thong before pushing it aside to freely caress me.

"Okay, we're off to our next stop!" the woman calls joyfully over the speaker system.

The bus crawls forward. The other couples on board shout and whistle excitedly. The aisle lights turn off, making it dark in the bus except for the bright lights from outside.

It's the most intoxicating, sensual moment of my life. I'm in my favorite city, doing something that's so wrong with someone who feels incredibly right.

Once I'm good and wet, his smooth fingers, soft and gentle against my tender skin, press up inside of me. I've been craving him for so long today that I already feel ready to climax. I bite down on his lip to keep from moaning loudly.

I gasp into his mouth instead, nearly forgetting to keep my own hand in motion. His breaths turn hot and heavy, becoming faster and faster with each of my carefully paced tugs. I feel his hips swaying ever so slightly with my strokes as he reaches the height of arousal.

My senses are electrified by his delightfully masculine smell, sounds of his raspy breaths, the delectable taste of his sweet tongue, the way his fingers brush and prod, the tender look on his face when I dare to open my eyes. I've never wanted anyone so badly.

"*Goddamn*," he whispers, biting at my ear lobe. "I really want inside of you."

I don't have to be told twice. Moving quickly, I shift my hips and yank his hand away to make room for me before he can protest. I'm so wet and primed for action that he slips inside of me without any problem, though I do let out a soft squeal into his mouth from the sheer girth of him. Adam gasps deeply. Rocking my pelvis with slow, precise movements, I push my hips down until I can feel his large tip filling me. He groans into my mouth, his clutch on my butt cheeks tightening. He frees a hand to cradle one of my breasts, kneading the nipple between his fingers.

Amidst laughter, animated conversations, and the overwhelming stench of booze, Adam and I have sex for the first time. It's so much better than in a hotel room or the back of the pickup where there's time for reflection and moments of pause. There's a hot kind of disconnection being out in public, and I love it. In this moment we are boundless, nothing more than lovers.

Adam Murphy has given me all there is to offer of himself, and it's every bit as amazing as my deepest fantasies could imagine.

I limit my thrusts, trying not to make what we're doing in the back of the bus so obvious. Our mouths sealed together dull the sounds of our enduring, passion-fueled cries. Adam's grasp on me becomes so tight, I know he's getting ready to explode.

He breaks the contact of our mouths to whisper with a gulp, "Damn it, I'm gonna come."

"It's good. I have an IUD." I add a harder thrust of my hips, allowing him to go extra deep.

He sucks hard on my bottom lip and trembles in my arms, releasing into me with a quick, stuttered breath before burring his face in the curve of my neck, panting. I let out a satisfied sigh and tangle my fingers in his thick hair, cradling his sweaty head against my chest.

"You just had sex on a bus," I whisper among a giggle. "How's *that* for your list?"

For the rest of the short ride, I snuggle against Adam, locking my right hand with his. He methodically rubs my arms, sometimes stopping to kiss the side of my head. The realization that I'm completely smitten with him washes over me. How can someone so beautiful and fun to be around be single, and all *mine*?

I wish there was a way to make time stop so this night would never have to end. Having sex with Adam ignited all the senses that have been asleep inside of me for so long. Although it wasn't sweet and tender, it's something I've been wanting to do ever since we first met, and we've made the kind of ultimate connection that can't be undone.

If anyone caught on to what the mysterious couple was doing in the back of the bus, they either don't let on, or just really don't care. Maybe they've seen it before. We exit among the other passengers without anyone gaping or stopping us, following the crowd into a low-lit Irish pub.

The raw, amped sounds of a live band are a total delight to my ears. The large pub, packed with patrons like sardines in a can, smells as if someone soaked old gym socks in whiskey. The line for the bar is at least three four in some places. Three redheaded waitresses dressed in tight blouses run back and forth beneath the flags of Ireland, taking money and passing out drinks with tight, stressed-out smiles.

I turn to Adam, as delighted as a school girl. "I do believe we've crashed a pub crawl!"

His eyes are missing their usual spark when he smiles back. "Can I get you a drink?"

"I'll take whatever's light on tap! I'm going to visit the bathroom! Meet you on the dance floor!" I kiss him and find my way to the restrooms at the back of the bar, behind where a dozen people dance to the three guitarists and a drummer playing an old David Bowie tune. After waiting for my turn to clean up in the girls' room, I weasel in next to a few girls around my age to dance along, feeling as if the weight of the world has just been lifted off my shoulders.

I had sex with Adam! And it was beyond amazing!

Instead of screaming happily, I throw my hands up in the air and shimmy around, giggling, allowing the middle aged woman at my side to press her fleshy butt into my bony hip. I can't remember the last time I danced, or even the last time I felt this incredible. I left all my inhibitions and worries back in Wisconsin with my over-doting parents and ghosts of my dead boyfriend's memories.

By the time the third song is over, I've made half a dozen dancing friends of all different ages, and I'm covered in sweat. The band starts into a slow song, breaking up our newly formed dance party.

I take cover in the corner to call Kelly, catching her on the second ring.

"You better be in an alley somewhere bleeding," she tells me. "You didn't call when you got to your hotel like you promised! I was ready to send search and rescue out for you guys!"

"Would you shut up a minute? Kel, he finally gave in! And it was so incredibly *hot*!"

"Hold on. You mean you *slept* with him? When? Where are you?"

"We're in New York! We skipped the other stops. I wanted to hurry things up and get here because he was acting weird about us, getting too serious and shit!"

"*Too* serious?" I hear her moving around like she's sitting up in bed. "But I thought you *wanted* things to happen with him."

I scan the crowd for any sign that Adam could be listening in, but I can't even see past the crowd to the bar in front. "I do. Or I mean, I did. I have a bad feeling about this secret of his. I don't want to get serious if there's some reason we can't be together."

"So you had *sex* with him? Jewels, are you taking your meds?"

"Hey, I gotta go! I'll call you later!" I end the call before she can launch into another lecture on how important it is to keep up my mental health.

With still no sign of Adam, I make my way back to the bar. He's not there either, so I send a quick text. He doesn't answer. I decide to wait where I left him, thinking he must've snuck back to the bathroom.

"You here alone?" someone asks. I turn to face a stout man with a thick mustache and goatee. His glossy eyes perk up. "Hey, you're on our bus tour!"

I nod reluctantly, hoping he doesn't recognize me as the one "getting it on" in the back. "Have you seen the guy I was with?"

"I was out for a smoke a little bit ago and he was standing by the bus."

"Thanks!" I say, touching his shoulder before springing to the door.

The cluster of smokers outside slowly part for me. I find Adam leaning against the bus, his head tipped back to watch the stars.

What the hell is he doing out here alone?

Telling myself not to make a big deal of it, I go to him, calling his name. His head bows down and he stares at me, throwing on one of the most forced smiles I've ever witnessed. I'm sure there's some kind of pain or maybe even fear behind it that demands to be heard, but he's too stubborn to let surface. Again I'm torn between wanting to know the truth and continuing on as a blissfully ignorant participant.

"Hey." He drags me to him and plants a kiss on my forehead. "I just had to catch my breath. That place is way too crowded."

"So everything's *okay*?" I ask, delivering a bite to my question, knowing he won't answer, or even address the fact that I'm irritated.

"It's been a long day. We still need to find a place to stay."

I rest my hands on his chest. "But it's early, and the band is crazy good. Plus, we're like a dozen blocks from the truck, and these cute little wedges aren't meant for actual use. If we don't take the bus, we'll have to grab a taxi. And I don't think messing around in front of a taxi driver will be nearly as fun."

He collects my fingers in his hands, looking irritated. "We can always go out another night. If it's always like this even on the weekdays, we'll have lots of time. I'm sure there will be more bands." His eyes drift to the traffic whizzing by. "Maybe we can even sign up for one of these pub crawls and actually *pay* our way on."

I squeeze his hand. "Hey, look at me."

Reluctantly, his eyes roll back my way, void of the compassion and endearment they held earlier.

"Are you mad because of what we did in the bus?"

"You mean *fuck*?" His bitter tone takes me by surprise.

"Was there something *else* we did that I'm not aware of?" I huff and pull away from him. "What's your deal?"

His hard gaze chills me down to my bones. "I told you I wanted to take things slow, remember? You made it cheap. Having sex on a bus is something sleazy that my brother would do, not me."

"Because you didn't have a good time? *Seriously*?" I gather my hair over one shoulder, suddenly feeling overheated from dancing with it down. That and my emotions are about to come to a boil. What's with his sudden Jekyll and Hyde bit? "What do you *want* from me, Adam? What is this *thing* between us? I thought we were on this trip to have a good time!"

"It's gotten too complicated." He twists the hair at the crown of his head. His shoulders fall. "C'mon. I don't want to do this with you. Let's go before we get into a fight." He leaves my side, disappearing to the street in front of the bus to hail a cab.

I stand on the sidewalk staring after him, feeling completely blindsided. I knew sex with Adam would be crazy hot. I just wasn't expecting the chill that would follow.

I WAKE UP ON THE BACK BENCH OF THE pickup with my muscles cramped from sleeping in the limited space. Adam's still in the passenger's seat, the back tilted as far as it would go, his beautiful lashes resting over his cheeks, mouth slightly parted. Staring at his peaceful face, uneasy swells fill my stomach. Sleeping in different places felt so horribly wrong, as if we're getting ready to part ways.

By the time we got back to the pickup, I was so angry by his rejection that I didn't want to walk around with him any longer in search of a hotel. He was reluctant to stay in a big city parking lot, but didn't seem eager to argue and caved in.

Looking down at my pretty pink dress all crumpled from turning on the bench in the night, I want to cry. Sure, the sexual chemistry between us is off the hook, but I shouldn't have let things get out of control on the bus. I should've waited like he wanted so our first time together could've been more like making love and not downright dirty.

But I can't let myself feel those kinds of things for Adam. Not when I know there's something horribly wrong with his life. Not when I know he could destroy me.

I've made so many mistakes in my short lifetime that I don't have room for any more.

Confused and ashamed, I quickly slip from the pickup with my purse and cell phone in hand.

Twelve

I RUN MY FINGER OVER ADAM'S CHEEK. "Wake up, pansy ass."

He makes a low, throaty hum. The same kind he made when we were having sex. He flinches when seeing me sitting in the driver's seat, and quickly tilts the seat back upright. "Where are we?"

"Home sweet home. At least for a couple weeks."

I point at the brownstone we'd seen pictures of online. In person it's ten times more charming, nestled in a picturesque neighborhood off 30th Street. The narrow buildings are painted a subtly contrasting hue, differently shaped windows and styles of doors making each of them unique. The street is mostly barren, some of the parked cars lined along it looking like they've been left indefinitely with numerous parking tickets on the windshield. A line of identical bikes for rent locked to a bar stand a ways down from our place. It's like something you'd see in a movie, or an episode of *Sex and the City*. The minute I first saw it, my heart took on a light, delightful beat.

Adam's eyebrows draw down. "I thought we weren't supposed to have the place until tomorrow."

"I called the owner. No one was renting it today, so he said he'd have the cleaning staff stop by this afternoon while we're off sightseeing." I open the door, wagging my eyebrows. "Are you ready to check it out, or what?"

He reaches for the backseat. "Where'd our bags go?"

"I already took them inside." I hop out of the pickup and wave him down with my hand.

I let a male jogger pass in front of our brownstone before lifting the gate and waiting for Adam to join me. His eyes light up at the sight of the green door atop the steps. "This place looks great."

"You really think I was going to let us stay in anything subpar?" I poke at his chest, clicking my tongue. "I thought you knew me by now, *Murphy*."

We race up the steps. I punch the code the owner gave me into the keypad, flinging the door open to the next flight of stairs. Adam passes me, hollering out excitedly when he reaches the top. "Holy shit! It's twice as big as it looked in the pictures!"

I skip to his side, beaming proudly. The small kitchen to our left, pimped out in faded marble countertops and black, distressed cupboards, has top of the line appliances, including a coffee maker and a pizza oven. A small island overlooks the living area where there's a giant stone fireplace and a three-piece sectional sofa filled with dozens of white, airy pillows. The marble floors continue on to a large square table and chairs, stopping at a patio door overlooking the backyard.

I nudge his elbow. "You gotta check this out."

He's back to his squirrelly self when he springs along with me. We step out to the small balcony overlooking the back side of the other buildings in the neighborhood. They each have their own little balconies similar to ours with a fire escape stairway running through it, some with plants, bicycles, patio furniture, and grills. Some of the ground-floor yards, each individually fenced off, have little plastic children's pools. One even has a swing. The place next door to us is like something straight out of a home magazine with a mix of expensive couches that looks like they belong indoors, and large Christmas lights draped overhead.

Simple wooden stairways lead up to the back door of some brownstones, while others are wrought iron with elaborate designs. Buildings of various heights and colored bricks stack together in the background like perfectly placed steps for a giant. It's an eclectic mix of different shapes and colors.

Our balcony has a cracked stone floor with a wrought iron table and chairs, their floral cushions worn and faded from the sun. It's all so incredibly charming. I feel as if I'm *home,* though in reality, I'm thousands of miles from where I grew up.

Adam rests his hands on the railing, grinning as he takes it all in. "Wow. This is awesome."

My chest warms to hear he's just as enchanted by the view. I can see us living together in a little place like this, close to the big city, yet in the midst of an intimate neighborhood, hanging out at night with the neighbors in their mismatched furniture beneath the twinkling lights. Adam did well in school before he dropped out, and as long as I work at it, I'm able to get decent grades too. We could each find a day job, and take classes at night. I picture myself cuddled up in his arms on this balcony, reading a book, or planning out our day.

Moments like those would keep me moving, giving me a new sense of purpose. I could forget all the past mistakes I've made, and live for a different kind of future. It'd be a clean slate. For both of us.

Realizing how far I've let my thoughts wander, I shake my head. They're too dangerous with all that still remains unknown between us. I need to keep moving.

"I know, right? Wait until you see the rest."

I don't wait for him to follow me back into the brownstone and past the kitchen. At the bottom of the narrow oak stairway leading to the next level, there's a small bedroom with two twin beds. I step inside and flip on the light. "This is your room. I already called dibs on the bedroom upstairs with the jet tub. Yours has a small shower and toilet."

Adam takes a deep breath, and his eyes morph with guilt. "Jewels—"

I spin around and walk back out the door, shaking my head and waving a hand through the air. "Don't worry about it. I had time to set up our stuff."

"Hey!" he calls out behind me. "Would you stop and talk to me for a minute?"

"I figure we can freshen up before we hit some tourist spots. The owner said there's a little bakery around the corner. You can grab some bagels or whatever while I'm getting ready." I flash a smile over my shoulder, not really looking at him. "See you in about an hour."

I'm halfway up the steps when the tears finally break loose.

THE CITY GIVES OFF A DIFFERENT KIND of heat from back home, sucking both the water and energy from your bones. We make lots of stops to try different foods from the vendors, grab water, even buy matching fedoras. Adam's filled with an unusual quiet that can only come from a tumultuous, internal battle, so I break the silence with constant chatter, telling him whatever facts I know about the area or stories of my other trips to the city. I avoid touching him at all costs, knowing any handholding or kissing will only complicate things and put us back in the same conundrum as before.

I'm just as charmed by the city as I was on my first and last visit, and find myself falling in love with it even more. The architecture, constant motion, endless restaurants and retail choices fill me with unbridled euphoria, making it easy to forget all about my complicated love life. Having Adam by my side, experiencing the city through my eyes, makes the trip that much more thrilling.

After a tour of the NBC studios in which the magic of *Saturday Night Live* is forever ruined when I see the miniature stage, we head to the top of the Empire State Building for Adam's first panoramic view of the city. He's thoroughly impressed, and takes his time drinking it in while I'm busy finding a spot against the building that doesn't make my head and stomach spin.

I feel the building swaying beneath me like it's far too high to stay upright. For some reason I don't remember being so terrified last time I looked over the city. My knees grow weak when I have a sudden bout of vertigo.

"How are you doing?" Adam holds his hand out with a sly grin. "Come over here."

"I can see perfectly fine from here."

"We can't check it off the list unless we do it together."

I finally give in, taking his hand. He leads me closer to the glass before wrapping his arms around me. I swoon with the familiar comfort of him, and forget about the terrifying depths below. The aerial view of Manhattan is spectacular, allowing for a stunning shot of Central Park one way, the Empire State Building and various skyscrapers in the other. The beautiful, blue sky stretches above the city, a slight haze of pollution drifting just below the scattered clouds providing a temporary relief from the relentless sun. It's mind blowing to see the hundreds of building structures jetting into the sky, and realizing they're all filled with residents of the city going about their daily lives.

As the wind pushes my hair away from my face, I realize how much I want this. I want this to be my life so badly that my heart aches. The excitement that New York City provides *and* the promises of Adam always at my side.

Adam's breath is warm and staggered against my ear. We stand like this for a long time, my hopes for any future together still staggering on the unknown, but knowing I can't give Adam up, no matter the price.

"I could stay up here forever," he whispers.

WE BRAVE THE SUBWAY SYSTEM BACK to Murray Hill, successfully finding our way to the neighborhood without getting lost, mugged, or murdered. For a Midwestern girl with minimal big city experience, I consider it a great accomplishment. Adam grabs a twelve pack of the most expensive beer from the convenience store around the corner before we return to the brownstone.

I sip on a beer as we stroll down the sidewalk leading to the brownstone. Two guys on bikes pass down the center of the quieter, narrow street. An older woman meanders along the sidewalk with a little black poodle that eagerly sniffs everything it sees. Three doors down from our place, a few middle aged couples have already gathered outside a little Italian bistro for an early dinner, their laughter light against the warm air. The smell of freshly cooked pasta drifts out the open door, making my stomach wild even though we just stopped for cannoli just an hour ago.

The charming neighborhood fills me with an inner peace that I thought I'd never feel again. I can't pinpoint exactly what it is about the area that stirs so much emotion in me, but it feels like home. Taking a deep breath, I grin to myself.

"Look at you," Adam says when I reach for the gate. "You're *beaming*. You really love this city, don't you?"

I gaze into his eyes, feeling my smile stretch even further. "It's pretty amazing, right? I think I could totally live here one day."

We're interrupted by a young guy with a high and tight haircut wearing an athletic tank top and gym shorts, his tattooed biceps glistening with sweat. With a clean-cut face, he's the type who could be accepted into the military by stereotype alone. White headphones strung around his neck blast hardcore rap.

"Hey! You must be the ones renting Sal's place for the next couple weeks," he greets us with an accent straight out of the Bronx. "I'm Theo. I live next door." He offers me his big, sweaty hand.

I take it, giggling. "Jewels."

"Sorry," he says, reclaiming his hand to wipe it on his shorts. "I just ran a 5k to blow off some steam."

"Aren't *you* ambitious," I answer.

His bright white teeth sparkle when he grins at me. I'll admit the guy is crazy hot, but he's also the type to sprinkle steroids on his breakfast cereal and crash beer cans with his skull. Not nearly half as alluring or naturally gorgeous as Adam.

Adam sticks his hand out to our new neighbor. "Adam."

While the two guys pump hands and size each other up, I perk to life. "Wait. Are you the one with the couches and twinkle lights?"

Theo's green eyes sparkle down on me when he drops Adam's hand. "My ex-girlfriend decorated it. I just haven't taken the time to tear it down."

"*That* would be a *waste*," I say. "It'd be a much better plan to have tons of parties to make her jealous."

"Yeah? You guys want to come over tonight and hang out? I can order in some of the city's best pizza from around the corner. Looks like you already have drinks, so..." His eyes lower, lazily passing my low-cut tank top to the beer in my hand before continuing down to my legs. "Come over, if you're up for it."

"We'd love to," I answer quickly.

While I don't miss the way he's undressing me with his eyes or the suggestive tone to his voice, I'm ready to do anything to avoid alone time with Adam in the brownstone. I'm not in the mood to revisit why he's mad I "took advantage of him" in the bus.

"Yeah, okay," Adam chimes in a second too late.

Theo's eyes don't leave mine. "Let me jump in the shower. You guys can either wait for me out back, or—"

I nod eagerly. Probably a little too eagerly since my mind is still wrapped around the vision of him standing naked in the shower with water rolling down his broad chest. Just because he's not my type doesn't mean I wouldn't enjoy the view. "We'll wait there. Sounds perfect."

"Awesome!" He touches the back of my arm, guiding me to his gate before holding it open for us. I feel his stare on my backside as Adam and I descend the stairs to the lower level brownstone.

Theo's place has a similar layout to our rental, although his furniture looks brand new, there's a ton of upscale artwork on the walls, his floors are a beautiful dark hardwood, and his counters are tan granite beneath mahogany cupboards. It looks as if a designer—or his ex-girlfriend—decorated the place, considering it's extremely tasteful. Then again, this is New York. Theo could be classy enough to have done it himself. I'm just accustomed to men who think a deer head and neon beer signs constitute good decorating.

Theo leads us into the living room area, pointing at the patio door. "Make yourself at home out there. I'll be done in fifteen."

As soon as he leaves, Adam darts out the patio door, his face tight with tension. I step past him to the first large couch, sinking into the batch of pillows and taking a long swig of my beer.

"This backyard kicks ass," I say, ignoring his spiraling mood. "I'm pretty sure I could handle a life like this. Can you imagine this *home*? Hanging out back here every night, living in a city where there's literally something going on twenty-four hours a day?"

Adam shifts the beer from one arm to another, glancing back into the brownstone. "Maybe you could see if *Theo's* looking for a roommate."

I roll my eyes. "No need to be *jealous*. I thought it'd be fun to see what the night brings. For all we know, the guy could be running Wall Street. Someone on TripAdvisor said these brownstones run from three to five million. Mark this night down as part of your adventure." Emptying my beer, I stand to take the box from Adam. "Sit down and relax. I'm going to put these in the fridge."

His eyes lock with mine when I reach for the beer. "*Jewels*," he whispers, pleading. His fingers brush against the back of my hand. "We still need to talk. You can't keep avoiding me like this."

My heart races with his touch. I want to kiss him and tell him I'm sorry. I want to break down and beg him to tell me his secret. Instead I take the box and head inside.

As I slip into the spotless kitchen, I hear the shower running. I'm surprised to find the fridge overflowing with fruits, veggies, and a ton of healthy stuff. "What, no energy drinks and power bars?" I mutter, shifting things around to make room.

Once I've jammed the box on a shelf and have grabbed another beer, I shut the door and head back to the hallway. I catch movement in the bedroom and turn to see a freshly showered Theo passing by.

Completely naked.

He stops dead center in the door frame, smirking. Pleased I caught him. "Oh, hey. I didn't hear you come in."

I give him credit for not acting embarrassed or surprised, though there isn't a single reason for him to be anything other than proud. He's every bit as muscular and *large* from head to...toe. Each individual stomach muscle can be counted, and ready to cut glass. The intricate tattoo covering his ripe shoulder continues down to his smooth pectoral muscles, dipping all the way down to his pelvic region where his deep tan continues on. As in, he tans in the nude.

I feel my jaw drop and hear myself inhale sharply, but I'm really not aware how intensely I'm staring at how hard he's become as we stand drinking each other in.

Wow. Just...wow.

His dark brows shoot up. "Can I get you...anything?"

"I'm...beer," I sputter, holding the bottle up. "I have beer."

He chuckles in a deep, hearty laugh. "So I see. I just have to get dressed and I'll be out in a sec."

"Clothes. Good call." I spin around as my cheeks grow warm. I have to actively tell my feet to move toward the patio doors where Adam's completely unaware of the not *completely* awkward encounter.

"Jewels?" he calls after me. When I look back he's still smirking, still naked. "Just so we're clear, you're welcome to stop over *anytime*."

INTENTIONAL PEEP SHOW ASIDE, THEO turns out to be a lot of fun. He plays a mix of hard rock over the speakers mounted underneath the roof as we work on depleting the beer supply. Adam and I both roll in laughter with his stories of the rather varied people of the neighborhood. And as he's busy playing host, I see a Marine Corps tattoo on his calf muscle.

While Adam's clueless to the exact level of comfort Theo has around me, I'm hyper aware of every sideways smirk or twinkle of his eye. It's awesome to have someone so hot obviously wanting to be more than friendly neighbors, but I have my hands full the way it is with Adam. And I can't stop staring at that damn tattoo.

Jason had one just like that.

The three of us are debating what flavor of pizza to order when a group of Theo's buddies stop by with enough booze to knock out an entire football team. And I can't help but wonder if that's exactly what they do for a living as they're all just as well built as our host.

"*Another* actress, or is this one a model?" one of the guys asks Theo, taking a swig of his mixed drink while wiggling his blond eyebrows at me. He's taller than Theo, though not quite as built or all-American looking. A scar over his eyebrow has the curious feel of many fights gone bad.

Adam stands up too quickly, his hand held out. "She's Jewels, I'm Adam."

The guy shakes his hand. "James. You new to the neighborhood?"

"We're renting the place next door for a couple weeks," Adam answers. It's great to see him being friendly with these guys, even if it is because he's becoming all Alpha male. Still, I'm beginning to feel the burn of gnawing guilt for dragging him over here without asking what he wanted to do.

James cups Adam on the back. "Welcome to Murray Hill. My man, Theo, will take real nice care of you while you're here. We've got a few house parties lined up this weekend. You'll have to join us." He tilts his head at me. "Where you from?"

"Wisconsin," I answer, standing to join them. "You know, the land of milk and cheese, and shit."

I waver on my feet, the five beers hitting me in a blanket of haze. Since hanging out with Adam I've hardly had any alcohol, and apparently it's made me a lightweight. But seeing Theo's tattoo had me pounding down more beers than I intended.

The three guys each move as if to catch me. Theo, being the closest, clutches my arm. "Whoa. Take it easy, beautiful."

"Hey, I'm from Wisconsin," I repeat, smiling brightly. "We drink beer for breakfast."

James cackles brightly. "You guys sound like news people."

I raise one eyebrow with an attempt of seduction. "You should hear me do the weather."

Adam cuts past Theo to take my other arm, pulling me from our neighbor. "Time to call it a night."

"She just needs something in her stomach," Theo decides, pulling his phone from his jeans pocket. "I'll order the pizzas."

Theo's buddies launch into a lively conversation on what flavors to order as Adam pulls me aside. "Enough with the beer. Let's go back to our place."

"*Our place*?" I ask with a drunken snort, lessening my eyes to small little slits. "I don't *think* so. *You* can go. I think I can manage to find my way back."

He rolls his eyes before pinning me down with a look that makes me want to hide in a corner of shame. "These guys are just like my brother—willing to take a girl any way they can get her, even if she's too plastered to know what she's doing. You really don't know me if you think I'd leave you here alone with them."

The guilt-inducing stare, the bitter tone of his voice, they're too much. The feelings I've been working so hard to keep at bay rise to the top like an army of Rottweilers. I lean in closer. "I once thought maybe I knew you, but I've decided I really don't." I stretch my arm from his reach. "You never talk about your family other than telling me your brother's an asshole. You won't explain why you quit school, or crash at your buddy's shit-hole of a house even though you have all this money. Then there's this big fucking secret you're so intent on keeping. So the answer is *I don't know. Would you* leave me here alone? You've had me, why not give some other poor bastard a chance?"

His eyes close for a long pause. They're internally bruised when they look back down on me. "I know you don't mean that. Let's not do this here."

"Yeah, I agree. I'm over it."

The weight of stares from the others falls heavy on my conscience. I turn to them with the same artificial pep that kept me going through my days of cheerleading. "Who's ready to do some shots?"

As the guys holler excitedly, I turn my back on Adam.

ALL PLANS TO KEEP MYSELF UNDER control go out the door with the third shot of Patrón. I'm usually a pro at holding my liquor, but anger, confusion, hurt, and every other crappy feeling that has swelled up inside make me a virtual mess. Rather than worrying about whether or not I'm crushing Adam's ego by flirting with the guys, I'm busy dirty dancing to the loud music with Theo, trying to forget Adam's only a few heartbeats away.

It isn't long before Theo slows his pace, slipping his bulging arms around my waist and pushing his hips against me. I feel it against my belly—the understanding that Adam and I aren't officially a thing, and his urgent desire to be with me. I hear it in his shallow breaths when he touches his rough jaw to my forehead. I can even smell it on him among the scent of expensive cologne and sweat pouring out in eager pheromones.

The promise of sex dangles in the air like forbidden fruit. The booze and provocative dancing have improved his appearance to a point that I'm incredibly turned on, clouding my usual impeccable judgment. I want to kiss him, even though I *don't* want to kiss him. It's still Adam I want to kiss, and love, and spend the rest of forever with.

But it doesn't seem like it will ever happen.

"So you and Adam..." Theo licks his full lips, fixing his green orbs with mine. Drinking me in. "Are you fair game?"

By dancing so intimately with Theo, letting him touch me in ways Adam has, I've wandered down a dangerous path, one that would forever destroy any chances of Adam and I being together. These are the kind of choices that define a person.

"No. I'm not. I'm sorry, I shouldn't—"

Sucking in a deep breath, I back away, nearly colliding with Adam. He's staring Theo down with a look that could land them both in the hospital.

"I'm taking her home," Adam finally says, not breaking the stare. "Thanks for everything. We'll let you know if we're still up for the party tomorrow."

Theo nods with a sexy, confident smirk. "Alright."

"Thanks," I add in a soft voice. "See you tomorrow."

Theo slings his arms around my neck, burying me like a little child in his massive hold. "Something tells me these are going to be an interesting couple of weeks," he whispers into my ear.

Adam takes my hand, pulling me away. I can feel anger rolling off him when he leans in to say, "Next time you can skip the shots."

Though I'm still conscious as I leave the party, strung around Adam and throwing goodbyes to each of the guys on our way out, the drinks pull me under like a dark, heavy blanket.

DULL POUNDING OF MY HEAD KEEPS ME from sitting up. On the nightstand there's a bottle of Advil and a glass of water dripping with perspiration. I roll over to wash down a few pills before swinging my feet off the bed, moaning. I'm still dressed in my outfit from the day before and smell the stench of tequila on my skin. After patting down my mangled hair, I realize Adam's standing in the doorway. Fingers stuck in his pockets, hair and clothes fresh as the morning, his loving eyes make me feel like a complete dirt bag.

"Get ready. I'll be waiting downstairs."

THE MOUTH-WATERING AROMA OF cinnamon drifts toward me when I head down to the kitchen, feeling like a new person after a long, hot shower. On the countertop there's a large slice of coffee cake and a Styrofoam cup with steam rising from its lid, my name scribbled on the side. Stomach rumbling, I reach for the goodies but freeze when I see Adam leaning on the balcony, overlooking the neighborhood with a quiet calm.

Ragged beats of my heart shake my entire body. I was a total ass to him last night. It all started because I didn't want to let myself feel this raking urge to be with Adam, not just for the sex, but because of who he is and who he makes me become when we're together. But I screwed up when I made the sex become a cheap thing. I screwed up when I let my hormones overrule my heart.

Only one of two things can happen at this point. We'll continue on as lovers, embracing our feelings that could possibly grow into something serious that will probably eventually destroy me, or we'll break apart and ruin the beauty our once friendly relationship created. The middle ground has disappeared among meaningful kisses and exhibition sex. Either way, it seems our relationship will end in disaster. It's an ultimatum I'd do damn near anything to avoid.

Why couldn't this be happening later on the trip, after we've visited Hawaii and enjoyed endless nights of wild sex and carefree moments? I'm not ready for this.

Adam whirls around, as if sensing my withdrawal, and tips his head.

My feet move toward him, though my heart cries for me to stop. We meet in the middle, my shins pressed against the couch. Adam reaches down for my hands, the intensity in his eyes stopping my breath.

"I'm sorry," I whisper, fat tears blurring my vision. "I don't...it's just...I didn't mean to hurt you. What you saw last night...that was me confused and afraid."

He looks ready to say something, ready to damn me or tell me everything's somehow miraculously okay, but he suddenly drops my hands to cradle my face, rushing in to cover my mouth with a long, sultry kiss.

I whimper against his mouth, bringing my arms around him and squeezing tight, resolving never to push him away ever again. Promising myself that I'll open my heart to him from this point on, allowing him to become my everything despite my fears, despite the fact I still don't know what's wrong with him or why he's reluctant to let me in.

The force of his lips about bring me to my knees as they suck and bend, his tongue eager and unyielding in between. I answer him with languid passion, wanting the moment to last forever, wanting the hard words I know are sure to come to stay deep down inside where they won't change us. The taste of my tears mix in with the sweet flavor of cinnamon and the familiarity of Adam.

His hands find their usual place underneath the sides of my shirt, caressing the skin above my hips, driving me mad for more. I pounce into his arms, propelling us back into the big squishy couch. As I straddle him, his kisses trail down my neck. I run my lips along the spot behind his ear, holding back my cries of angst and words of destruction. I break past his hold, reaching for his shirt, ready to jerk it over his arms.

"Wait!" he yells, trying to fight against me.

But it's too late.

I discover the reason he never removes his shirt, the reason he avoids letting me touch him.

Pink, puckering scars circle around his navel. A larger one starts near his breast bone, stretching all the way down beneath his boxers. Some of the scars have faded, some are darker red as if from more recent times. Numerous procedures mar his beautiful belly, although hardened and defined from obvious dedication to the gym. It looks as if he's been to the butcher shop. When I run my fingertips along the ugly scars, he winces.

"Is *this* your secret?" I ask in a mere whisper. "Is this what you don't want me to know? What happened?"

There's shame in Adam's eyes when he nudges me from his lap and turns away, running his hands through his hair. "This trip was supposed to be fun, without all these complications," he mutters, as if talking to himself and not me. His hands are still locked behind his head as he stares at the floor. "You were so hot, and funny, and full of this unbridled energy. I wanted to be around you as much as I could. You made me forget all the shitty things in my life. I didn't know I'd fall so hard for you. I never should've let this happen."

He sniffs, his shoulders trembling.

Is he *crying*?

I debate whether or not to stroke his back, and tell him whatever it is, everything's going to be okay. Because it obviously won't be, not ever again. Still, my heart stutters wildly in my chest. He *"fell hard"* for me. It wasn't all imagined on my part. Half disturbed by whatever is still bothering him, and half thrilled that we may have a chance after all, I fight off a confused smile.

"Hey." I reach for him, but decide against it, folding my hands in my lap instead. "Will you please tell me why you have so many scars?"

Still looking down, he rambles on to himself. "Try to understand why I did this, why I invited you to come along. I promised Zach I would try. Right before he died, I told him I'd go out without any regrets."

"*Go out*?" I repeat, warding off a chill. In the past week he's talked more about his best friend's death, how it was slow and painful for him in the end. But what does Zach's death have to do with us? I frown, shaking my head. "I don't understand."

"I'm sick, Jewels. This list...the need to get out and do these things, it's because I'm dying."

Thirteen

SOMEWHERE IN THE DARK CORNERS OF my mind, I knew this moment was coming, although I tried to pretend it wasn't real. I kept telling myself the weight loss and extreme exhaustion were only my imagination. I purposely denied myself the masochist thoughts that would bring our little fantasy world crashing down. But I never once guessed that he was actually *close to death*.

"Sick with *what*?" I manage quietly, my head spinning. "How long have you known?"

Staring at his feet, hands folded, elbows resting on his knees, he sighs. "I've been sick pretty much all my life. Type one diabetes. That's why I met my best friend in the hospital. That's why my parents kept me sheltered and wouldn't ever take me anywhere. That's why my brother was always the successful one in the family, even though he's a spoiled jerk. That's why I felt this need to go out and see things. That's why I created the list."

He finally looks up, his beautiful eyes reflecting with overwhelming hurt. "I spent nearly six solid years of my life in a hospital. I've had *three* transplants. Two pancreas and one kidney. My body rejected all of them. I don't even *have* a pancreas anymore. I'm what they call a 'brittle diabetic' because my blood sugar is particularly hard to control.

A couple weeks before I met you, I was told my remaining kidney isn't working properly. Rather than go through the hell of another surgery and probable rejection, I chose to go on this trip with you. I've been crashing at my buddy's to avoid my parents. They said if I refused the surgery it'd be like walking out of their lives. But I'm tired of being in the fucking hospital, having feeding tubes and ports stuck into me, being incredibly weak and sick for months on end. I'm lucky I've made it this long without dying from an infection, or from the wrong mix of medications, or a thousand other complications I've faced over the years."

He wipes at his face. I know it devastates him that I'm seeing him this way; weak and broken down. And it kills me to hear of the horrors he's faced. I want to wrap him in my arms and cry with him, but I'm still struggling with the shock of it all.

"*Damn it*, Jewels. I don't have much time left. I saw this trip as a chance to do one big thing before I go out. One real shot at being *normal* for as long as I can, without doctors and surgeons poking at me. It's easier to pretend when I'm with you that nothing's wrong. I didn't purposely set out to break your heart. I didn't know I'd fall in love with you."

A million little holes pierce my heart.

He loves me and he doesn't have much time left.

Angry and dejected, I bolt to my feet. "I don't understand what you're telling me. You could live if you had the surgery, but you've just decided to give up? You're not even going to *try* to get another transplant?" Sobs wrench my throat, coming out in more of a pained wail. He reaches out to comfort me, but I fight back, swatting at him with my hands. "I knew your secret was monumental, but why would you hide something that your life depends on? How could you just refuse to do something that will save your life? We have to get you to a hospital!"

"You don't understand what it's like, going through the surgeries. The pain that comes after I've been sawed open, or having to get around in a wheelchair after because I'm too weak to even walk across a driveway. Waiting for my body to reject it, then getting sick from the drugs they pump into me trying to reverse it. It's total hell. I wouldn't wish this kind of life on anyone. Not even my worst enemy."

He sits motionless on the couch, looking totally broken. I thought he was getting a bit thinner, but I was lying to myself and pretending I didn't see all the other signs. Rimmed red eyes, pale skin, it's almost as if he's close to disappearing.

"I'm sorry," he repeats, seeming out of breath.

"Don't be *sorry*! Being sorry won't help anything! You can't *do this*, Adam! You can't just give up! We need to fly home and get you to a doctor!" I jump to his side, crashing into his arms. "I need you! Don't you understand?"

His lips press to the side of my head. Do they feel more delicate, or is it my imagination kicking into overdrive? "I can't go back. I spent most of my life in a hospital. I don't want to die there, too. I'm just ready for it to all be over."

I lean away to look him in the eye, trying to understand how he can simply give up on something that could save his life. "You made me believe you wanted to do this because of your best friend's dying wish."

"That part is true," he says with his lips against my ear. His hands trail up and down my back, filling me with a false sense of comfort. "We met two years after I was diagnosed and practically lived in each other's hospital rooms. I used to think I could beat this because Zach had it even worse than me. He was two years older and had gone through three pancreas transplants before we even met. His mom had to home school him after third grade. A few weeks before his heart gave out, he went blind and he couldn't eat food because his stomach nerves were shot from all the surgeries. We went through a lot together. He made me promise I'd live life to the fullest while I still could, and I swore I wouldn't let him down. After he died I couldn't make sense of it all. I decided it isn't worth fighting this hard when eventually I'll die from the disease anyway."

Looking into the depth of his eyes, I see an old soul inside, one who's experienced the highs and lows of life. Something I could probably never understand. But I want to. I want to help him fight this and be his shoulder to cry on.

I harden my gaze. "When Zach told you to do those things, I guarantee he didn't mean for you to give up in order to make it happen. I'm so sorry your friend died, Adam. I don't know *what* I would do if something happened to Kel. But do you think she'd just stand back and say 'okay' if she knew I was blowing off my chances of living to screw around? Do you think Zach would've turned down another surgery that could've cured him?"

He turns away, his eyes wet. "You didn't know Zach."

"I don't have to know him. I know *you*. You're an amazing, good, incredibly sweet guy with a lot to live for. If you let me take you back, I'll stay by your side as long as it takes for the surgery and your recovery. I'll stick with you like you did with me after I was roofied. I'll help you through it, because that's what people who love each other do. I'm not going to let you just give up. It's not just *your* fight anymore! You have to do this for *both* of us! I don't care if it sounds selfish of me to say that. It's true. If you really do love me, you'll let me take you home. I tried to pretend I didn't feel anything for you because losing Jason destroyed me, and I couldn't let that happen again. But I was lying to myself. I care too much about you to walk away."

The corners of his mouth twitch with a smile that never comes to full form. He rubs away my tears with the side of his hand, shaking his head.

"I'm sorry to put you through this. But I decided long ago that I can't go through it again. You saw my scars. You must understand what the surgeries do to me. I get why you're angry, and I'll understand if you leave. I still can't say that I regret any of this. Meeting you, going on this trip, it's been the best time of my life. It's better than I ever imagined. I'll always be grateful you agreed to come along."

For the first time in my life, I really want to punch someone. Probably not Adam, who apparently has enough to worry about without his girlfriend *or whatever I am* going crazy, but someone, *anyone*. I burst from the couch, trying to pace my breaths to keep from hyperventilating.

"So you're just going to fucking sit there and tell me goodbye?" I spit. "You're not even going to *try* to fight this so we can be together? What am I supposed to say to that? It's been nice knowing you? Good luck with your journey into self-deprecation? You can't just fall in love with someone and not give a shit what it does to them! You can't let me fall for you and then push me away! That's not how love works!"

His eyes fall flat, although filled with tears. "We both tried to stop it from happening. I knew that night on the bus it was just your way of trying to make things mean less between us. Please believe that I never wanted to hurt you."

"Too fucking late!"

Everything becomes a tinged, watered down red when I fly to the steps that will take me outside, away from the brutal truths and broken reality.

WANDERING THROUGH THE STREETS OF New York, I never really get the feeling I'm actually lost. On our last trip, my mom and I were able to navigate our way through the grid system, so I always have a glinting sense of exactly where I'm located. I catch slivers of the Empire State Building to my left, and the gleam of the Chrysler Building far ahead to the right. Around four blocks down, however, I realize I not only forgot my phone in the brownstone, but I only have $10 in my pocket. Even better yet, it begins to sprinkle.

I duck into the heavy wooden door of the first Irish pub I come across. It's relatively quiet inside with only two other patrons sitting at the bar. Probably not surprising for an early Friday afternoon. The bartender, washing glasses behind the bar, flashes me a bright grin when I settle on a stool in the middle.

"Mornin', sweetheart. What can I get ya?" He's tall and slender with carrot orange hair and an accent so thick it takes my brain a moment to catch up. The man and woman sitting separately at the bar glance at me for only a moment before their interest waivers and their eyes return to the TV.

I pat the corners of my eyes, wondering just how much of a wreck I look after crying. After Adam broke my heart. "Something with caffeine. Diet Coke?"

"Comin' right up."

The bar displays the same collection of liquor in two sections, divided by a decorative mirror and TV where a soccer game plays. Like the bar from the other night, dozens of flags from Ireland are displayed near the ceiling. My spirits sink lower with memories of the night I gave myself to Adam.

The bartender sets a glass of pop on the bar in front of me. "It's on the house. Ya look like ya could use a pick me up."

I smile artificially, deciding I'm not in the mood to share my twisted problems with a total stranger. "Thanks."

I sip on the drink, my eyes trained on the TV as fresh tears spill down my cheeks. Of all the things Adam confessed, telling me he's giving up was the worst. Hearing him say he won't even try for *my* sake makes me wonder if he really does love me, or if he was just saying it to make me feel better among the string of shitty news. I know so little about diabetes. I don't really understand the function of a pancreas, and didn't know you could function on one kidney. How long does he have left?

After a few minutes I feel movement of someone claiming the bar stool next to me, smell their heavy, musky scent of an expensive cologne or aftershave. Feel their big hand brush against my back.

"Jewels." Theo grins down on me, dressed in a slightly rumpled suit and bright red tie that look oddly perfect on his hulking frame. "What are you doing here alone? Where's Adam?"

Blame it on the alcohol still in my system, blame it on the fact that we shared a jaded form of intimacy the night before, blame it on Adam for dumping his destructive secret on my shoulders, but I burst into a heaping mess in my hot neighbor's arms.

SITTING IN THE PRIVATE BOOTH AT THE back of the pub, I gather my hair over my shoulder and collapse against Theo's side. He rubs my shoulder in a way that's more sympathetic than sexual. It's exactly the right kind of comfort I'm craving, considering Kelly is thousands of miles away.

I left the brownstone over an hour ago. In Theo's arms, I was finally able to release the feelings I've been harboring for so long to have a good, proper cry. Theo didn't push me to tell him what was wrong. He just held me against his chest and let me cry it out until I was able to talk. Other than the fact that I probably ruined Theo's designer suit and freaked him out for a little while, it felt amazing.

I glance at the clock mounted above the bar. "He's probably going crazy about now. I should go back." I look up at Theo, my shoulders slumping. "What am I going to do?"

"The way I see it, there's only one solution to this mess," he tells me, his chest vibrating with each word. "I saw the way he looked at you last night when he wanted to leave. The guy's a total goner. And considering you love him back, walking away isn't going to work. If he's set against having the transplant, trying to force him into it will only make him angry. You're going to have to ride this trip out with him, Jewels. Make sure he doesn't spend whatever time he has left alone, feeling rejected."

I wipe at my running nose with a napkin and huff. "That's all you got?"

His shoulder lifts behind me. "Love can't always be about what *you* want. Sometimes it's about letting the person you're in a relationship with know that they're the center of your universe, even if you have to give up something to be with them."

"This sounds suspiciously like a lesson you've deduced on your own."

"Thanks to Brooklyn, the ex-roommate. She was studying to be an actress. I got tired of her going to parties where she hoped to get noticed by some sleazy producer or studio exec. My schedule wouldn't always allow me to go along, so I acted like a dick and told her it was the parties or me. It was hard not to get jealous. I loved her, but it wasn't enough. Now I wish I would've made different choices. Not because she was featured on *Saturday Night Live*, though the after parties would've been *so* kick-ass, but because I miss her. She could be pretty bossy and high maintenance, but I miss everything else and would do anything to get a second chance. I guess I took advantage of having her in my life. I actually thought we'd end up getting married one day."

I lean back to study Theo's handsome features, a wide grin spreading across my lips.

I never would've guessed this insanely hot guy would turn out to be so sweet and big-hearted. There must be different degrees of love at first sight because I've fallen for him as a friend nearly as fast as I fell for Adam sexually and soulfully the very first time we met.

"You seem like a pretty stellar act." I pull on his crooked tie, pretending to straighten it. "I'm sure it won't be long until you find at least *one* keeper among the millions of women who live in this city."

"Are you absolutely *sure* you're in love with this guy?" He narrows his eyes, lit with mischief. "You and me...just *imagine* the possibilities! Our children would be one tier above the greek gods."

"If only we had met a few months ago. Then *maybe*, although I apparently have a thing for the sickly type." I rest my hand on his chest with a sad smile. "It means a lot that you were here for me. Really. If you hadn't showed up for me to slobber all over your shoulder, who *knows* where I would've ended up."

"You seem like a good kid. It'd be a shame to see you fall apart over this guy." He pulls a sleek, leather wallet from inside his suit jacket, leaving a $10 bill on the table for his last beer. "I'll walk you back. You let him know you're in this for whatever it's worth. If you can work it out, I'd still love to take you both out tonight. The party's going to be off the hook, I promise."

"Okay, now that I've cried on your shoulder, it seems like we can bypass the polite talk." I tilt my head. "What *exactly* do you do for a living?"

"I'm a producer for AMC."

"Seriously?"

He gestures to his suit. "If I was joking, I wouldn't be able to afford this suit."

I scoot over to kiss his warm cheek.

His eyes widen in surprise. "What's *that* for?"

"Just...thanks."

He stands, holding his hand out for me with a bright smile. "Better wait to thank me later, *after* I've shown you the time of your life."

THE BROWNSTONE IS DEAD SILENT, AS IF there's a shroud of gloom spread across it. My feet squeak against the wooden stairway as I climb to the top, calling Adam's name. When he doesn't answer, fear pulsates through my veins. What if he ran off? What if he thinks I left him for good? What if he collapsed somewhere?

"*Adam?*" I call out again, my voice elevated with panic. "Adam, where are you?"

I check his bedroom. He's not there, but his things are still scattered everywhere. At least he didn't pack up and leave. Maybe he's out looking for me.

I don't know why I didn't think to look on the balcony, but that's where I find him, red-eyed, staring out at our diverse neighborhood. His head hangs low, his shoulders slumped. He looks awful, but I'm still glad to see him. I'm glad he stayed.

"Hey," I squeak from the doorway, popping my head out.

His head darts in my direction, his eyes closing in a silent prayer of thanks.

"I'm sorry I ran off without telling you where I was going. You dropped quite the load on me. I just needed time to think, and...*deal*. Can you come inside for a minute?"

Standing slowly, he dips his head before following me inside. I hear the door close and wheel around, rushing at him. I stop when we're only a heartbeat apart, staring at him for a moment, hoping he can see in my eyes the compassion ripping through me. I pull at the bottom of his t-shirt, and he doesn't stop me. I'm careful when I pull it over his arms, lifting it off over his head. His hands return to his side.

I run my fingers over his scars, touching him lightly as if he'll break from my touch. I hear his shuddering breaths, but my eyes don't leave the evidence of traumas he's endured. I lower down, holding his hips as my lips brush over each incision with soft resolve. His fingers settle inside my hair, cradling me to his trembling stomach. I stop to look up at him, one hand pressed to his wounds and the other reaching for his hand.

"I *love you,* Adam. I tried to pretend that it was nothing more than casual sex between us, but I care about you so much I feel as if I'll burst every time you look at me. If you won't let me help you, it won't change anything. It won't change the fact that you're branded in my heart forever. It won't change the fact that I want to be with you, however long you want that to be. I'm yours."

He brings me back to my feet. Our eyes latch as he brushes my hair behind my shoulders then cradles my face in his hands. The kisses start slow and gentle, each of us tenderly touching the other with meaning and grace. I try to lose myself in the smell of his sweet breath, the caress of his tongue, the taste of his mouth, but I can't stop wondering how many times we'll have left to do this, how many days before he becomes too sick to continue on. Soon I'm crying softly against him.

Adam pulls away slowly, drying my tears with his thumbs. "Do you want to stop?"

"I want you to make love to me," I whisper, shaking my head. "For *real* this time."

He scoops me up into his arms. There's a strained look in his eyes, reminding me he's weak. I loop my arms around his neck and kiss him as we pass the kitchen and enter his room.

He lowers me to the mattress, breaking the connection of our mouths to undress me. His fingers are tender and slow as they remove my shirt and shorts, then my frilly panties and laced bra. Once I'm completely naked, exposing all my imperfections for him to see for the first time, he takes me in like I'm an art piece at a gallery. His hands follow my every curve, sending my nerves on edge. He stops to kiss every part he touches. His lips circle each of my breasts, the tip of his tongue teasing my nipples before he sucks them in gently.

His mouth continues down, covering each pocket of cellulite I've stressed over, the stretch marks at my thighs from when I lost my freshman fifteen. His mouth hovers between my legs, pausing before giving me a kiss down there that's warm and light. Soft moans fill my throat when his tongue dances against me. My hips rise and fall with his kisses and my fingers curl up inside his supple hair.

"*Adam*," I purr softly. "*Please*. I want all of you."

He stops all at once, staring up at me from between my thighs. "You're so fucking beautiful."

I bring him up to unbutton his shorts and remove them along with his boxers, pushing them down his legs. I push him on to his back, taking my turn to touch and kiss every part of him as he did to me. He's already hard from exploring my body, but I don't want to rush things. I don't want this intimate moment between us to turn so hot that we're only repeating the steamy scene on the bus, even though it was pretty damn good.

"Has anyone else ever seen all of you like this?" I ask, my fingertips brushing over his scars.

The lump in his throat bobs before he shakes his head. "Only you."

I lean down to kiss them again, as if my lips could somehow heal them. If only we lived in a world filled with real magic. If only there was a way to fix Adam, cure him of his diabetes and give us a fighting chance. I'd even settle for a way to make him realize the transplant is worth the risk, to give us more time together.

"These scars, they don't matter. They don't change the fact that you're still the most beautiful man I've ever laid eyes on. Seeing you here...now...I can't believe this is really happening. I can't believe you're mine."

"You have my heart, too, you know," he manages, tenderly brushing his fingers against my cheeks.

I crawl back up to him, pressing my lips to his mouth. He rolls me over to take the top position, stopping to kiss the curve of my neck, the hollow of my collar bone. "I love you," he whispers against my skin. "So much it hurts."

I bring his mouth back to mine. The kisses go on for an eternity, but they're still never enough. Every moment I have left with Adam will never be enough. Preparing to make love to him feels like just one of many goodbyes that are to come.

He stops to grab a condom from his shorts on the floor. I stroke his thighs and watch as he rolls it on. I'm holding back tears when he positions himself over me, waiting for my permission, waiting for me to accept him for what he is. Loving and broken.

"Yes," I plead, digging my fingers into his back. "I can't wait any longer."

And then he fills me, slowly, drawing the motion out as we watch each other. No one has ever looked at me the way Adam does, so compassionate and filled with respect. I've never felt love so deep it literally steals my breath. I gasp when he thrusts into me, hard and eager. His mouth covers my lips over and over, as if to breathe life back into them.

"I love you," I say, cupping his face in my hands. "Nothing will ever change that."

Tears run from my eyes into my hair. Adam brushes them away as he rocks against me, over and over, his eyes never closing, never looking away unless he's trying to kiss my tears away. Kissing my forehead. Kissing my eyelids. Kissing my cheeks. My mouth. Keeping his kisses gentle, both his tongue and strokes languid.

He groans into my ear as he climaxes, his muscles tense as he quivers in my arms. I bury my face in his chest to cry privately, but he won't let me rest.

"I want you to finish, too," he says, sinking his face back down to my tender spot. Though he takes his time just as he did when we made love, I'm nearly there and it doesn't take long before I buckle beneath him, crying out his name and finding my own euphoria.

As I lay in Adam's arms, I'm filled with love, and ecstasy, and a peace that comes with loving someone so wholly who loves me back, knowing I've given him everything I have to offer. The only thing left to do is hope he'll come to his senses and realize our love is worth fighting for. I can't help but wonder, knowing what lies ahead, if I've made a colossal mistake by giving him my heart. Because unless I can convince him to undergo the surgery, going back from here will be impossible.

Fourteen

ONCE THE PRETENSES ARE DROPPED and we've resolved to be together no matter how things will end, there's a hesitant vibe created that we try our hardest to ignore. Whenever I try to bring up the transplant or ask questions about his condition, he withdraws. Whenever I show concern over how he's growing weak, he gives me the cold shoulder. I learn to hold the subject as taboo despite my nagging resolve to make him change his mind.

The next couple of days we go on a whirlwind tour of the city with Theo as our guide, hitting some swanky and rather obscure places I hadn't heard of. He surprises us the first day with a private helicopter ride over Manhattan and the other four boroughs. While I don't hate the stunning aerial view it provides, the heights thing has me clutching Adam's hand so tightly that I leave indentations in his skin. The next day we tour through an old underground tunnel that was once occupied by pirates and street gangs, then check out the public library before catching a high-end burlesque show in which an ex-girlfriend of Theo's is the star.

Having Theo along, acting a buffer so I don't have to engage in small talk with Adam, turns out to be delightfully accommodating since it's downright impossible to carry on like nothing's out of sorts with the recently revealed truth hanging over our heads.

The next day Theo's too busy working to play tour guide, so I'm left in charge. I admit it's probably out of sheer panic to avoid the truth when I grab us a taxi to Central Park, and announce we're going to crash as many activities we come across as possible. We spend the day sampling more than one birthday cake, playing semi-professional frisbee, walking dogs, hanging in random couches by the large fountain, and learning how to play acoustic guitar. The constant action is enough to make us forget our worries, even smiling and laughing with each other.

The following day when we visit Coney Island, it starts out like a dream date. It's hard not to get caught up in the excitement of the crowd enjoying the sun and sand. We hit each of the amusement park rides, and I eat cotton candy until I'm sick to my stomach. Adam wins me a stuffed puppy by scoring a basket through an undersized hoop, and we spend an excessive amount of time hanging out underneath an umbrella on the beach. Then the fun takes a spiral nose dive when Adam nearly passes out. He won't let me do anything, and shuffles to a vending machine for a can of pop, downing it in nearly one swallow. I stand by watching him, horrified. I noticed earlier that he was sweating and his hand felt rather clammy, but didn't say anything, knowing it would only set him off.

In the days to come, Adam grows increasingly weaker. Our days end sooner and involve rides through the city on the red double decker buses. We still make love in the brownstone at least once per day at Adam's insistence, even though he seems completely wiped and I'm majorly conflicted, questioning why I continue to go along with his denial. It's a dangerous line between caring and knowing I have to back away if I don't want to scare him off. It's a dangerous line between letting him live his life and watching him throw it away.

Theo invites us over nearly every night. We drink beer under the twinkling lights in his backyard, sometimes with his buddies and their girlfriends. One night the three of us even fall asleep there during the early morning hours, Adam and I nestled together in the couch across from Theo. It's easy to pretend this is our life and that everything's going to have a happy ending unless Adam has a particularly bad day, or I see the dullness creeping into his gaze, reminding me our time is limited.

I keep in touch nearly every day with Kelly through FaceTime and texts, and call my mom as often as it takes to appease her, continuing with the lie that I'm a counselor at Kelly's family camp. It takes every ounce of willpower not to break down and tell Kelly everything, beg for her help or advice. But this is the kind of conversation that should be held in person, so I keep up the front that everything's okay and we're having a grand time in the big city.

Pretending I'm okay and Adam's okay begins to wear on me our second week in New York. Before we're to go on a bar run with Theo and James our last night in the city, Adam heads upstairs for a nap. I lay with him for a while before wandering over to Theo's place.

"I gotta hand it to you," Theo says, shaking his head as he opens the door wide. "You're a lot tougher than you look. I would've thought by now you would've broken down instead of playing into Adam's lie."

"I need a beer," I say, brushing past him.

Theo shuts the door behind me, chuckling. "Go, sit out back. I'll bring you one."

His backyard has become an oasis, a place for me to relax and think. The building tension from the week easily fades away just at the sight of it. I sink into my favorite sofa of the three, closing my eyes and wishing things were different. Wishing Adam was healthy and this was *our* place. Wishing we didn't have to go to our next stops and, eventually, back home. I didn't mean to fall in love with the city any more than I fell in love with Adam. It's going to be hard to leave for our next destination, especially when I'll be all alone with Adam without the instant support from Theo.

Theo hands me a beer before settling on the couch at my side. "Are you sure you want to keep going? Maybe you stay here for a few more days. You can crash in my guest room until you've got things figured out."

I take a long swig and sigh. "Adam wants to keep going."

"Everyone can tell he's growing weak. James asked me yesterday if he was sick. What would you do if he just collapsed behind the wheel? Do you even know what he needs?"

"He doesn't want to talk about it. Now that he's no longer hiding it, he isn't as secretive about testing his blood sugar and giving himself insulin shots. I've seen him do it enough times that I think I could help if there was an emergency. Whenever he naps, I spend the time doing as much research on his type of diabetes as possible. But...I don't know anymore. I thought I could pretend everything's okay and go along with this. Just watching him waste away...I'm starting to wonder if I have it in me. It's killing me to see him like this."

Theo sets his hand on my knee. "I know I told you that you might have to give up a little bit of yourself if you want to be with him, but at some point you're going to have to draw a line. The guy cares about you, even if he decides to throw his own life away. If he's going to continue to be stubborn, maybe you should tell him it's time to return home."

I stare at Theo's Marine symbol on his calf. "I made the mistake of pushing someone I loved away once before, for all the wrong reasons. It didn't end well." I wipe at my sudden bout of tears. "I can't walk away from Adam, no matter how moronic he's being, or how much he infuriates me. I love him more than anything. I'm in this for as long as he'll put up with me."

"Hang in there, kid." Theo folds me in his arms, setting his chin on my head. "Things would be so much easier if you had just accepted my offer the first time we met."

I burst out laughing.

I INSIST ON DRIVING TO WASHINGTON, mostly because I'm afraid of Adam passing out after my talk with Theo. It was hard to leave our new friend behind. I almost took him up on the offer to stay with him a few days longer. But Adam was ready to go bright and early, chatting on excitedly about seeing the White House and the chances of catching Obama while there.

As expected, Adam takes a nap as soon as we check into our room, even though he slept a good part of the way. Our hotel is within walking distance to many of the tourist attractions, but knowing it would completely wipe Adam out, I sign us up for a tour bus while he's sleeping.

My heart isn't in our trip to Mount Vernon the next day, although I try to genuinely smile for the pictures Adam insists on taking at each stop. I'm too worried about how he's feeling, watching his every move, debating whether or not to follow Theo's advice and call off what's left of the trip. Whether Adam can sense this or not, he continues on like nothing's wrong, despite his much slower rate and dampened spirit. He's become frail, like an old man in a young guy's body. It reminds me of Johnny Knoxville doing his *Bad Grandpa* skit.

When we return to our hotel that night, he buckles onto the bed so quickly I wonder if he's passed out. Then he tilts his head up, grinning. "Want to make reservations for dinner somewhere? I found some great steak restaurants in the area."

"Let's just order in," I suggest, curling up at his side.

He's suddenly over me, kissing my neck, running his hands up and down my legs and stomach. "I like the sound of that plan."

As much as I want to get into the moment with him, there's a cloud of anger surfacing over the unfair situation. He's basically resolved to a form of suicide. Why should I have to go along with it? Any *sane* person would try to talk someone down off a ledge. Why should this be any different?

Maybe this is what it feels like to finally cross the line. I've humored Adam for as long as I can, even though I know it's wrong and it goes against every instinct. I still love him and probably always will, but I can't do it anymore. I can't pretend this hasn't become out of control.

I nudge him to slide off the bed. It's way too easy to push him away, and I suddenly feel guilty for doing it. Just how easily can I accidentally hurt him? "I have to go to the bathroom."

He watches me with a wounded gaze. "Everything okay?"

"Fine. I just...I don't think that burrito from lunch agreed with me."

"Oh." His eyes grow wide. "What can I order that will agree with your stomach?"

"Just a sandwich, maybe." I shuffle to the bathroom and lock myself inside, running the water to hide my cries of anguish. As much as I'm relieved that I've finally unlocked the emotions that will allow me to cry again, I wish there was a way to shut them off.

THE NEXT DAY IS PRETTY MUCH THE same. I watch Adam with weary eyes while he pretends nothing's wrong, and becomes excited over everything we see. We make it to the White House, but the President is out of the country on peace talks. We visit the Lincoln Memorial and the reflecting pool, but there's a dark overcast that duplicates our sullen mood. By the time we reach the wall honoring the Vietnam Vets, it's down-pouring.

The city seems to be crawling with tourists, many young children in groups or with their families. The culture is so different from New York—suits and ties, wider streets, slower paced, less people, uptight—that I find myself mourning the fact that we're no longer in my favorite city. I miss the energy and inspiration that came with strolling through our neighborhood, the various street-side cafes, and the convenience of the subway that would get us anywhere we wanted to go.

For dinner I allow Adam to take me to a five star restaurant where the linens cost more than my dress, and nothing on the menu is under $50. It's beautiful and lit with low candles that make it terribly romantic, but Adam sees the light has gone out of my eyes. After we're done eating, he takes my hand over the table.

"I was thinking today...we still have to get tattoos."

The tattoo thing was my idea, and kind of a joke, but Adam wrote it down. "We don't have to do *everything* on the list," I say with a shrug.

"Let's go, right now. There must be a hundred parlors in this city. One will have a walk-in appointment available."

Though getting tattoos was once one of the things I had looked forward to most, since it's one of the few things *I* haven't done, the fun of Adam's list has diminished with our doomed future. It's beginning to feel pointless, even if it is a list of things he wants to do before he leaves me forever. "We haven't even decided what we're going to get."

The smile he gives me doesn't look right against his tired eyes. "I know just the thing." He throws the signed receipt on the table and stands, still holding my hand. "Let's go."

IT'S EXTREMELY DIFFICULT NOT TO giggle each time I catch the tattoo artist giving Adam a sideways look. When they're done and he's covering the fresh ink with saran wrap, Adam catches me smirking. "What?"

I hide my mouth behind my hands with a burst of laughter. "I think Rooster's trying to understand why you went for a...*girly* tattoo. Am I right?"

The heavily tattooed, hulking man with piercings in places I didn't know you could pierce just looks at me and shrugs. "I've seen everything by now. Guys will get anything when they're in love."

Adam comes over to me, hooking my heck inside his arm. "It's not *just* for her. It's also for my love of the greatest band on the planet."

He holds his bandaged yellow star on his forearm up to mine. I'll admit, having matching tattoos makes it feel final, like we've openly professed our love for each other. Yet I've already decided it will be a permanent memory of our trip together. My memory of *him,* once he's gone.

"Whatever, man. None of my business." Rooster stands, tossing his plastic gloves into the trash. "You can pay your other three hundred bucks at the desk."

I make an "o" with my mouth. "Wait, you meant three hundred a *piece*?"

Rooster smiles, his eyes flat. "Welcome to the big city."

"These are officially the most expensive, nickel-sized stars ever known to man," I say to Adam. "We need to call Oprah! We're going to be *famous*!"

Rooster's face clouds over, unamused.

Adam pulls me away with him, waving Rooster off. "It's not a problem, I got it."

After paying the rest of our ridiculous bill, we step outside into the fresh night air, laughing. Adam rests his arm around my neck again and kisses my temple. "I should've gotten a tattoo of your name with a heart. I'm sure our buddy Rooster would've *loved* that."

"I think the stars are perfect." I stop to entwine my arms around him, gazing up into his eyes. "I really do love you, you know. I'm trying. It's just...hard."

Adam nods slowly as he bends down to meet my lips, literally sweeping me off my feet as we kiss on the sidewalk in the middle of loud drunks and rambunctious teens out past their curfew. For a moment I forget that he's sick and giving me no other choice than to let him die and get caught up in the feel of him.

With our lips still attached, I hold my hand out to grab the next available taxi. We stop long enough to get in and give the driver directions to our hotel before we're all over each other in the backseat.

I'm too busy losing myself in the idea of getting as much of Adam as possible to care that we're most likely being watched by the old man driving. I crawl into Adam's lap, thrusting my tongue deeper into his mouth, rocking my hips above him. I feel his hardness through his cargo shorts and position myself directly over it, letting his pulsating tip press up through my cotton panties. His hands, hidden underneath my dress, slide up to stroke my butt checks, guiding me as I continue pushing him up as high as the stiff material of his shorts will allow.

Adam's lips break away to trail down my neck and back up. "God, I want you," he whispers against my ear. "Every inch of you."

I tip his head up to face me, stealing long, breathless kisses before stopping to stare at him, holding his face in my hands. My heart shatters with the sincerity of his beautiful gaze. Beyond the exhaustion and wear to his body, he looks up at me with so much love and expectation that I don't know how I could ever stand to be in another relationship again. Even after he's gone. He's all mine, only I don't get him for long. I kiss him again.

If time was a thing you could bottle away to forever place on a shelf to be admired, this would be a moment I'd never want to forget. I can't shake the gut-wrenching feeling that everything will go downhill from here.

THE NEXT MORNING WE'RE BOTH incredibly glum, only laughing when we apply lotion to our fresh tattoos in campy unison.

Adam doesn't offer to take my bags, nor do I expect him to. He's so drained I have to resist the urge to help him back into the pickup. He's so quiet and still as we drive out of the city that I lean over to check for a pulse. At first I'm sure he's dead until I find it. It's slow, but there.

At the first available rest stop, I race out of the pickup to call Theo, sobbing so hard I can hardly form any words.

"Theo, he's so weak! I think he's...I can feel him leaving me! Jesus, I'm not ready for this! I don't know what to do with him! A minute ago I had to check for a fucking heartbeat!"

"Jewels, it's going to be okay," Theo coos from his end, waiting until I'm calm enough to continue. "Listen. I'm going to find the airport nearest you and fly you two back here for the weekend. There's a big party tomorrow night I can't miss for work, but you can tag along. The three of us will go out tomorrow, have a good time, and try to talk some sense into Adam together on Saturday. I'll help you get through this."

"You're going to just 'fly us out'?" I repeat, brushing at my tears. "Who *does* that?"

"Don't worry about that, I can afford it. I'll find a way for you to pay me back later."

Despite the teasing in his tone, I recognize Theo for the amazing friend he's becoming and thank my lucky stars we met.

IT ISN'T UNTIL I'VE HAD TWO SHOTS OF Patrón and four beers that I realize I haven't taken my depression meds in a couple days. By then I'm on top of the world—or rather on the top of an elite high-rise apartment overlooking the twinkling lights of Manhattan with the man I love at my side. He's weak, but he's alive.

The party buzzes with low jazz music paired with excited conversations of the guests wearing trendy cocktail dresses and designer button downs. Theo only introduces us to a few of the other party-goers, but I recognize more than one from a distance. We're partying with some of Hollywood's big shots. I start to feel wildly out of place in my dress from the clearance rack.

Adam doesn't know about the shots, of course, but from the look in his eye I think he's on to me. "You alright?" he asks, slipping his arm around my waist. He's the one who looks like he needs someone to hold him up.

Our last round of wild sex the night before took a lot out of him. But every touch lights me on fire, every look sets me ablaze with desire. I want more of him. I almost feel remorse over my hormones that have taken control of my psyche when I drag him close, wrapping my arms around his neck and covering his mouth with a probing, telling kiss.

"The host is starting to wonder if you two are porn stars he should look into," Theo says beside us. Adam pulls back, his head low in embarrassment.

I giggle, slipping my hands through Adam's. "If you'd given us a little heads up that you were so tight with half of Hollywood, Mr. Big Shot Producer, maybe we would've worked a bit more on our audition for your friends."

Theo wiggles his eyebrows, handing us each another bottle of beer. "Then I would've been worried you wanted to hang with me for the fame and not my smoking hot body." He waves at someone in the crowd. "I'll be right back. Have to rub noses with the rich and famous."

Adam stiffens beside me, watching Theo walk away.

"Okay, you need to stop with the jealousy bit," I whisper, standing tall to playfully nip at his lip. "You *know* that's just how he is. And *you're* the one who told him you'd like to experience what it's like to have his job. This is his way of letting you in, giving you a little glimpse of the glamour involved. Besides, I'm yours. No refund. Remember?"

"You're sure he got the message? I mean, I appreciate that he's become a good friend of ours and all, but I still don't understand why he was so amped about flying us back—"

I cover his mouth with another kiss. "I guarantee he got the message, loud and clear. And he knows damn well you're all mine. If you need a little reassurance, we could go find somewhere quiet."

"Here? On the *roof*?" he asks, his voice shooting up half an octave.

I lick my lips and grin, reaching down to fondle him, letting him know I'm serious. "Another thing to add to the old list. What do you say?"

A deep hum vibrates through his chest. "You're going to kill me."

He couldn't have come up with a worse choice of words, but I don't call him on it. I've become so desperate to share whatever intimate moments we have left together that it's like I'm possessed by desire.

I look away, grabbing his hand and pulling him along to the dark side of the roof. We find a concealed spot behind the air conditioning unit where I don't have to see the city below and worry about controlling my breathing.

Adam has only had one drink that I know of, but I feel the alcohol's hold on him in his clumsy moves, taste it on his bitter tongue. I want to stop him and ask if brittle diabetics should be drinking. Doesn't it mess with his blood sugar? Could it shorten whatever time he has left?

The minute his fingers find me and he realizes I'm not wearing underwear, I know the sex won't last long. He unzips his pants and groans loudly into my mouth as he enters me, the notion of finding a condom lost with the whims of our passion.

The sex feels borderline dirty, and I'm almost ashamed. I have to bite down on his lip to keep from crying with each of his half-hearted thrusts. He pulls out rather than exploding inside of me, leaving his mark hundreds of feet high on a roof in New York.

Drunken giggles fill me as I try to drag him back. "I want to do that again!"

Adam hushes me, touching my mouth with his hand. "Not so loud."

"C'mon, baby," I say, trying to make my voice sound sensual. "Fuck me again. Who knows how many times we have left?"

Adam recoils like he's been slapped and his expression hardens. "I'm calling it a night."

I know I've stepped over the line. The whole point was to get a reaction out of him. Make him feel some kind of guilt for the situation he's forcing me into. Still, I hate to see the hurt in his eyes.

"Don't be mad," I plead, reeling him back in. "Please, don't be mad. I love you. It's not my fault you've turned me into a sex vixen."

He tilts his head back and sighs before returning to plant small kisses on my shoulder and neck before running up to my mouth. "I'm not mad, baby. I just don't want you to feel like shit again in the morning. I'm excited to see whatever else you have to show me." He gently sucks on my lower lip, his excitement returning to match mine.

"I have to show you my world," I whisper, breathing heavy against his mouth. "Just one more time. I know you've got it in you. Let's own this night and make it one we'll never forget."

He gives in, making love to me for a third time in the course of twenty-four hours. The whole time I feel as if I'm breaking inside.

EARLY MORNING I WAKE ALONE IN THEO'S guest bed. Immediately, I begin to panic. What if something happened, and he's lying collapsed downstairs in a puddle of his own blood or *whatever* it is that would happen to a diabetic who is in need of a transplant? What if his heart gave out like Zach's had?

Again, I'm plagued with the same set of questions I don't have an answer to. What if he needs insulin? Has he been properly monitoring his blood sugars? What if the alcohol affected his system? Is he past the point of caring about any of that?

I shoot upright. How have we gone this long without him telling me *something* about his condition, or any of the danger signs?

Then I find a note propped on his pillow:

Out for bagels and coffee. Back in 10.

Curling up into a ball, the note clutched in my hands, I cry until the tears won't come anymore.

By loving Adam unconditionally, I haven't fully considered the perils I've agreed to.

Here's the thing about falling for someone who's already given up; there's no promise of tomorrow. There aren't any words of comfort that can be said, no glimpse of a positive change. Every moment, every thought could be their last. It's like you're helplessly walking into quicksand, waiting for the muck to cover your mouth and eyes until you can no longer find a way to breathe. No, it's more like jumping from a high bridge without the promise of water underneath.

And I fucking *hate* heights.

Finding a home phone number for Adam's parents is even harder than I guessed. There must be a hundred Murphys living in Milwaukee, and I don't even have an idea of their first names. I lock myself in the attached bathroom and run the water while searching through his limited list of friends on Facebook, hoping for enough privacy to get the job done.

Then I come across a name that stands out above the rest. *Cora Stone*. I've heard Adam mention Zach's last name a time or two, and know the two must somehow be related. She's young and beautiful with long, dark hair and large, brown eyes, possibly still in high school or recently graduated.

It takes four tries before I come up with the right message to send her.

Fifteen

"YOU LOOK *INCREDIBLY* HOT THIS morning," Adam greets me as I emerge freshly showered twenty-some minutes later. He swings me into his arms and plants an extra long kiss on my lips. Like the other day, he tastes strangely fruity, and his lips feel uncharacteristically dry.

I stiffen under his touch, wondering if there's something he's neglecting to taste so strange and act so exuberant. His arms aren't as strong, and I swear I can feel more of his ribs with my touch.

"Maybe you should take my internal temperature," I say with a wiggle of my brow.

I'll play his game as long as I can. I just pray that Adam's parents will be in touch with me soon. Before it's too late.

He hoists me up into his arms, setting me on top of Theo's spotless counter. "Sounds like a formal invitation." He kisses me hard, his breath already rapid, although I don't feel his arousal against my wandering hands.

I want to push him away, make him stop. It's beginning to feel too much like I'm taking advantage of a sick person. Thankfully, my phone vibrates behind us. I reach for it with my mouth still attached to Adam's.

"Let it ring," he whispers, catching my lower lip between his teeth. He reaches underneath my shirt to cradle my breasts. "I have bigger plans for you."

I brace myself against him. "My mom's mad that she hasn't been able to reach me the past two days. I have to answer it." The screen shows an unknown 414 area code. *Bingo*. I hop off the counter and head for the stairway leading outside. "I'm so not talking to her with you standing there fondling me. I'll be back in a sec."

I slide my thumb across to answer the call before it's too late, and pause until I'm safely outside. "Hello?"

"Is this Jewels?" a girl asks, her high voice pensive.

"Yeah. It's me. Is this Cora?"

"Yeah." She pauses. "Adam's mom isn't...I gave her the message like you asked. She told me to call you."

"I know they're upset that he won't go through with the transplant. He won't listen to me either, but he's really weak. I don't know anything about diabetes. I want to take him to a doctor, but he refuses to go. He says he's done with doctors and surgeries. I'm afraid..." I stop to choke on a small sob. "I don't know what to do. I can't just stand back and watch him die."

"Look, I don't know you, and it's not my business anymore what he's doing in New York with you. But you have to find a way to bring him back. He's going to die without a new kidney. You have to convince him he has no other choice." She stops, sucking in a deep breath. "They have a donor waiting. You *have to* bring him home. *Please.*"

There's raw fear and desperation in her voice. *It's not my business anymore.* Cora was once in love with Adam, or maybe even still is. And she's afraid.

It takes me a minute to recover from the unexpected blow. "Yeah...I mean, of course. I'll do whatever it takes to get him there."

"Please, hurry," she says with a catch in her throat.

I DRUM MY FINGERS AGAINST THE BAR down the street, bouncing my leg and feeling as if I'm going to puke all over. The bartender doesn't miss this and casts borderline surly looks my way every now and then. Finally, Theo strolls in, wearing his running gear, covered in sweat. I was lucky he had his phone so I could catch him during his morning run.

There's a twinkle in his eye and a curve to his lips until he sees my face. "What is it? Did something happen to Adam?"

I shake my head, fighting off tears. "I need your help. I have a plan."

STORMING INTO THEO'S BROWNSTONE, I pass a wide-eyed Adam and head for the guest bedroom on the top floor. "Where are you going? Where have you been?" he calls after me, trailing behind.

"We have to go!" I say, rummaging through my clothes and throwing them into a heap on my bed. "I have to get the fuck out of this city. Let's go to Texas! Or we could catch a flight to California and be there in no time! It's crazy awesome, you'll love it! We don't have to stay there long though. A night or two would do. We can switch our tickets to Hawaii and be there by the end of the week! We can get your cousin's pickup on our way back!"

I latch on to him for desperate, needy kisses. The sad part of the act is that I remember how it feels to have an attack of mania. After Jason's death I was mostly stuck in the depressive mode for months on end, and didn't cycle too often. But when I was up, I was out of control, getting crazy drunk and sleeping with whatever guy caught my attention. It was when I met Levi that the medicine finally leveled my moods.

The dangerous part is that the downward spiral feels real. I almost don't know where the lie begins and where the manic part of me has really taken over. Was that the reason I couldn't get enough of Adam on the rooftop party? It's almost too easy to slip back into my old ways.

Adam peels me away. "*You're* the one who wanted to come back here. Why are you freaking out?"

On cue, Theo calls out from downstairs, "You guys still here?"

My eyes widen. "Shit, we have to leave!"

Adam shakes his head. "What's going on?"

"Don't go down there!" I plead, clinging to him.

"Jewels, you're scaring me. You have to stop and take a breath."

I shake my head, pulling on Adam's arm. "They can't make me go back!"

"Be down in a minute!" Adam calls back to Theo. He folds me in his arms, planting sweet-smelling kisses to my temple. "Hey, no one's making you go anywhere. I'm going to see what Theo wants. Just sit tight for a minute. We'll talk when I get back."

"Please," I whisper, squeezing his shirt in my hands. "Don't leave me."

"I'm not leaving you, Jewels, I promise." He removes my hands from his shirt and kisses me on the lips. "I'm just going to talk to Theo. Whatever's upsetting you, we'll figure it out. Together."

As soon as he's down the steps, I sneak to the end of the hallway, hoping to catch snippets of their conversation, but I hear the front door close. Adam wants to talk to Theo where I can't listen in.

TIME TICKS BY SLOWLY. I NEARLY FALL asleep while waiting for the two guys to finish talking. Finally, I hear the click of the front door followed by Adam's footsteps ascending up the stairway. I race into the bathroom.

He pauses in the doorway. "Jewels?"

I drop the open bottle of pills, watching them scatter across the stone floor. As expected, Adam comes racing into the bathroom. Seeing my hand filled with pills, he approaches me carefully, as if I'm made of dynamite. It reminds me all too well of the way my mom looked at me when I had my first break. "What are you doing?"

"I...I just needed something to help me calm down."

He bends down to pick up the empty bottle, reading the label. His eyes flicker up to mine. He knows I'm lying. "Theo just told me about a conversation he overheard you having when he came back from his run."

"He's a liar," I hiss, stepping back. I fall to my knees and reach for the spilled pills. "He just wants in my pants. Lucky for you there's only one person I'll let in."

"That's bullshit and we both know it." Adam's expression turns sad, disheartened. He stops my frantic hands, wrapping them inside his. "Baby, I need you to tell me the truth. Do you take those pills for depression?"

I need to strategically place my lies so I don't give in, but don't lead him astray. So far he's playing beautifully into my plan. As much as it hurts to lie to him, it has to be done. My expression clouds over. "That *bastard*. How much did he overhear?"

"A lot. He said you were arguing with your mom about where you really are, and why you haven't refilled your meds. He said you told them if they called the cops...you'd hurt yourself." His eyes are watering over when he strokes my face, nudging my chin so I'm forced to face him again. "Is any of that true?"

"Why do *you* care if I hurt myself?" My lips tremble. "You're going to leave me anyway! I get that you're scared and I get that you've been through total hell, but I'm not enough for you to want to live. I'm not enough for you to want to continue on and fight. Why should I go on living this bullshit life without you?"

I'm no longer playing into the lie, I'm becoming it. The pain of losing Adam is unimaginable. I've envisioned what it would be like to be at his funeral, to sit in a cold church and stare at his casket, knowing I'll never see him again, just like Jason.

Adam scoops me into his arms, holding me tight. I feel his heart racing against my chest. "That's not true! You *are* enough. You're *more* than enough. I love you so much, Jewels, I don't even know how to deal with it sometimes. Every time I look at you, I feel this burning need to touch you or kiss you. And I hate every minute we're apart. You've become the only thing in this world I care about. Refusing the surgery has nothing to do with you."

"Just like these pills have nothing to do with you," I mutter into his neck. "You wouldn't be around to mourn me for long after I'm gone."

He pulls me back, his eyes wild and fraught. "Please don't say those things. Jesus, don't ever say that. I'm sorry, I never would've asked you to come on this trip if—"

"If *what*?" I challenge. "If you knew I was bat-shit crazy? Then you probably wouldn't have loved me either, right? You're saying I tricked you into caring for me?"

"I know you're not crazy. You told me about losing Jason, and you told me you had a rough time after he died. I just didn't know how bad it was." He steps closer, wrapping his hands around my wrists. "You didn't trick me into anything. I love you unconditionally, regardless of whatever demons you're battling. I'm here for you. Whatever you need...I'll help you through this."

I twist away, seething for *real*. Nothing he can say will offer the comfort, or ease the worry that he won't live to see another day.

"You say that now, but you're growing weaker every day! What happens when you're too sick to be there for me? What happens when you're gone and I'm battling this all alone? You say you love me, but you won't fight for us! You can't fucking stand there and pretend you'll always be there for me!" I swat at the tears rolling down my cheeks, feeling my face turn a deep red. "I should just leave and let you die here all alone. You've already given up on yourself. Why should I keep trying to pretend everything's okay? Would *that* make you happy?"

"No," he whispers, a lone tear spilling from his lashes. My words have pierced his heart, just as intended. "*You're* what makes me happy. *You're* what I want."

"I don't believe you!" I cross my arms. "You're just saying that so I won't take all these pills and make the pain disappear!"

"I'll prove it to you." He brings me back into his arms, kissing the side of my head as his arms tighten around me. "I'll do whatever it takes to show you how much I love you."

FIGHTING WITH ADAM IS BRUTAL AND feels the most unnecessary of evils. Each time he tries to hold my hand, or bring me closer to lean against him, I refuse, playing into the part of unwilling participant in the plan. The entire plane ride back to Wisconsin, we only share a few short conversations filled with tension.

Because I'm supposed to be mad that he's forcing me to go home to face my parents.

Theo took the keys to the pickup and promised he'd take care of its return. I didn't get a chance to talk to him in private, to thank him for helping me dupe Adam into returning, though he did give me an extra squeeze when we hugged goodbye. I'd like to think it was his "way to go" pat rather than another attempted perversion.

Kelly waits in her mom's Jeep on the curb right outside the luggage carousel, looking uncharacteristically sullen. I gave her an abbreviated version of the truth from the women's bathroom in the JFK airport, and of course, she was eager to help in any way she could. Luckily it's the weekend and she's on break from her duties as camp counselor. She greets me with a hug. I'm a mere rag-doll against her.

"You'll get through this," she whispers before kissing the side of my head and taking my bag. Adam hugs her next, mumbling something into her ear before we slide together into the backseat of her car.

Kelly asks non-invasive questions about our flight, if we've had anything to eat, and so on. Adam answers her questions easily, as if it's just another night of the three of us hanging out, looking for something fun to pass time.

As the miles to my house lessen, an anxious rush to turn around constricts my chest like the onset of a heart attack. I silently thank Kelly for driving, because I don't think I could've gone through this alone. Once Adam realizes this was a trap to bring him back, I could lose him forever whether he finally agrees to the surgery or not. I keep glancing over at his steely blue eyes, trying to convince myself it's the only way. Even if he becomes angry with me, at least he'll have a chance to live a longer life.

"It's going to be okay," he whispers, kissing the side of my head.

I wish I could believe him.

As soon as he sees the sparkling white BMW parked in my parents' driveway, he knows. He drops my hand without saying anything. He doesn't need to. I can see the ugly realization of my betrayal flash across his face.

I MAY BE A LEGAL ADULT INVOLVED IN A complicated grownup relationship, but it doesn't stop my parents from treating me like I'm sixteen all over again. My mom claims it's because I went against our agreement when she takes the cell phone away that they pay for. She tells me I'm mentally unwell when they condemn me to their house indefinitely. She says it's because I put Adam's life in danger by sneaking away with him when she forbids me to see him ever again. She says it's because I'm not ready to be on my own that I'll spend the rest of my summer working under her unyielding supervision.

Once the storm has passed, Kelly comes by my house early the next morning. I'm amazed when my dad actually lets her up to see me. She strolls in casually, her eyes traveling across my childhood possession of cheerleading trophies and worthless nicknacks still adorning the bookshelves along the bubblegum pink walls. She's been here a dozen times, but I don't think she'll ever get over just how Barbie-licious my bedroom remains from high school.

I tell her everything that happened after she left the night before. Appearing afflicted by my list of punishments, she flops down beside me on the king-sized mattress, our feet hanging together off the side. "At least you don't have a *car* for them to take away."

I huff in agreement, wiping at my swollen eyes. "I'm surprised she didn't offer to buy me one just so she could."

"They'd have to get a court order to make you stay, you know. You're old enough to just walk away."

"It would only encourage them to try harder."

Her bracelets clink together when her hand covers my arm. Her unyielding support takes me back to the rough months when I was freshly mourning Jason's death and the way she was always trying to cheer me up even though I had hit the bottom depths of a crippling depression. "Have you heard from Adam?"

"Although I'll be old enough to legally drink in a few weeks, I'm not allowed a cell phone, remember?"

"I still don't understand what the guy has against social networking. Even my *grandma* has a Facebook account. At least he has *my* number. He'll call when he's ready to talk and can't get in touch with you."

Angst wraps around my heart when I remember the cold shoulder he gave me, the way he shot me a blank stare while his parents laid into him, the way he pretended I didn't exist when he rode off in the back of their car. I may as well have actually taken those damn pills that day in New York. Especially if he won't ever take me back.

Tears roll down my face. "I'm not so sure about that, Kel. I doubt he'll ever want to talk to me again."

Her fingers brush up and down my arm. "Do you think he'll at least agree to the surgery?"

"I hope so. If I lost him, it better be for a good reason." I dab at the tears in my eyes, sighing. "You know the worst part? I was doing really well in New York. For the first time since Jason died I was seriously happy and functioning like anyone else. We made friends there. I envisioned myself living with Adam in a place like the one we were renting. My mom thinks I had a mental breakdown, when in fact I've never been healthier. So not only have I probably lost Adam, but I'm back to having to earn my parents' trust all over again."

"Did you tell them that?"

"They don't believe me. They thought running away with Adam without telling them meant I must've relapsed. They thought it was an impulsive thing to do, just to defy them."

Kelly sits at my side, perking to life as if an actual light bulb has been lit above her head. "Come with me back to camp! There's an opening for another counselor! You can get away from your parents and make a little more money so we can get a place together this fall like we planned!"

"Kel, I can't just *leave*. It'll be like you said, they'll try to get a court order to make me stay." And that could easily lead to another commitment in a mental ward, even though I'd continue to insist I'm okay. I couldn't deal with everyone treating me like I'm insane again.

"So *let* them. You can prove to the court that you're not sick. You'd pass all the tests. Anyone can see you're mentally stable. No offense, but your mom has her head too far up her ass to see the truth half the time. She's really controlling, Jewels. You're never going to get ahead if you're *grounded* like a teenager for the rest of the summer. You're always saying you have no idea what you want to major in, so who cares if they cut off your funds? Spend a few years working and then get your shit together so you can finish with whatever you eventually decide on. Nothing is holding you back to stay here. You can start over wherever you choose."

I stare back at her, wide eyed. "Do you comprehend the level of shit I'd be under if I were to take your advice? We're talking forehead deep, *at least*."

"I'd say you better start looking for a snorkel to wade through it." As a smile crosses Kelly's face, I realize she's laid out the path I've wanted to take, but was too afraid to venture onto.

Maybe there are risks in a life without Adam still worth taking.

DESPITE MY RESOLVE TO EXECUTE Kelly's plan, my parents' threat for a court order never comes to light. I basically have Theo to thank for unexpectedly showing up on our doorstep a few days later with the pickup we left in DC. With his irresistible charm that must come with being a producer, he's able to convince my parents I was healthy while living in New York, and the "manic episode" was just the lie I claimed it to be in order to bring Adam back for medical care.

After the drama with my parents subsides, I take Theo out for dinner downtown before he checks into his hotel for an early morning flight. He's every bit a gentleman, opening doors and leading me around the way Adam always does, a big grin implanted on his face the entire time.

"You realize that we're doing this as *friends,*" I warn when he pushes my chair back to the table. "I mean, I owe you for driving all the way here, but under no circumstances will there be any sexual favors exchanged."

"Damn! Foiled again!" He chuckles as he sits in the chair across from me. "Do you want to know the *real* reason I drove your truck across the country?" His eyes are bright with an untold truth.

I clap my hands together, feigning the kind of excitement I've decided I may never feel again. At least as long as Adam refuses to talk to me. "Your friend decided to cast me for an upcoming porn flick?"

"Adam called me."

My shoulders collapse. "Oh."

"He's having the surgery, Jewels." He reaches across the table to squeeze my hands, suddenly stony-faced. "He checks into Mayo tomorrow."

"Wow." I take a deep breath. "That's...great." My dad agreed to drive me up to the camp Kelly's family manages after Theo flies out in the morning. Rochester, however, is in a completely opposite direction, assuming Adam would let me visit.

"He said you should bring the truck back to him."

"Oh." I nod, my eyes drawing down. "Makes sense. His cousin probably wants it back."

"No, *bonehead,* Adam wants you to come see him before the surgery." When I look up, a giant grin has spread back across Theo's sexy lips. "You may be smoking hot, but you sure can be dense sometimes."

I bite my lip to keep from smiling. "You drove it thousands of miles just so I could take it across the border to see him? You do realize going into Minnesota is not like crossing into Mexico, right?"

"No, I drove it thousands of miles to deliver an important message for a good *friend*. It's like you said that night the three of us fell asleep in my backyard. Some people come into your life when you least expect it, sometimes for reasons we'll never understand. As much as I'd like to think you and I met because we were going to be a *thing*, it seems I had a bigger purpose to serve."

Tears brim my eyes when I squeeze his hands. "If Adam and I ever get back on our feet and survive this thing together, we're totally coming out to thank you for everything you've done. And we fully expect another backyard party while we're there. Maybe this time you could invite your pals Jay and Beyoncé."

Theo laughs merrily. And for the first time since we tricked Adam into coming back to Wisconsin, I'm hopeful that everything may be okay.

MY DAD'S THE ONE WHO CAVES INTO giving me my cell phone back when I say I'm not sure of where I'm going in Rochester and hope I don't get lost. He makes me promise not to tell Mom, but I think she's already agreed to restore all my privileges after Theo's visit. There's a string of complaisant texts and missed calls from Adam, the last voicemail message telling me his building and room number. His voice is rather tranquil for someone about to undergo a major surgery he was once dead set against.

As I near his room, my pulse races. I stop to lean against a wall across the hallway, catching my breath. I must've restyled my hair half a dozen times and changed my clothes at least a hundred. I settled on wearing my hair down in loose curls with the pink dress I wore the night we had sex on the bus, remembering how much his eyes came to life when he first saw me.

It's only been a few days since we returned from New York, but the hours stretching between the days feel like a lifetime. Whatever happens between us today, I'm glad he's agreed to the surgery and I'm glad he's asked me to come see him. It should be enough, but deep down I know it isn't. I want him to declare that he's still in love with me and wants us to be together once he's back to normal, or as normal as he can ever be with his serious condition.

I run my fingertips across the star tattoo, remembering the hot night in the taxi after we got our matching ink, and the way Adam looked at me. Even if he's still upset by what I did, there must be something between us he sees worth saving.

A high, piercing giggle catches my attention. I peer into the room where I'm to meet Adam just as he embraces a skinny girl with long, dark hair, holding her tightly the way he's held me many times. They draw apart and he leans down to kiss her forehead, his eyes closed. I watch them, slack jawed.

Adam doesn't have a sister.

Maybe it's a cousin. Or a really flirty nurse.

They exchange a few more words and gleaming smiles before the girl spins to her side, squeezing Adam's arm playfully. I immediately recognize her from her Facebook profile.

It's Cora Stone, Zach's sister.

I scamper away before they catch me watching.

Sixteen

SITTING AT A TABLE IN THE MIDDLE OF the quiet hospital cafeteria, I flip through the various texts from Adam asking if I'm lost, if I need directions, and finally if I'm okay. I'm definitely lost, and directions wouldn't do me any good. And I'm certainly nothing close to okay. It's been half an hour since I was to meet him in his room, since I saw him embracing the girl who sounded so heartbroken on the phone as she pleaded me to bring him home.

Someone calls my name. I look up to see the stunning, long-haired brunette who was waiting at my home alongside Adam's dad the night we returned.

It's easy to see how Adam got his crazy good looks when I gaze back at his mom, taking in her regal stature and kind blue eyes. She wears loose fitting black pants and a long-sleeved black cardigan, as if she's too frail to endure the air conditioning, or just too classy to wear shorts and a t-shirt. The diamonds in her ears look to be at least two carats each, sagging slightly on her lobes. When she smiles at me, the deep creases around her eyes make her appear at least a decade older than my parents.

"What are you doing out here all alone? Did you and Adam—"

"No," I interrupt, standing. "I just needed a minute before I went in to see him."

She closes the distance between us and surprises me by leaning in for an awkward hug. Stunned, I set my hands on her back. She smells like a giant floral shop without a window and feels incredibly delicate underneath my hold.

"I didn't get a chance to talk to you the other night. I want to thank you for bringing Adam back to us. I know it wasn't easy, but you did the right thing." She draws back, taking my hands in hers. The huge diamond on her ring finger spins around, pinching my fingers. "You have to understand his father and I...we tried everything we could. Adam shut us out. We never thought he'd take it as far as he did. We figured he'd come to his senses once he realized his life depended on this surgery. Whatever you said to him, it was the only thing that convinced him that going through with the surgery was his chance at another life. No one else was able to do that to him, not his father, or myself, or even Cora."

I want to smile back, but Cora's name sends my stomach into a series of dips and menacing dives. "I never did ask her...is Cora Zach's sister?"

"Yes, she is. Thank God for Facebook or you may never have found us and my son probably would be dying in some New York alley by now."

"I wouldn't have let it go that far," I insist quickly, shaking my head.

"I know you wouldn't, dear. Adam has nothing but sweet things to say about you."

If he's still casting me in a positive light, maybe I overreacted when I saw him with Cora. Maybe she's like a little sister, nothing more.

She squeezes my hands again. "Do you want me to show you to Adam's room? I was just on my way to see that Cora settled in her room, but I can make a pit stop with you."

I frown, feeling like I'm going to be sick. "Cora's room?"

"No one told you?" The smile on Mrs. Murphy's face grows. "Cora's Adam's donor. She's giving him one of her kidneys."

Hole. E. Shit.

So maybe I didn't overreact.

Cora's giving him a part of her *body*. I remember the sound of her voice on the phone, laden with the kind of affection that can't be denied. Begging me the desperate way I'd beg someone to save Adam if it came down to that.

I feel the blood drain from my face.

"Jewels, are you okay, sweetheart? You don't look so well. Do you need to sit down?"

"I'm fine," I lie, standing.

What I saw in that room...it could've been a girl with a crush and a man with a thankful heart. Or it could've been something more, and Theo could've misinterpreted Adam's directions for me to return the truck.

"Let me buy you a water before we swing by Adam's room. He's eager to see you again."

Although the thought of putting anything into my stomach doesn't seem like a good idea, I let her do it. Because she seems dedicated to make things right with the girl who convinced her son to accept the life-saving surgery, even though I'm not the one who's going to save his life.

THE MINUTE I STEP INTO ADAM'S ROOM at his mom's side, his eyes fill with light and his adorable dimples pop. Aside from that, he looks tough. Seeing him wearing the hospital gown, sitting in the mechanical bed somehow makes him look smaller, like a child rather than a man. I guess once you strip a man of their style and masculinity, they all tend to look vulnerable. I mean we're all subject to harm, so it shouldn't be such a shock. Still, it throws me for a loop to see the guy I've been so intimate with so many times looking so beat down.

I'm so jilted by his looks that I hardly notice the smartly dressed guy in khaki shorts and designer button-down standing beside the bed. With his broad shoulders, square face, and sharp cheekbones, no introduction is necessary. Other than his lighter brown hair, Adam and his brother are nearly clones of each other.

"Look who I found," his mom declares brightly, setting her hands on my shoulders.

"Mom, you shouldn't have," Erik tells her, his blue eyes lighting up. When he smirks, a dimple like Adam's appears on one side. "My birthday is still *months* away."

"Don't be *rude.*" Their mom gives him a tight smile before looking back to Adam. "I'm going to check on Cora. I'll stop back in a little while to see if you kids need anything." She points at Erik. "Come along and give these two some privacy, sweetheart."

"Thanks, Mom," Adam tells her before she disappears from the room. He throws a bright smile my way. "Hey. I'm glad you're here."

Erik's eyes bulge as he gives me a once over that's so incredibly awkward considering he's my boyfriend's little brother. "*You're* the new girlfriend?" He nudges Adam with a barking laugh. "Holy shit! Talk about a score! I didn't think you had it in you, bro, *especially* being so close to death and all! *Damn*!"

"Wow," I tell him with a plastic smile. "You're just as *charming* as I imagined you'd be."

Adam glares at his brother. "Time for you to leave."

"Jesus! Alright!" Erik throws his hands up at his sides. "I'll get out of here before your hot girlfriend discovers who's the *real* man in this family." He starts toward me, his dimple flaring. "I'll still be around if the two of you don't work out." He throws me a cringe-worthy wink.

I wink back as he passes me for the doorway. "And I'm going to pretend you didn't really just say that."

Once he's gone, Adam rubs at his neck. "God, I'm sorry. He flew in this morning. I don't even know why he bothered coming."

"You really weren't kidding about him. I don't think the two of you could be any more different." I continue to stand in the doorway, unmoving.

"Jewels, I've been trying to call you ever since I got here with my parents."

"I didn't have my phone." I offer a stiff smile. "Turns out there's no age cap on when a person's parents can ground them."

"I wanted to apologize. I should've told you I was sick the day you told me about Jason. You'd been through enough already. " He tips his head back with an exasperated sigh. "Would you *please* come over here?"

I take small, tentative steps toward him, although not close enough for us to touch.

"I've been going crazy thinking about what you said to me in New York. You're right, it wasn't fair of me to tell you that I love you, and then say in the next breath that I was giving up. Theo called to tell me the hell I put you through the past couple of weeks. It was wrong to force you to go along with my decision not to have the surgery. I don't know how to start telling you how sorry I am...for all of it. I'm ready to do whatever it takes to make things right between us. I'll understand if it will take time for you to trust me again. I just don't want to lose you. I'm not going to give up on us." He pauses for a few moments, running a hand through his hair. "Say something. *Anything*. Tell me I finally deserve to call myself an asshole."

Unsmiling, I fold my arm against my stomach. As heartfelt as his apology sounds, there's still something he kept from me. "Who's Cora?"

He flinches with my words. "My mom told you?"

"She told me she's your donor. I already knew she's Zach's sister. Dead friend's little sisters don't go through a potentially lethal surgery for nothing. What is she to you?"

"Remember when you asked about my past girlfriends and I told you I had one for a few months?" When I nod, he closes his eyes. "That was Cora. We...bonded after Zach died. Things started to get a little intense. She wanted things I couldn't give her. She eventually broke it off when I refused to accept her kidney."

I know I can't be mad that he's accepting a kidney from an old girlfriend, especially when I'm the one who forced him into the surgery to begin with, but *really*?

Fresh tears prick my eyes. "How could I ever compete with someone who gave you a freaking *organ*? Do you still love her?"

"In a way, yeah, I do. She's my best friend's sister. We went through a lot together, and now she's giving me a 'freaking organ'. There's no way I'll ever be able to repay her, even if I live to be an old man." His impossibly serious gaze burns through me, penetrating right down to my soul that aches to return to him. "Do I love her in the way that I want to kiss her, and make love to her, and see the world with her, spending endless nights at her side in whatever life I may have left? *No*. I have someone else in mind for that role."

"Anyone I know?" I ask, crossing my arms. I tilt my head back and sigh. "Adam, come on. It's a *body part*."

He reaches out to gather me in his arms and pulls me back onto the bed with him, laughing. Pinning me down on the mattress, he kisses me. At first his lips are light and playful, but they quickly turn eager and meaningful. He breathes heavily through his nose, gripping the sides of my face as if I'm his life preserver while his tongue and lips work on making their mark, claiming me.

I wrap my hands in his hair, finally feeling at peace. At *home*. His health problems will never go away, but they'll just be a part of what defines the strength of our relationship. Because no matter what will happen next, I'll never let him go. And with the urgency he's using to kiss me back, I get the feeling he feels the same. The seal of our lips breaks free, and his lips cover my cheeks, my eyes, the spot beneath my ear.

"Maybe someday if I survive this and my body will allow for it, you can carry my baby," he whispers. "There's no competition for that."

"Whoa, big guy." I push on his chest. "We're both homeless. We need to figure out some kind of life plan before we bring offspring into the picture." I kiss him again, reaching for the slit in the back of his gown. "We've got more pressing matters at hand, like whether or not we should add a hospital bed to our *growing* list. Pun most definitely intended."

He shakes his head, laughing whole heartedly. "God, I love you."

I clamp my hand around his jaw, glaring into his steel blue eyes. "Just *promise me* you're going to come out of this surgery, and you'll be there for me. I mean it, no wussing out on me again. You can't just give up. You have to fight for our future now. Understand?"

"You were still raw from losing your first love, but you trusted me. And I let you down.

I'm so sorry, Jewels." He kisses my nose and brushes his fingers against my cheek. "Now that I know your little episode was just a ploy to get me home, I still can't forget all those things you said about leaving you all alone. I realized that I could never do that to you. I'm ready to do whatever it takes to be with you for the rest of my life. I'll do whatever it takes to keep you from getting hurt again. I love you...more than you'll ever know."

"*That's* what I wanted to hear." I nod and kiss him deeply, making sure he has something to look forward to once he's out of surgery. We're well past second base when we're interrupted by a startled nurse.

IT FEELS LIKE A LIFETIME THAT I SIT WITH Adam's parents and obnoxious brother in the lobby, waiting for updates. Luckily Erik is bright enough to understand that I'm not in the mood for small talk, and finally leaves me alone with my thoughts when I don't really respond to his questions.

Finally the white-haired surgeon emerges to announce that the transplant went as well as they had hoped. I'm so relieved that I burst into tears and throw my arms around him.

Adam's still groggy when I finally get to see him, but he's full of kisses and slurred devotions of his love. "This is my girlfriend," he tells the nurse with a dopy grin. "My Jewels. Isn't she the most beautiful thing you've ever seen? I'm going to marry her one day."

The middle aged nurse stops adjusting his IV to peer over at me, giggling. "You've got yourself a real keeper."

A few hours later, I visit Cora. When I enter her room with a dozen red roses, she's half propped up in the bed, drinking from a straw a woman holds for her.

"Can I come in?" When she nods, I place the roses on a table where two smaller bouquets already stand. "These are from me and Adam. Me being Jewels, by the way. I just wanted to stop by and see how you're doing. And, well, thank you for saving Adam's life. Sending a card didn't seem adequate."

"Finally, Jewels!" The older woman offers me her hand. "I'm Cora's mom, Tammy." It makes sense as she's a graying, rounder version of her daughter with deep wrinkles set around her eyes.

I take her warm hand, nearly crumbling when I think of all this woman has been through with her children. "I'm so sorry about your son. Adam talks about him all the time. Sounds like he was a great guy."

"He was a wonderful boy." She smoothes the skin across Cora's forehead. "Just like my Cora's a wonderful girl, putting herself through this for her big brother's friend."

Cora smiles up at me, showing a beautiful row of straight, white teeth, but the smile stops at her lips. Her eyes are listless. "I had to do it, you know. I mean, we were in love when I first offered it to him, but just because we're no longer together doesn't mean I wanted to take it back. I don't think it's something you really *can* take back. Once you've offered to save someone's life, it just seems like a douche-y thing to void the offer."

"It was a really non-douche-y thing for you to do," I agree.

"He's *really* in love with you. He loved me, too, but not in the sappy way he's completely head over heels for you." Her eyes roll to the ceiling. "It's almost embarrassing. You should teach the boy a little something about self-respect."

I nod, feeling a smile ease across my lips. "Noted. No one likes a sap."

"I just wanted you to know that. I mean, why I did it. I'm sure it's hard to accept his ex will forever have a part of her body inside of him. If you really think about it, it's even worse than having to deal with ex-wives and step-children.

I mean, a part of me will *always* be around, no matter what he does or where he goes. There will be no getting rid of me."

"Hadn't really thought of it *that* in depth...but yeah, I see where you're coming from. The only thing worse would've been if he had needed an eye transplant. Then you would've been always *watching* me. That would've been awkward as hell."

"Adam said you were pretty chill, I just wanted to test it out on my own. Make sure you're not one of those blonde cheerleader types who's all fake and clingy."

I reach for a strand of my hair, twirling it between my fingers. "Considering I once *was* a cheerleader, I think I should *totally* be offended somewhere in that statement," I answer in a mock bimbo tone.

Tammy ticks her tongue as she pulls at Cora's sheets, tucking them in around her body like she's a five-year-old. "If Adam heard you girls going on like this...I think it would warm his heart to hear you getting along so well."

"Don't get too comfortable with it," Cora warns her mom. "I plan to harass them at their wedding, and teach their children horrible habits, maybe give them obnoxious toys that make really loud noises."

"Us or the kids?" I ask, breaking out in a deep grin.

Cora returns my grin. "I do think we're going to be friends, *eventually*. I need a little time for you to grow on me."

I walk to her side and lean down to hug her in that only awkward way a hospital bed will allow. "Thanks. You know. For being non-douche-y."

This time when Cora smiles back, her eyes twinkle. "I'd say anytime, but I think I'll need my other kidney."

WHILE ADAM RECOVERS IN THE hospital, I drive the hour commute to Rochester from home, a couple nights staying curled in his hospital bed at his side when our favorite nurse lets us by with the violation of hospital rules, and his family isn't around trying to mend their relationship. In the time I spend with his parents, I learn Adam's incredibly handsome dad is kind, and has Adam's good humor, but he's soft spoken and easily manipulated by his eager to please wife. They treat me like I'm some kind of hero for saving their oldest son, and go out of their way to make sure I'm well fed and rested. Hopefully their affection for me never wears off.

At Adam's request, the only visitors allowed are his parents and brother. I can't say I'm anything other than relieved when Erik takes off after only one day, although when he announces he's heading back to New York, my jaw drops to the floor. Adam told me his brother just finished his freshman year of college. It never came up *where* he was going to college. I can't believe Adam didn't say anything while we were in the city. I don't bring this to Adam's attention, however, because it never seems like the right time.

Eight days later, the doctors clear Adam to go home. Adam's cousin, Davis—the one who loaned us the pickup truck—offered his spare bedroom to us so Adam could make his regular follow up appointments for the next month. At first my parents weren't totally thrilled with the plan that involved me living with two men, but I think they eventually accepted that Adam would need my help. I think they finally understand I'm going to do whatever I want at this stage of my life.

When we show up on the doorstep of Davis's modest apartment, it comes as no surprise that he's handsome like the other Murphy boys I've met. He's much taller than Adam and his messy hair is a shade of sandy blond, but he has the same square jaw and a slightly darker shade of baby blues. From the moment I first lay eyes on his relaxed posture and grunge-inspired wardrobe, I know he's bound to be just as laid back and friendly as Adam.

He reaches out to slap Adam's hand in greeting. "What up, cuz? Looking pretty tough. One of these times they should just install a zipper for all these surgeries they keep putting you through."

Adam lets out a small chuckle. "Don't I know it. Thanks again for letting us crash here. Beats staying in a hotel for however long it takes."

"Anything for my brother from another mother." Davis's eyes fall to me. "Jewels. *Finally!*" He flashes a row of perfectly straight white teeth. "I've been dying to meet the girl who finally talked some sense into my boneheaded cousin."

"And I've been dying to meet the kind soul who loaned us his pickup." I don't know what else to say to him, because just like the rest of his family, Adam had very little to say about Davis.

"Hey. Getting to drive his sweet ass Challenger around for a few weeks? *Totally* worth it." He takes our duffle bags from me and opens the door farther. "Make yourself at home. You guys are welcome to crash here as long as you want. It's not the Hilton, but I managed to score a queen mattress from a buddy at work."

It's obvious the minute we step inside that Davis is an artist. The couch, television, and kitchen table are all covered with paint-splattered sheets. Murals in progress are everywhere, cans of spray paint lining the tile floor beneath them. The apartment feels smaller than it should because of the total chaos.

Davis returns from a room in the hallway without our bags and catches me taking the place in. He laughs. "Sorry about the mess. As you can see I'm a graphic designer. I just got back last night from a show in New York and haven't had time to clean the place up."

"New York, huh?" I turn to Adam and cross my arms. Adam shrugs back at me, oblivious to my interest in his cousin's trip.

Davis begins to roll up a large mural. "After you two are settled in your room, I'll cook up whatever Adam can eat. Until then, let me know if there's anything else I can get you."

"Thanks," I say as Adam pulls me to the hallway. "It's awesome of you to take us in like this, really."

The first doorway leads to a small room with a mattress on the floor among more artistic supplies. Our bags sit in the corner. "At least you can paint pictures of me when you can't sleep," I tease, collapsing to the bed. "By the way, you forgot to mention your brother goes to school in New York. Seems you're the only one in your family who hasn't been there."

Adam shuts the door behind him and slowly lays down at my side, careful not to jar his healing wounds. He hooks me with his arm, pulling me close. "I wasn't going to waste our time out there trying to meet up with him. We don't even get along, so it would've been pointless. Besides, he would've told my parents where I was hiding out."

I roll my eyes and breathe out an exasperated sigh. "It would've saved me the trouble of tricking you into coming home."

He runs a finger across my cheek, his expression solemn. "I get the feeling it's going to take me a lifetime to make it up to you."

"Yeah, pretty much." I lean in to kiss him deeply, reminding myself not to take it too far. Then I lean away, grinning. "As soon as you're properly healed, I know of a few ways you can make things right."

He runs his fingers through a strand of my hair. "If you keep kissing me like that, I'm going to have to sleep on the couch until I'm cleared for physical activity."

"We could go back to the no touching rule." I lift my eyebrows.

"No way." Adam brings me back up against him, planting another long, soulful kiss on my lips. When we part, my toes tingle in anticipation. "I'll never make that mistake again. I don't plan on letting another day pass without getting to touch you."

I snuggle up against him, my hormones lit like a blazing torch. Soon I hear his light snores beneath me.

AS ADAM WORKS ON HIS CONTINUING recovery, I put in some hours at one of my mom's stores in Rochester to build on my depleted savings. Although the surgery leaves him incredibly weak, sometimes even requiring the use of a wheelchair when we go places like the mall or the grocery store, Adam's doctors are upbeat that he won't reject the new kidney. But there's no guarantee. And I have to remind myself during our heated make out sessions to be gentle with him.

On August 4th we celebrate my twenty-first birthday with my parents at a swanky hibachi grill in downtown Rochester. They give me a card filled with more than enough money to make it through the rest of the summer. I'm relieved when they keep the conversation fairly light rather than asking questions on what Adam and I expect to do next. I've spent hours on the phone with my mom since staying in Rochester, and we agreed to take one day at a time. My dad only met Adam for a brief moment when his parents came to retrieve Adam from our house, but Dad seems impressed, and even shakes Adam's hand with a genuine smile when it's time to go.

Adam and I end the night on the backside of a grassy reserve in Davis's pickup with champagne and chocolates for me, bottled water for Adam. It's surreal to be in the back of the pickup again, bringing both good and bad memories of our road trip flooding back like the opening of a flood gate. He even breaks out the worn dinosaur blanket again, finally confessing it was something the nurses at the hospital gave him after he was first diagnosed.

I provide the tunes, of course. Nothing could be more perfect as we gaze up at the stars, jamming to Coldplay as they rock what is officially now known as "our" song.

"Just think," I say, running my fingers over his healed tattoo as the song ends, "if you hadn't listened to me, I'd probably be picking out tunes for your memorial service instead of getting to do this."

Before he can yell at me for saying "I told you so" or being so morbid, I spring over him to press my lips to his, sucking on his bottom lip, then his neck, and letting my hands wander down to his shorts. We've both been eager to have sex for the first time since his surgeon finally gave the all clear.

He groans, holding onto my head while delivering kisses to my jaw. "Keep that up and it will be an extremely fast reunion." He slips my tank top strap off to the side, giving his mouth free range at my collarbone.

I find my way inside his underwear and reach for his hardness. But I find something fuzzy and square instead. Dazed, I pull the object free.

It's a black velvet box.

My tongue freezes in my mouth and my eyes pop wide. I love Adam, and I definitely want to spend the rest of forever with him, but...*oh shit*. Are we ready for *marriage*? Would he expect me to cook and clean for him? My level of expertise in the kitchen involves boiling ramen noodles. And he's already mentioned kids a few times, but I definitely know I'm not ready for that responsibility. It would probably be best to start out with something small, like a goldfish, to see if I'm even capable of keeping another thing alive.

Adam breaks out in a maniacal laugh, taking the box from my hand and kissing me among chuckles. "Ahhh, it was so worth it to see your face just now. I knew you wouldn't be able to resist reaching for me the minute we had a green light. Don't worry, I'm not proposing marriage. At least not *yet*."

He pops the box open to reveal a house key.

"Aw, you're giving me the key to your heart? How incredibly cheesy of you."

He rolls his eyes to the dark sky. "It's the key to our new brownstone." He brushes his lips over mine and pulls back with a grin. "Happy birthday."

My eyes grow wider. "You mean a brownstone in *New York?* For *us*? Who did you murder to acquire such a thing? Should I be concerned for Theo's whereabouts? I think I liked the tacky metaphor better."

Laughing, he brushes my hair away from my face before resting his hand against my cheek. "I may have neglected to tell you I have a good-sized inheritance that kicked in when I turned twenty-one. My parents froze it when I was too stupid to consider someone worth living for may come along. It's not as nice as the place we rented, but it's a start anyway until we find something better." He slides the key into my hand, beaming. "So, how 'bout it? I know we haven't been together long, but I've been thinking." He pulls on my head until he has full access to devour my lips. "We can move to New York and give this happily ever after notion a go. See if it suits us. Do the college thing, or whatever—"

I kiss him with everything I've got. There aren't any other words he could've chosen that would be any more perfect. Nothing else he could've given me for my birthday would've resonated so much love in my heart. I melt into him, knowing every choice I've made in the past few months, each time we felt a spark between us or looked into each other's eyes, have all led to this one, untouchable moment of pure bliss.

He pushes on me, gasping for air. "So that's a yes?"

"Of course it's a yes." I kiss him long and hard before breaking away, grinning. "Has anyone ever told you that you talk too much?"

We make love underneath the stars. It's awkward and slow as I'm afraid every movement will hurt him, but his desire takes over and we quickly fall into our usual rhythms and pleasures.

Life doesn't always have a happy ending. Adam most likely will never be totally healthy again. We'll always have to monitor his blood sugar. He's getting an insulin pump soon, and he may even need another transplant one day. I know there are probably even more health-related obstacles to come.

As I ungracefully scream out into the endless starry night with a toe-jerking orgasm, I know a lifetime of these priceless moments with Adam will never be enough.

For more information on Type 1 Diabetes and ways you can help, visit www.diabetes.org

To hear the songs intended to accompany *Adam's List*, visit
www.AuthorJenniferAnn.blogspot.com

Acknowledgements

A special heartfelt thank you to my cousin, Hope, for sharing with me what it's truly like to be a Type 1 diabetic, having to endure so many surgeries and procedures. After hearing more in-depth the horror stories of her battle, I can't imagine having to face all the life-threatening obstacles that come with the awful disease right at the prime of your life. She's one tough cookie. Her story is truly an inspiration, reminding me when life seems hard or unfair that there are much bigger things I could be struggling with.

Venturing out of my YA paranormal niche was challenging, exciting, and at times a bit scary. Thank you to the NA authors (especially those at NAAU) who were so willing to accept me into their community and lend a helping hand! I'm so lucky to work among such amazing people who are always ready to help the "competition!"

A big thank you to all my friends and family who cheered me on throughout this ride, and continue to support me no matter what genre I take on. I feel incredibly blessed to have so many amazing people in my life, even though I have yet to meet some of my closest friends in person! Special shout out to Corrie Hanson, Lauryn April, Maria Monteiro, Danielle Sibarium, Laura Howard, S.J. Pajonas, P.K. Hrezo, Kaitlyn Stone, S.T. Bende, Sydney Aaliyah, Leigh Talbert Moore, and Ilsa Madden-Mills for all your help (and being such amazing peeps I can always count on)!

To my stunning cover model Brooke Chavie who is beautiful on both the inside and out and has a bright future ahead of her, thanks for being a friend!

Thanks to my copy editor, Eileen Proksch, for her hard work, and my substantive editor, Christopher Vondracek, for his dedication and wisdom that helped *Adam's List* become the best version of itself.

To each and every one of the bloggers who took on the cover reveal of *Adam's List* and supported the story in its infancy, a mere "thank you" doesn't seem adequate. I appreciate that you took a chance on a "new" author, and had such great things to say about my somewhat twisted love story!

About the Author

Jennifer Ann is the pen name young adult paranormal author Jen Naumann uses to write new adult romance novels intended to spice up your life and pull at your heart strings. When not writing from one of the 10,000 lakes in Minnesota, Jen is either helping her husband farm, or chasing down one of their four active children.

For the latest on Jen's work, visit www.JenNaumann.net

Also by Jennifer Ann

Keep reading for a preview of the second book in the NYC LOVE series, *Kelly's Quest*!

Jewels Peterson

BEFORE NOW I DIDN'T HAVE A FULL understanding of what the saying "walking on clouds" meant, but I'm about to move into a brownstone in New York City with the love of my life, so...yeah.

For a Saturday morning, our small neighborhood tucked away in Murray Hill seems relatively quiet; the mixed odor of the city and summer smells thick in the stifling air. The little Irish pub on the corner, lined with dark hardwood inside like most of the others we've visited, doesn't open until noon, though I've heard it doesn't draw in much of a crowd during normal party hours. The constant hum of traffic along Park Avenue still takes some getting used to, but I wouldn't want it any other way. Aside from a few joggers, dog walkers, and residents going in and out of their brownstones, my best friend and I are the only two around.

I've only been here a few times since Adam first surprised me with the news that he purchased us our very own piece of New York with an inheritance he received from his beer mogul grandfather. We were quick to pack our things in Wisconsin and move into a rental for a few weeks while the final papers were processed for the brownstone. We spent the last few weeks picking out a college, findings jobs, and shopping for furniture as neither of us has owned so much as our own mattress outside of our childhood homes.

My face nearly splits in two when I take another long look at our new home. The narrow, tan building blends in with the others sandwiched beside it, but the dull shade of red I chose for the front door gives it a subtle kick from the other lower-level entrances. Our wrought iron gate is tall and rather heavy, giving me an extra sense of security even if the gate is only for show.

Inside is a work in progress with leaky faucets, cracked plaster, floors that need refinishing, and a kitchen that's a complete eyesore. But it's ours, and we plan to fix it up over time. The ground-level backyard is exactly the kind of getaway I've been dreaming of since I took the road trip to the city with Adam earlier this summer.

My best friend, Kelly, wipes at her sweaty forehead from the unrelenting heat the morning already brings. The incredibly short shorts and low-cut tank top she wears fit her curvaceous body like they were custom tailored for her. Without a stitch of makeup, she looks younger and exhausted. Her large brown eyes show the stress of the grueling weather wearing her down. She twisted her long brown hair into a sloppy bun this morning, but pieces have already fallen out around her supermodel-like cheekbones. Only Kelly could make natural look incredibly sexy. Whenever I try that kind of look, I resemble Whitney Huston during her days on crack.

I was somewhat thrown off when Kelly insisted on flying out to help us move. When I reminded her moving meant doing physical labor, she mumbled something about getting away from her sisters. After spending her summer as a counselor at her family's camp, I think the restrictions of being around her overbearing sisters really wore her down.

Kelly pushes her pouty lips out farther than usual. Moments like this I see why all guys seem to be drawn to her. "Does Adam seriously expect us to stand here and do nothing until he gets back? I don't understand why we can't just go in. I swear I've lost ten pounds in sweat."

I nod, feeling my ratty Alice in Chains t-shirt cling to my chest. "You're right. Let's take a few things in. I'm sure it won't hurt anything."

I slide in next to her and unlock the back gate with the keys Adam had me hold on to until his return. The van is filled with a few dozen boxes, a bed for the guest bedroom, an armchair, and the dresser from my childhood. Most of our furniture was newly purchased, thanks to Adam's inheritance, and should be delivered later in the afternoon. All I care is that we have our bed up by the end of the day. Tomorrow's my fourth day working at the market down the street, and I want a good night of sleep. Standing on my feet all day has been particularly draining, considering it's been over a year since I last worked at one of the clothing stores managed by my mom.

The first tangible object within reach is Adam's flat screen. Together, Kelly and I wriggle the monstrosity free and shuffle toward the steps.

"Don't even think about it!" a voice yells out. Theo, my relatively new friend, swoops out of nowhere to my side, grabbing my end of the

TV. "You had strict orders not to go inside on your own, remember?"

I turn to him, smirking. He's so predictable. In running clothes soaked with sweat, headphones blasting hardcore rap, it's like looking at the same temporary neighbor we met just months ago in these same streets when Adam and I were renting a place and still trying to figure out what to make of our tumultuous relationship.

Considering Theo hit on me, buck-naked, mere minutes after we first met, it's actually a small miracle to think just how good of a friend he's become to both me and Adam. And I still laugh every time I see him dressed in designer suits for his swanky job as a television producer.

"Look who finally decided to show up to help," Kelly snorts, struggling with the TV on her end. "Pretty sure you could manage to carry this whole thing on your own, big guy."

Theo moves his hand down the flatscreen further until her face relaxes with relief. "That better, or you need me to carry you, too?" he teases with a playful smile.

Kelly rolls her eyes to the sky. "Back it down a notch. Not everyone is automatically charmed by your massive muscles."

"Oh, I can charm the pants off anyone, Cavenaugh. All you have to do is ask."

I moan, shaking my head. This has become their usual banter since they first met two days ago. Theo flirts, and Kelly pretends she's not interested, although I caught her giving him some pretty dopey-eyed glances. I think a part of her is afraid of what will happen if she lets herself fall for him since she lives in Wisconsin. I'm secretly hoping something will happen between them so maybe she'll decide to move to New York. It's going to be hard not having my best friend around, considering she's always been the one I can count on when things turn to shit.

Theo and Kelly disappear down the narrow steps to our newly acquired brownstone, just four streets down from Theo's. Taking a deep breath of the heavy air, I study the peaceful neighborhood. A warm rush of pride and excitement fills my gut. Until now, I've never felt like I was exactly where I'm meant to be. My life suddenly feels right on track, like this is exactly how things are supposed to play out.

Theo and Kelly emerge from the ornate door, her bright giggles endless. Theo catches me smiling like a goober at the building behind the van and folds his massive arms. "Where is Loverboy this morning? I think this is the first time I've seen the two of you more than five feet apart in the last two weeks. Shouldn't he be helping us?"

I snap from my trance and reach for the pile of blankets that were covering the TV, throwing them into Kelly's arms. "It's not like he can actually carry stuff anyway. And he had to meet with a professor."

Dealing with Adam's Type I diabetes was at first incredibly stressful on our relationship, especially when he was ready to accept possible death over being with me. By the time we met he'd been through so many surgeries and awful procedures—leaving him regrettably scarred and broken—that he didn't have the mental strength to endure any more. Though he insisted that we'd never be anything more than friends, we fell in love and he realized our relationship was worth fighting for. He's come a long way on his recovery, yet it's still slow going.

Kelly snorts as she heads back to the steps with her arms full. "Who meets with professors on the weekends? He's such a nerd."

"He's trying to make sure all his credits are accounted for before fall semester starts," I scold her.

Kelly scoffs before disappearing. Theo crawls up inside the back of the van to sort through our sparse belongings.

"You should probably stick to the lighter stuff until James gets here," I suggest to him. "I'd hate to see you develop a hernia while Kel is in town."

Luckily, Theo wasn't the only overly muscular, tattooed friend we made in the city. His buddy, James, was quick to volunteer his help when he heard we were moving.

Theo peers around the corner of the van, his expression broad with hope. "Are you saying she is into me? I mean, she's a total knockout, and any friend of yours has to be worth my time. C'mon, give me something to work with."

I shrug coyly. "I never said anything of that sort, though she did make a comment about your perfect ass, and the only time I've really heard her giggle is when she's around you. If you say anything to her, though, I'll totally deny it. I can't have you breaking my best friend's heart."

"I don't plan on breaking her heart, I just want to get to know her. C'mon, throw a guy a bone here." He crouches down until we're closer to eye level. "How can I impress her so she'll agree to go out with me?"

A familiar pair of arms slip around me from behind, molding against me like it's where they're meant to be. "Offer to take her on a trip across the country. It worked for me."

I whirl around in my gorgeous boyfriend's arms. I didn't see him sneak out of the rental this morning, but it's no surprise he's looking as hot as ever in a button-down that matches the hue of his steely blue eyes. His hair doesn't have the usual spiky flip going, which is typical when he has to get up early. He's growing stronger with every day and has more of the boundless spirit from when we first met. I lace my fingers through his hair and drag him close, pressing my lips to his for a deep kiss.

Theo coughs behind us. "You'd think that'd grow old eventually."

Adam stops kissing me to beam at Theo. "Once you find the right one, it never grows old, my man. You wait. You'll figure it out one day." He kisses the tip of my nose. "Have you been inside yet?"

Theo jumps down onto the street with a big box in hand. "No, she hasn't, and you can thank me. I caught her just as she was trying to sneak in."

"I wasn't trying anything," I say, rolling my eyes with feigned annoyance. "The man's a chronic liar."

Adam's eyes sparkle. "Are you ready for your surprise?"

I lean in to kiss him again. And again. "Does it involve locking Kel and Theo out to give us a little privacy?"

"I'm sure we could make that happen." Adam smirks before sucking on my bottom lip.

"I've developed a whole new level of sympathy for your new neighbors!" Theo hollers over his shoulder.

We follow him inside, hands held, my excitement skyrocketing through the roof. The first level of our new place looks halfway decent sized without any furniture, but I know as soon as the couch and deep armchair we picked out arrive, the living room will shrink back down quickly. The wooden floors, bleached and cracked, just need a little TLC once we've saved up a bit more money. The kitchen, however, could use a wrecking ball. The crooked cabinets have rotted out in places, and small chunks of the laminate countertop are missing. It's unattractive, but at least Adam was able to afford something in this neighborhood. After we've fixed it up, we'll probably come out ahead if we ever decide to sell.

Adam's adorable dimples flare when he pulls me toward the drapery-covered patio door, past our friends playfully arguing on their way back outside. Before Adam pushes the doors open, I already have an inkling of what I'm about to find.

What was once a small area with short, chain-linked fencing and the world's saddest patch of grass has transformed into a backyard wonderland. Dozens of twinkle lights are strung beneath a draping canopy that does an excellent job of filtering the sunlight. Three outdoor sofas with red cushions circle a stone fire pit inside a new, walnut stained fence. Ornate stone covers the ground inside the intimate gathering area in a swirling pattern, with a patch of fresh sodding in the far back. It's incredibly charming. I can't believe it's ours.

"Ohmigod, Adam!" I drag him over to one of the couches, sinking back into the giant pillows. When he collapses on top of me, I kiss him. Hard. "It's exactly what I pictured! When did you have time for all of this?"

His lips trail down my neck. "Davis was only visiting as a ploy to keep you busy while I had to put in 'extra time' in therapy."

I spent the better part of the last week running around the city with Adam's cousin from Minnesota. He's an artist and has been in New York dozens of times for shows, so he actually showed me some of the insider tips

I've missed. "So he really isn't thinking of moving out here?"

"I think deep down he's actually considering it, but you never know with him." Smirking, Adam bends in to cover my neck with kisses. "Want to know the best part about this setup?" His hands wander down my thigh before reaching up my shorts to gently stroke the part of me that will always want him. I inhale sharply, delighted. "With this ingenious cover over our heads, I can do whatever I want, whenever I want, to my girlfriend in the privacy of our backyard." He kisses my lips. "Just don't let out one of your screaming orgasms, or the new neighbors will likely call the cops."

"Could you be any more amazing?" I cling to him, dusting the tip of my tongue against his lips. "We better send Theo and Kel away. I have a feeling we're going to be back here a while."

"By all means, don't let me stop you," someone calls out sarcastically.

Adam and I turn around at the same time to find the very last person we'd ever expect to see standing in our new patio doorway.

It's almost impossible not to acknowledge that Adam's brother, Erik, is just as hot as my boyfriend. Their square faces have the same exact shape and angles in addition to their eyes being nearly the same beautiful shade of blue. Even their hair is styled in a similarly precarious way. Last time I met Erik, I wondered if I'd be able to tell the difference between them in the dark, aside from Adam's surgery scars marring his otherwise smooth stomach.

But Erik's abrasive personality makes him a thousand times less charming. He reminds me of one of those preppy assholes in 80s movies with his turquoise designer polo and striped khaki shorts. The arrogant smirk against his full lips is something I've come to expect, even though we've only met once before. I've heard Adam call him a "prick" or "asshole" enough times to know he's a piece of work. Plus there were the inappropriate comments Erik made about me being too hot for Adam and how he'd be around if things didn't work out just seconds after we were first introduced. Needless to say, the brothers aren't close, and very rarely communicate.

I scramble to adjust my clothing and hair before Erik can make some kind of gross comment about what he caught us doing.

"What are you doing here?" Adam yells, pushing me off his lap. "How did you know where to find us?"

"I hired a PI," Erik says, shrugging one shoulder.

Adam bolts to his feet. "You what?"

With a jolly chuckle, Erik strolls toward us. "Holy shit. Back it down a notch, bro. I'm not that interested in finding you. Mom gave me your address. I was passing through on my way home and thought I'd stop by." He sinks into the other couch beside me, stretching his long arm across the back as he assesses our backyard. His musky cologne makes my eyes water. "Nice pad."

"Thanks." I reach up to pull Adam's hand until he's back down on the couch at my side. All the muscles in his upper body are tight with tension. I lace my fingers through his and squeeze. My gesture doesn't seem to take the edge off as I had hoped.

"Don't make yourself too comfortable," Adam tells his brother in a low, almost threatening voice. "Next time you should considering calling before making a surprise visit."

Erik rolls his eyes with an arrogant flair. "I would if you actually gave me your number. I figured you would've reached out to me sooner, considering we're only living minutes from each other now."

Theo sticks his head out the patio door and nods at Adam. "Delivery truck is here. They need your signature." His expression changes when he tips his head at Erik. "Hope it's okay that I sent him back. You didn't mention you had a brother, but I figured there's no way he's lying since the two of you could pass as twins."

"I'm not exactly his favorite person," Erik replies smartly, a tight smirk curling his lips.

Adam turns to kiss my cheek. "I'll be back in a minute." When he stands, he passes a poisonous look to his brother. "Be nice to her. I mean it."

"I'll be a perfect gentleman," Erik insists, crossing his legs. He throws me a sickening wink as Adam joins Theo in the doorway. Once they're out of sight, Erik leans in closer, his eyes narrowed. "It seems you have my brother whipped. He nearly blew his entire inheritance on this place. My parents don't seem too concerned, but they're idiots. Give me one good reason I shouldn't think my big brother has snagged himself a little gold-digger."

My jaw drops. I figured his rude side would rear its ugly head eventually, but hitting me with a 2 x 4 would come as less of a surprise. "I...are you high?" When his suspicious gaze doesn't change, I cross my arms. "I seriously can't believe you just said that. You don't know a thing about me. And whatever Adam chooses to do with his inheritance isn't any of your business."

A low chuckle rumbles in his throat. "So you're not going to deny it, then?"

Both flustered and appalled, I bring my hands up to cover my face and moan. Just when it feels as if things couldn't possibly become any more awkward, Kelly comes skipping out to join us. "Jewels, what'd you think? Isn't this fucking amazing?"

"Hello, beautiful," Erik sings, popping to his feet. He offers his hand to her, using a sudden charm that makes him almost appear civil. "And you are?"

She takes his hand with a suspicious gaze. "I'm Kelly, and you must be mistaking me for someone who is easily charmed."

I stand at his side with a wide-eyed stare, hoping to pass a silent message. "He's Adam's brother, Erik."

Kelly's eyes also burst wide when she understands. "Oh! The infamous brother. Right." She drops his hand like a hot potato. "What are you doing here? I thought you and Adam weren't simpatico."

"He's just leaving," I say, crossing my arms.

"Do you live in the city?" Erik asks Kelly, unfazed by my blatant hint. "We should really meet for drinks sometime."

Kelly runs her fingers along the torn hem of her shorts, suddenly looking peaked. "Actually, I..." Her voice trails off and she wets her lips, glancing back at me, her brown eyes perplexed.

I know my best friend's mannerisms better than my own. There's something she's holding back because she knows it will upset me. I'm wrecked with guilt. She's had to walk on eggshells ever since my high school sweetheart was killed in Afghanistan last year, sending me into a deep depression. Before I met Adam, my life was a total mess. Kelly was always there to pick up the pieces.

"Kel, stoping making that face. What's going on?"

"Shit. I've been meaning to tell you since I got here, I just haven't found the right time, if there even is such a thing." She lowers her head like a scolded puppy. "I bought a one way ticket here. I'm staying indefinitely." Her jittery hands raise to the sky, and she smiles in mock enthusiasm. "Surprise."

CPSIA information can be obtained
at www.ICGtesting.com
Printed in the USA
LVHW010958101119
636874LV00021B/2472